Player's Handbook   Rules Supplement

The Complete Druid's Handbook

by David Pulver

Table of Contents

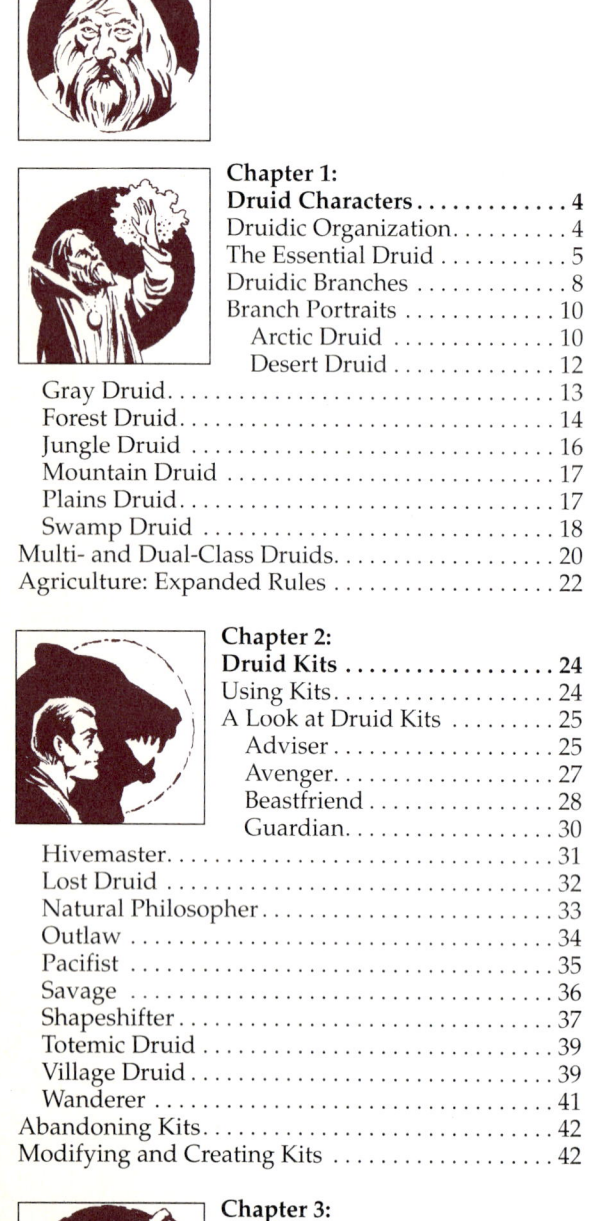

Introduction 3

Chapter 1:
Druid Characters 4
Druidic Organization. 4
The Essential Druid 5
Druidic Branches 8
Branch Portraits 10
   Arctic Druid 10
   Desert Druid 12
   Gray Druid. 13
   Forest Druid. 14
   Jungle Druid 16
   Mountain Druid 17
   Plains Druid. 17
   Swamp Druid 18
Multi- and Dual-Class Druids. 20
Agriculture: Expanded Rules 22

Chapter 2:
Druid Kits 24
Using Kits. 24
A Look at Druid Kits 25
   Adviser 25
   Avenger. 27
   Beastfriend 28
   Guardian. 30
Hivemaster. 31
Lost Druid 32
Natural Philosopher. 33
Outlaw 34
Pacifist 35
Savage 36
Shapeshifter. 37
Totemic Druid 39
Village Druid. 39
Wanderer 41
Abandoning Kits. 42
Modifying and Creating Kits 42

Chapter 3:
The Druidic Order 43
The Circles 43
High-level Druids 45
The Shadow Circle 53
Creating a
   Druidic History 56

Chapter 4:
Role-playing Druids 58
Druidic Faith 58
The Neutral Alignment 59
A Druid's Responsibilities. 62
Character Strategy. 69
Relations with Others. 73
Personality Types 76
Diplomat 76
Gardener 77
Idealist 77
Mysterious Figure. 78
Nurturer 78
Rustic 79
Traditionalist 79
Fanatic 79
Misanthrope. 80
Druid Campaigns 80

Chapter 5:
Druidic Magic. 86
New Spells 86
   First-level 86
   Second-level. 87
   Third-level 90
   Fourth-level 90
   Fifth-level 93
Sixth-level 95
Seventh-level 96
New Magical Items. 98
Herbal Magic. 103

Chapter 6:
Sacred Groves 107
Features of a Sacred Grove . . . 107
Stewardship. 108
Sanctifying and Awakening
   a Grove 111
Magical Sacred Groves 112
Defiled and Cursed Groves . . . 115
Standing Stones. 117

Appendixes:
A: AD&D® Original
   Edition Druids 119
B: Bibliography 124

**Druid Character
   Record Sheet** 125

Druid Kit Record Sheet 127

Introduction

Tables:
1: Farm Rating 22
2: Farm Random Events 23
3: Lesser Grove Powers 112
4: Greater Grove Powers 114
5: Properties of Cursed Groves 115
6: Powers of Standing Stones 118
7: Original Druid Experience Points 120
8: Original Hierophant Experience Points ... 121
9: Elemental Conjurings 122
10: Druidic Spells by Class and Level ... 123

CREDITS

Design: David Pulver
Editing: Sue Weinlein
New Black and White Art: Jeff Easley
Color Art: Larry Elmore,
Keith Parkinson, Alan Pollack
Typography: Angelika Lokotz
Production: Paul Hanchette
Special Thanks: Peter Donald, Chris Murray,
Bruce Norman, and Tim Pulver.

TSR, Inc.
POB 756
Lake Geneva,
WI 53147
U.S.A.

TSR, Ltd.
120 Church End,
Cherry Hinton
Cambridge CB1 3LB
United Kingdom

ADVANCED DUNGEONS & DRAGONS, AD&D, DRAGON, SPELLJAMMER, DUNGEON MASTER, FORGOTTEN REALMS, and WORLD OF GREYHAWK are registered trademarks owned by TSR, Inc. PLANESCAPE, MONSTROUS MANUAL, and the TSR logo are trademarks owned by TSR, Inc.
All TSR characters, character names, and the distinctive likenesses thereof are trademarks owned by TSR, Inc.
© 1994 TSR, Inc. All Rights Reserved. Printed in the U.S.A.

Random House and its affiliates have worldwide distribution rights in the book trade for English language products of TSR, Inc. Distributed to the book and hobby trade in the United Kingdom by TSR Ltd. Distributed to the toy and hobby trade by regional distributors.

This material is protected under the copyright laws of the United States of America. Any reproduction or unauthorized use of the material or artwork contained herein is prohibited without the express written permission of TSR, Inc.

Mysterious guardian of a sacred grove, wise counselor to monarchs, cunning master of many shapes, friend of animals, and terrible defender of unspoiled Nature: This is the druid of the ADVANCED DUNGEONS & DRAGONS® game.

Although the priests of the Celtic tribes of Western Europe in the time of Rome called themselves druids, the druids of the AD&D® game are not Celtic priests, nor do they practice the bloody rites that made the ancient druids infamous in the eyes of Rome. Rather, these druids more closely resemble creatures of Victorian romance and modern fantasy, Merlin figures who revere Nature and wield power over plants, animals, the weather, and the elements.

This book is designed to illuminate the many abilities of druids and show how the neutral and "unaligned" druid can best adventure with a party of predominantly good characters. It also reveals what a druid does when not adventuring and demonstrates how a druid can become the center of a new and exciting campaign.

The Complete Druid's Handbook adds numerous options to the druid class from the *Player's Handbook*, including druids from regions other than the woodlands, and introduces many specialized druid kits. Also included are new spells and magical items, as well as rules for a druid's sacred grove.

Those using this book with the AD&D Original Edition game should know that page references correspond with the AD&D 2nd Edition *Player's Handbook* (*PH*) and *DUNGEON MASTER® Guide* (*DMG*). The original druid class appears here as an appendix, with some material from the AD&D Original Edition reference book *Unearthed Arcana*.

CHAPTER 1

Druid Characters

The traditional druid is a guardian of the woodlands. Nature, however, is vast and diverse; thus the druids detailed in this book might live their lives protecting jungle rain forests, arctic tundra, or even the subterranean Underdark. As a result, several distinct branches of druid are presented here, each essentially a new subclass built around the basic concept of the druid class. As a player, choose your druidic branch right after deciding to play a druid character.

Druidic Organization

The basic druid as described in the *PH* is referred to here as the "forest druid." The names of the other branches reflect their geographic specialty: arctic druids, desert druids, and so on.

Members of all the branches of the druidic order have the same alignment—true neutral—and worship Nature. They share one ethos and owe at least nominal allegiance to the world's Grand Druid. But, as befits the infinite diversity of Nature, every branch differs in details and approach to its mission. The granted powers and spells that Nature finds appropriate for a druid in one region are often inappropriate for a druid from a very different climate and terrain.

For instance, while the forest druids described in the *PH* have major access to the Plant sphere of priest spells, the branch of desert druids has only minor access to that sphere, reflecting the less abundant plant life in the desert. Similarly, while a forest druid's ability to pass through overgrowth is very useful in the woods, it has much less utility

for a desert druid. Instead, the branch of desert druids has granted powers enabling them to survive in arid country.

Some rivalry exists between the different branches of druids. On most worlds, the forest druids belong to the dominant branch. However, on a few worlds (such as one in the midst of an ice age) another branch might wield the most power. For more details on rivalry between branches, see Chapter 3: The Druidic Order.

The Dungeon Master can restrict some branches to nonplayer characters (NPCs) or even prohibit them to suit the background or direction of a campaign. For example, the Dungeon Master (DM) might decide that the gray druids of the Underdark would make exciting adversaries for the characters. Since having player characters (PCs) as gray druids would water down the impact of the gray druids as foes, the DM can prohibit players from choosing that branch. Later in the campaign, after the party has encountered the gray druids, the DM might open the branch to players.

Similarly, some druid branches simply may not seem very logical or useful in certain campaigns. A wise DM would discourage players from selecting the arctic branch for their druid characters in a campaign set in a jungle.

The Essential Druid

Some characteristics and limitations apply to *all* branches of the druidic order. The following section expands on the rules for druid characters in the *PH* (pgs. 35–38).

Alignment and Ethos

All druids are of neutral alignment and share an ethos devoted to protecting the wilderness and maintaining natural cycles and a balance between good and evil (*PH*, pgs. 37, 47). For a detailed discussion of the neutral alignment and the beliefs of druids, refer to Chapter 4: Role-playing Druids.

Experience and Hit Dice

All druids must use the druid column of Table 23: Priest Experience Levels (*PH*, p. 33). Druids, like other members of the priest group, use eight-sided Hit Dice (HD), gaining one die per level from 1st through 9th level. After 9th level, druids receive an additional 2 hit points per level, but gain no special bonus for high Constitution.

Proficiencies and Crossovers

Druids gain proficiencies just like other priests (*PH*, p. 50), starting with two weapon and four nonweapon proficiencies.

It is strongly recommended that you, the player, use the optional nonweapon proficiency rules when creating druid characters with this book. The various branches of druids (and the druid kits described later) make extensive use of the nonweapon proficiency system to differentiate among types of druids.

Note that druid nonweapon proficiencies come from the general, priest, *and* warrior groups. Druids have access to the warrior group (even though many other priests do not) because it contains many of the proficiencies associated with outdoor skills the druid needs to operate in the wilderness.

Money and Equipment

Druids start with 3d6×10 gp, which they can use to purchase equipment. All but a few coins (less than 1 gp) must be spent prior to entering play.

If using the optional druid kit rules described later in this book, both the initial money and the equipment allowed might vary depending on the kit.

Magical Items

Druids use all magical items normally permitted to priests, with the exception of written items (books and scrolls) and those types of armor and weapons that are normally forbidden them. (The weapons and armor permitted to members of each branch and kit do vary, but they remain similar to those allowed to druids in the *PH*.)

Thus, a druid who finds magical chain mail may not wear it, since druids must use only nonmetallic armor. Similarly, a druid cannot wield a magical mace, since maces are not among the permitted druidic arms.

The Secret Language

All druids can speak a secret language in addition to other tongues they know. Using the optional proficiency system, the secret language does *not* require a proficiency slot.

> The secret language of the druids has its roots in British tradition. A language called Thari, derived from Celtic roots, apparently was spoken as a secret tongue throughout the British Isles by a small number of traveling folk such as tinkers and bards. It later was adopted by some Gypsy clans in addition to Romany, their own Indic language. Thari may predate the Dark Ages, and some claim fluency in it even today. Certain researchers seeking the roots of Thari as a language distinct from Gaelic have linked its origins to both ancient Celtic craft guilds and to the historical druids. If the DM wants to name the druids' secret language, Thari possesses some historical relevance.

Not only can druids use the secret language to provide passwords, they can speak this private tongue when they wish to baffle nondruidic eavesdroppers. It is a precise tool for discussing Nature; a druid can say "dense, old-growth pine forest" in one word rather than a whole phrase.

The secret language has a specialized and detailed vocabulary limited to dealing with Nature and natural events; beyond this sphere, it is very basic. A druid could use the secret language to talk about the health of a person, animal, or plant; discuss the weather; or give detailed directions through the wilderness. The language also can describe druidic spells, ceremonies, powers, and any natural and supernatural creatures known to the druids. However, it contains no words for sophisticated human emotions, for most tools or artifacts (beyond those used for hunting, farming, or fishing), or for weapons and armor (other than items druids use). The language also contains few words that refer to concepts peculiar to sentient beings, like *property, justice, theft,* or *war.* Tense distinctions blur in this secret tongue; usually the concepts druids express bear a certain immediacy or timelessness.

Finally, the secret language of the druids remains a purely spoken tongue. A few simple runes or marks (symbolizing *danger, safe water, safe trail,* and so on) exist for marking paths and leaving messages, but the language cannot communicate actual sentences and complex ideas in writing.

Here's an example of how the secret language works in practice. Suppose two druids are discussing a magical item and want to converse entirely in the secret language, using no words borrowed from other tongues. One druid wishes to say:

> This magical long sword was a gift to Melinda, wife to King Rupert, from Rupert's court wizard Drufus. The mage gave it the power to throw lightning bolts. But then King Rupert grew jealous of Melinda. He had her executed and

took the blade for himself. After Rupert died, the sword was left buried in the dungeons under his castle.

In the secret language, the story might come out something like this:

> This magic scimitar was for the Tall Golden Female, mate of the Man-Leader, from the Wielder of Magic from the Vale of the White Eagles. He put the *call lightning* power in it. But the Man-Leader wanted it. He killed the Tall Golden Female and took it for himself. He died. The scimitar stayed in the cave under his big stone man-den.

See the difference? There's no word for *long sword*, so our druid has substituted "scimitar." (All druidic weapons have names.) The idea of a *gift* is described in more basic terms. In addition, the concept of naming has no place in this Nature-oriented language; people and creatures are known by description, status, or place of origin.

Wizard becomes the more generic "wielder of magic." *Lightning*, a natural phenomenon, has an equivalent in the secret language. But the secret language cannot convey a human emotion such as Rupert's *jealousy*, so the druid has had to substitute less precise phrasing. Similarly, the private tongue does not cover *execution* or *murder*, so the druid used the more generic "killed." Finally, no druidic term corresponds to *dungeon* or *castle*, so the druid has had to use other words—"cave under his big stone man-den"—to convey that image. Of course, a druid not worried about being overheard might mix the secret language and normal speech in a single sentence.

The secret language helps bind the worldwide druidic order together. Druids from different circles (See Chapter 3: The Druidic Order) or branches all speak the same secret language. However, they may have developed their own regional accents or dialects. These could enable a listener to identify the region the druid comes from, or provide a clue to the speaker's branch.

In a SPELLJAMMER® or PLANESCAPE™ campaign and through the use of certain spells and magical items, druids from different worlds can meet. The DM should decide whether their secret languages resemble each other enough to allow communication.

Finally, the druid's secret language, while private, is not supernatural—theoretically, others can learn it. However, because the tongue provides druids with code phrases or passwords, they simply *will not* teach it to nondruids. The great druid of the region will punish any who break with this tradition.

Shapechanging

Characters belonging to almost all druidic branches (discussed later in this chapter) can shapechange into various animal forms upon reaching 7th level. For more than the following guidelines, consult the description of a particular branch's granted powers.

Normally, the druid can assume only a limited number of shapes each day, depending on the character's branch; the choice of branch usually restricts the types of forms the druid can assume.

Shifting shape takes one round, during which the druid cannot take other actions. The druid can remain in the new shape indefinitely—the duration of a form ends only when the druid turns back to the original shape or assumes another one. A druid can shift from one shape to another without returning to human form first.

Upon assuming a new form, the druid heals 10% to 60% (1d6×10) of all damage. (Round fractions down.) For example, a druid who has suffered 15 points of damage rolls a 3 on a d6. Therefore, the character regains

30%×15 hp, or 4.5 hp. This value becomes 4 hit points after rounding.

The animal form a druid assumes can vary from the size of a bullfrog or small bird to that of a black bear. Unless noted otherwise, the druid can assume only the form of a normal (real-world) animal in normal proportions. A druid in animal form takes on all the beast's physical characteristics— movement rate, abilities, Armor Class (AC), number of attacks, and damage per attack. The druid retains original hit point and saving throw values.

The druid's clothing and one item held in each hand also become part of the new body; these reappear when the druid resumes normal shape. Generally, a druid in animal form cannot use such items, but in particularly challenging campaigns, the DM may allow protective devices, such as a *ring of protection*, to function normally.

A shapechanged druid radiates strong Alteration magic.

Turning Undead

No druid has the granted power to turn undead. Such creatures are not of the living world—the only world that concerns druids—so members of this class have no control over them.

Higher-level Druids

The worldwide organization of the druids allows for the existence of only a limited number of 12th- or higher-level druids, assigning them special titles, servants, and responsibilities. Druids who gain enough experience to reach 12th level can advance only if they find a vacancy within the Order's ranks or wrest a position from another druid through the challenge. (See Chapter 3: The Druidic Order.)

Only one 15th-level druid exists in any campaign world: the Grand Druid, chief of all druids in the world. The Grand Druid can come from any branch, though on many worlds this position requires a member of the usually dominant forest druids. A Grand Druid who retires and continues to gain experience can become a hierophant druid, of which a world can have any number.

The rules for druids of 12th and higher levels described in the *PH* on pgs. 37–38 apply to all druidic branches. For more details on the hierarchy of druids and the special responsibilities of higher-level characters, see Chapter 3: The Druidic Order.

Druidic Branches

Each branch within the druidic order operates, effectively, as a separate priest class under the standard druid rules. Here's how the pages that follow describe the characteristics of each branch:

Minimum Ability Scores. The druidic prime requisites of Wisdom 12 and Charisma 15, or slightly modified scores, serve as the minimum ability scores necessary for a character to choose a particular branch.

Races Allowed. Standard (forest) druids are usually humans or half-elves, but members of other races can choose some druidic branches. (Details on these options appear in *The Complete Book of Humanoids*.) A number in parenthesis shows the maximum level these characters normally reach; they can achieve higher levels only with high ability scores, as stated in the *DMG*, pgs. 14–15.

Armor and Weapons Permitted. Most druids wear natural armor (leather) and use wooden shields. Other armors, especially metallic kinds, are forbidden to all druids.

Most of the weapons permitted to druids of a particular branch resemble tools used in herding, hunting, and farming, or hold symbolic meaning to the druid. For instance, the curved scimitar and khopesh represent both

The Complete Book of Humanoids offers four new races for use as druid PCs: alaghi, centaurs, saurials, and swanmays. Other non-humans can become druids, at the DM's option, though details on these characters should be carefully worked out within the guidelines of *The Complete Book of Humanoids*. Possible allowable races include:

Dryads. A dryad is quite shy and unable to travel far from her home tree. Unusual circumstances might allow a dryad PC to become a druid and travel within a large forest using magical items that link her with her home tree, but it remains unlikely that the dryad will advance beyond 4th level in ability. DRAGON® Magazine (#109, "Hooves and Green Hair") has suggested that half-dryads (born of a union of human male and dryad) might reach 7th level or higher. Dryads and half-dryads always become forest druids.

Elves. The AD&D Original Edition *Unearthed Arcana* reference book allowed elves to become druids. Only sylvan elves may achieve druidhood, perhaps in remote areas such as lost islands or other worlds. Sylvan elf druids can reach 12th level (like regular clerics) and can take the Herbalist kit from *The Complete Book of Elves* (pgs. 83–84). They always fall under the forest druid branch. Interested players might develop a druidlike priest kit for an elf, such as the halfling's Leaftender. Though drow cannot become druids, half-drow (like all half-elves) can; these almost always become gray druids.

Giant-kin. Firbolgs and voadkyn, described in *The Complete Book of Humanoids*, might become forest druids in certain remote regions of a campaign. They could reach the 7th level of ability. Again, players could develop a druidlike priest kit for this race.

Halflings. The AD&D Original Edition game allowed halflings to reach the 6th level of ability as NPCs; *Unearthed Arcana* allowed halfling druid PCs to reach higher levels. In the AD&D 2nd Edition *Complete Book of Gnomes and Halflings* (pgs. 119–120), halfling priests gained the Leaftender kit, which strongly resembles the druid class. Leaftender priests normally may achieve 8th level. If halflings become true druids, they can reach 8th level, too, usually in the forest or plains branches.

Lizard Men. A civilized group of lizard men on a world in the SPELLJAMMER setting might have druids among them. Though some lizard men aboard the ship *Spelljammer* (detailed in *The Legend of Spelljammer* boxed set) achieved high levels of clerical ability, most lizard man druids would not advance beyond 7th level. These beings become jungle or swamp druids.

Satyrs. As a rule, satyrs concern themselves too much with having fun to bother with the serious side of a druid's life. Satyr druid PCs should not gain levels above 4th. An article in DRAGON Magazine issue #109, "Hooves and Green Hair," allowed half-satyrs (born of human women and satyrs) to reach 6th level or higher. Satyrs and half-satyrs always belong to the forest druid branch.

the sickle used in the harvest and the crescent moon, which stands for birth, death, and rebirth in the cycle of Nature.

The standard druid can use the following weapons: club, sickle, dart, spear, dagger, scimitar, sling, and staff (*optional:* scythe).

Use of metallic weapons and tools usually remains unrestricted, but local availability can prove a problem, especially in areas like the arctic tundra. Nonmetallic materials can make effective weapons, with the following modifiers (compared to similar metallic items):

Bone: 30% cost; 50% weight; –1 damage; –1 to attack roll.

Stone: 50% cost; 75% weight; –1 damage; –2 to attack roll.

Wood: 10% cost; 50% weight; –2 damage; –3 to attack roll.

The damage modifier reduces the damage normally done by the weapon, with a minimum of 1 point of damage. The attack roll modifier does not apply to missile weapons, as the attack roll reflects the character's aim and is not a function of the material used to make the weapon. Damage modifiers do apply to missile weapons, however.

Enchanted nonmetallic weapons must overcome the negative modifiers, too; thus a *bone dagger +1* works just as well as a normal steel dagger.

Whenever a nonmetallic weapon inflicts maximum damage in combat, it has a 1 in 20 chance of breaking and becoming useless. (The DM rolls a d20.)

Nonweapon and Weapon Proficiencies. A druid of a particular branch must have certain proficiencies *required* by the branch. *Recommended* proficiencies are only strong suggestions. If the DM permits the optional druid kits from the next chapter, select the druid's proficiencies only after you, the player, have chosen a kit, since kits have their own proficiency requirements.

If the DM prefers to use secondary skills rather than nonweapon proficiencies, choose appropriate druidic skills from Table 36 in the *PH,* p. 53.

The *scythe* is a weapon available to many druidic branches. Its large curved blade, sharp only on its inner edge, attaches to a handle 5 to 6 feet long. A harvesting tool used to reap grain, the scythe costs 5 gp and weighs 8 lbs. This medium-sized (M) weapon must be used two-handed. It causes piercing/slashing (P/S) damage with speed factor 8. A scythe inflicts 1d6+1 points of damage vs. small or medium-sized opponents, or 1d8 vs. large opponents.

Spheres of Influence. Each branch allows its members access to different clerical spell spheres. (An asterisk indicates a sphere to which branch members have only minor access.) Druids gain bonus spells for high Wisdom.

Granted Powers. A druid has a wider variety of granted powers than a standard cleric, an advantage balanced by a druid's more limited sphere selection and inferior armor.

Special Limitation. Some branches suffer from unusual disadvantages. For example, heat debilitates an arctic druid.

Holy Symbol and Grove. Many branches of druids use plants as holy symbols and spell components—mistletoe, for instance, symbolizes the forest druid. In habitats where mistletoe is not available (such as deserts or arctic regions), druids use other symbols.

Forest druids worship in groves of ancient trees, which have become sanctuaries, meeting places, and sites of power for them. Alternate worship sites can replace groves for branches whose primary terrain does not foster tree growth. (See Chapter 6: Sacred Groves.)

Branch Portraits

The following section of this chapter describes the various branches of druids that might exist in a campaign world. The DM may freely create other branches as desired, such as wildspace druids (from unusual worlds in the SPELLJAMMER campaign), aquatic druids (tending ocean life on the continental shelves), aerial druids (living on semisolid cloud islands), and so on. Note that kits function within and in addition to branches.

Arctic Druid

Description: Arctic druids feel at home on the frozen polar tundra or on the slopes of snowcapped mountains and ancient glaciers.

They even venture at times across lifeless ice fields to assist lost animals. If an Ice Age took place in the distant past, arctic druids may very well claim to belong to the oldest druidic branch, tracing their ancestry all the way back to the days when humans huddled within caves.

Glydo, a typical arctic druid, (illustrated above) concerns himself more with animals than with plants. Guardian of caribou herds, penguins, auks, seals, polar bears, and other arctic and subarctic animals, he relentlessly pursues those who exploit animals out of desire for profit. However, he faithfully befriends hunters and trappers who respect the land and take from it no more than they need.

Minimum Ability Scores: Wisdom 12, Constitution 13, Charisma 15.

Races Allowed: Human, half-elf. *Optional*—alaghi (11).

Armor and Weapons Permitted: Leather armor, wooden shield; club, dagger, dart, harpoon, knife, sling, spear, staff. Arctic druids can use metallic weapons if they find them, but mining is extremely rare in arctic areas, making such items rare as well.

Weapon Proficiencies: *Recommended*—knife, harpoon, spear.

Nonweapon Proficiencies: *Required*—(general) fire-building, weather sense; (warrior) survival (arctic); *Recommended*—(general) animal handling, animal training, direction sense, fishing, swimming; (priest) ancient history, healing; (warrior) endurance, hunting, mountaineering, tracking.

Spheres of Influence: All, Animal, Divination*, Elemental, Healing, Plant*, Weather. (The arctic druid's minor access to the Plant sphere reflects the less abundant plant life in arctic climes.)

Druid Characters • 11

Granted Powers: An arctic druid like Glydo has the following granted powers:

• Receives a +2 bonus to all saving throws vs. cold-based attacks.

• Learns the languages of intelligent monsters whose natural habitats are tundra, arctic, and subarctic regions. The arctic druid gains one extra proficiency slot for this purpose every three levels (at 3rd, 6th, etc.). Such languages include those spoken by ettins, frost giants, ice toads, selkies, werebears, white dragons, winter wolves, verbeeg, yeti, and others.

• Ignores the effects of freezing weather upon himself at 3rd level.

• Identifies with perfect accuracy arctic plants and animals, thin ice (ice that would give way under the weight of a person or a sled), and pure water at 3rd level.

• Passes over ice and snow without leaving a trail and can move over such terrain at full movement rate at 3rd level.

• Shapechanges up to three times a day at 7th level. The druid can assume the form of a land mammal, marine mammal, or bird that dwells in arctic and subarctic climates: a caribou, penguin, polar bear, seal, reindeer, snowy owl, wolf, wolverine, and so on. The druid can't take the same animal's shape more than once each day.

Special Limitation: An arctic druid is used to a cold climate and suffers a –1 penalty to attack rolls, saving throws, and ability checks in environments with temperatures above 80 degrees Fahrenheit.

Holy Symbol and Grove: Glydo, as an arctic druid, uses as his holy symbol a bone of an arctic animal that has been carved into the shape of a knife, whistle, flute, or other instrument. If the druid dwells beyond the arctic tree line, he chooses as his "grove"— usually near a glacier—an ancient cave whose walls are covered with prehistoric paintings of animals.

Desert Druid

The deserts prove as inhospitable to most normal plant and animal life as the arctic regions. However, deserts remain vital to the worldwide order of druids.

Desert druids such as Otaq (pictured on p. 11) are either members of native nomad tribes or hermits who have moved to the desert to escape civilization. Valued for their abilities to heal sick animals (and people) and to find or create pure water, they normally remain on good terms with desert nomads. Although desert druids revere all the flora and fauna of a desert, from cacti and scorpions to vultures and camels, they most fiercely protect the few fertile oases, which house their sacred groves.

Desert druids also may reside in semidesert areas, hot scrub lands, and chaparral. Unless a DM sets a campaign in actual desert land, this branch best suits an NPC the party may encounter traveling through the wastes. Many desert druids live as hermits, not fond of disturbances, and can be short tempered or downright eccentric. However, no one can top their knowledge of their own desert area. If a party seeks something in the trackless wastes or finds itself lost, facing a sandstorm, or running out of food or water, a chance encounter with a desert druid like Otaq may spell salvation.

Minimum Ability Scores: Wisdom 12, Constitution 12, Charisma 15.

Races Allowed: Human.

Armor and Weapons Permitted: Leather armor, wooden shield; club, sickle, dart, spear, dagger, khopesh, scimitar, sling, short bow, staff.

Weapon Proficiencies: *Recommended*— scimitar, short bow, staff.

Nonweapon Proficiencies: *Required*— (general) direction sense, weather sense; (warrior) survival (desert). *Recommended*— (general) riding (land-based); (priest) healing, local history; (warrior) endurance, tracking.

Spheres of Influence: All, Animal, Divination*, Elemental (air, earth, fire), Elemental* (water), Healing, Plant*, Weather.

Granted Powers: A desert druid like Otaq has the following granted powers:

• Receives a +2 bonus to all saving throws vs. fire or electrical attacks.

• Goes without water for one day per level without suffering thirst. Regaining use of this power requires the druid to have resumed a normal intake of water for a time equal to the days of deprivation.

• Learns the languages of desert-dwelling intelligent creatures (brass dragons, dragonnes, lamias, thri-kreen, etc.), gaining one extra proficiency slot for this purpose every three levels (at 3rd, 6th, etc.).

• Infallibly identifies desert plants and animals and pure water at 3rd level.

• Sees through nonmagical mirages at 3rd level and gains a +4 on any roll to save against illusions cast within a desert.

• Crosses sands and dunes on foot without leaving a trail and at full movement rate at 3rd level.

• Senses the distance, direction, and size of the nearest natural water source (well, spring, oasis, sea, etc.) if one lies within 1 mile per level. This power, gained at 3rd level, is usable once per day.

• Shapechanges up to three times per day at 7th level, once each into a normal mammal, reptile, and bird. The druid can shapechange only into animals whose natural habitat is the desert. Common desert-dwelling animals include camels, eagles, hawks, lizards, mice, rats, snakes, and vultures. Otherwise, this power functions identically to that described in the *PH*, p. 37.

Special Limitation: None.

Holy Symbol and Grove: A desert druid's grove normally lies within a beautiful oasis in the deep desert. Branch members use as their holy symbol a vial of water from a sacred oasis, filled under a full moon.

Gray Druid

The rare gray druids inhabit and tend the shadowy realms of the hidden life that exists without sunlight—fungi, molds, and slimes—and the nocturnal creatures that dwell in lightless, subterranean realms. Gray druids are more closely associated with the earth than with other elements of Nature. While many of them live in underground caves or ruins (especially in the Underdark), they are found any place fungal life grows abundantly, either above or below ground.

Gray druids tend to oppose dungeon delvers, especially dwarves, who they believe defile and exploit the underground environment. They have very good relations with deep gnomes and passable relations with drow, who they feel show more appreciation of the beauty of the Underdark than most dwarves or men.

But the gray druids don't always oppose surface dwellers. Suppose a maze of caverns has developed a complex ecology: fungi, slimes, rust monsters, subterranean lizards, purple worms, and so on. Then an evil wizard and his ogres move in and begin "clearing" the caverns, destroying the monsters in preparation to establish an underground stronghold. In this situation, the gray druid Rybna (pictured on p. 11) might recruit a party of adventurers—not to loot the caverns (though the PCs may take the wizard's treasure) but to defeat the wizard's forces—and in so doing, save the local ecology from destruction.

Minimum Ability Scores: Wisdom 12, Charisma 15.

Races Allowed: Human, half-elf (drow).

Armor and Weapons Permitted: Leather armor, wooden shield; club, sickle, dart, spear, dagger, scimitar, sling, staff.

Weapon Proficiencies: *Recommended*—dart, scimitar.

Nonweapon Proficiencies: *Required*—

Druid Characters • 13

(general) direction sense; (priest) herbalism; (warrior) blind-fighting. *Recommended*—(general) animal training, fishing; (priest) ancient history, healing.

Spheres of Influence: All, Animal, Divination*, Elemental (earth, water), Elemental* (air, fire), Healing, Plant, Weather*.

Granted Powers: A gray druid like Rybna has the following granted powers:

• Identifies with perfect accuracy pure water, fungi, subterranean animals, and all slimes, puddings, jellies and molds (including monster types) at 3rd level.

• Learns the languages of subterranean creatures (orcs, goblins, troglodytes, xorn, etc.), gaining one extra proficiency slot every three levels (at 3rd, 6th, etc.) for this purpose.

• Controls fungi, jellies, molds, oozes, puddings, and slimes (nonintelligent or of animal Intelligence) at 7th level. The druid can use this power once per day to control 1 Hit Die of creatures per level. It affects only a 30-yard radius around the druid. For instance, Rybna, a 10th-level druid, could control two 5 HD slimes or one 10 HD pudding. The creatures receive no saving throw, but remain controlled only as long as they stay within 30 yards of the druid. An uncontrolled creature reverts to its normal behavior patterns. A gray druid like Rybna will not send a controlled monster to its death unless by doing so she can protect the subterranean ecology. This power does not animate a stationary entity or grant it any new abilities. (Rybna could command a shrieker to shriek or be silent or move, but not to sing or speak.) Control lasts for one turn per level of the druid.

• Shapechanges into a normal reptile, a normal mammal, or a nonpoisonous giant spider at 7th level; the druid can assume each form once per day. The druid can change only into a reptile or mammal that dwells underground, such as a mole, badger, tunnel snake, etc. The ability is otherwise identical to druidic shapechanging in the *PH*.

Special Limitation: Gray druid Animal sphere spells affect only animals native to subterranean environments. So, Rybna could cast *animal friendship* on a rat, a huge spider, or a badger, but not on a wolf or horse.

A gray druid has a –2 penalty on saving throws against spells creating bright light, such as *continual light*.

Due to long enmity, dwarves react to gray druids at –2. (The reverse is also true.)

Holy Symbol and Grove: Gray druids use a puffball mushroom grown and harvested in complete darkness as their holy symbol. They usually take part of an underground cavern—a thriving subterranean ecosystem—for a grove.

Forest Druid

The forest druid—the druid described in the *PH*—serves as the guardian of both the great forests of the wilderness and the smaller woodlands and orchards that lie next to cultivated fields in flat lands, rolling plains, or wooded hills. Forest druids hold trees (especially ash and oak) sacred and never destroy woodlands or crops, no matter what the situation (although a druid could act to change the *nature* of a wood enchanted with evil, for instance, without destroying it). The forest druid acts as a living bridge between the wilderness and those humans—such as hunters, loggers and trappers—who dwell on its borders.

As the player, you can choose to role-play one of two kinds of forest druids: one from a temperate deciduous forest, or one from a subarctic conifer forest. The former type is better known and more numerous on most worlds; though conifer forests grow to vast sizes, they exist within often hostile environments and lack the great variety in wildlife of warmer forests.

For quick reference, the information on the temperate-forest druid branch is repeated

here, along with suggested proficiencies. Unless otherwise noted, information applies to both temperate- and cold-forest druids.

Minimum Ability Scores: Wisdom 12, Charisma 15.

Races Allowed: Human, half-elf. *Optional*—alaghi (11), centaur (14), saurial (9), swanmay (12). (Only humans, half-elves, alaghi, and centaurs can become cold-forest druids.)

Armor and Weapons Permitted: Leather armor, wooden shield; club, sickle, dart, spear, dagger, scimitar, scythe, sling, staff.

Weapon Proficiencies: *Recommended*—any two of the above weapons.

Nonweapon Proficiencies: *Recommended*—(general) animal training; (priest) healing, herbalism; (warrior) animal lore, survival (forest), tracking.

Spheres of Influence: All, Animal, Divination*, Elemental, Healing, Plant, Weather.

Granted Powers: The forest druid has the following granted powers:

• Receives a +2 bonus to all saving throws vs. fire or electrical attacks.

• Learns the languages of woodland creatures (centaurs, dryads, elves, satyrs, gnomes, dragons, giants, lizard men, manticores, nixies, pixies, sprites, treants, etc.), gaining one extra proficiency slot for this purpose every three levels (at 3rd, 6th, etc.). (The languages of cold-forest druids include those of the giant lynx, giant owl, pine treants, and cold-dwelling groups of centaurs, elves, gnolls, gnomes, etc.)

• Identifies plants, animals, and pure water with perfect accuracy at 3rd level.

• Passes through overgrown areas at 3rd level without leaving a trail and at full movement rate. For instance, the temperate-forest druid Garon (pictured above) can move with ease through dense thorn bushes, briar patches, pine trees, tangled jungle vines, and

Druid Characters • 15

so on. He also is immune to poison ivy, poison oak, and similar irritating plants. When using this power, Garon must be on foot, not riding an animal.

• Has immunity to *charm* spells cast by woodland creatures such as dryads at 7th level. The druid's immunity does not extend to *charm* spells cast by creatures who merely happen to be living in or passing through a forest, such as a woods-dwelling human mage or vampire.

• Shapechanges into a normal, real-world reptile, bird, or mammal up to three times per day at 7th level, exactly as described in the *PH*. Each animal form (reptile, bird, or mammal) can be used only once per day. The druid cannot assume giant forms.

Special Limitation: See "Holy Symbol and Grove."

Holy Symbol and Grove: The grove of a forest druid is just that: a stand of hallowed trees. Druids of this branch—such as Gatha, a cold-forest druid (illustrated on p. 15)—use mistletoe as a holy symbol. For full effectiveness, Gatha must gather the mistletoe by the light of the full moon using a golden or silver sickle specially made for this task. If a spell requires a holy symbol and Gatha only has mistletoe harvested by other means, halve the damage and area of effect (if any) and add +2 to the target's saving throw (if applicable).

Jungle Druid

The protectors of tropical rain forests, jungle druids usually grow up in tribes, as jungle pests, vegetation, and climate discourage farming, herding, and city-building. Because most tribal members live closely attuned to the natural world, jungle druids have a greater likelihood of involving themselves directly in the affairs of humans than other druids might. In fact, a jungle druid like Sima (pictured on p. 15) usually holds a position of power and respect, wielding great political authority.

However, jungle druids do not associate themselves with a particular tribe or people, as do most tribal priests or witch doctors. Instead, they adopt a neutral position, mediating intertribal feuds and handling relations between human tribes and jungle-dwelling humanoids, demihumans, or intelligent monsters. In some cases, a great druid becomes a virtual "king of the jungle," wielding power over a coalition of several tribes, nonhumans, and animals.

Minimum Ability Scores: Wisdom 12, Charisma 15.

Races Allowed: Human. *Optional*—saurial (9).

Armor and Weapons Permitted: No armor, wooden shield; blowgun, club, dart, knife, spear, staff.

Weapon Proficiencies: *Recommended*—blowgun, knife.

Nonweapon Proficiencies: *Required*—(priest) healing, herbalism. *Recommended*—(general) animal taming, weather sense; (priest) local history; (warrior) survival (jungle), tracking.

Spheres of Influence: All, Animal, Divination*, Elemental, Healing, Plant, Weather.

Granted Powers: The jungle druid has the following granted powers:

• Passes through overgrown areas, such as thick jungle, without leaving a trail and at full movement rate.

• Learns the languages of tropical forest and swamp creatures (couatl, lizard men, naga, tasloi, yuan-ti, etc.), gaining one extra proficiency slot for this purpose every three levels (at 3rd, 6th, etc.).

• Identifies plants, animals, and pure water with perfect accuracy at 3rd level.

• Shapechanges into a normal (not giant) reptile, bird, or mammal up to three times per day at 7th level. The druid can use each animal form (reptile, bird, or mammal) only once per day and can choose from only those animals that make their normal habitat within

jungles or tropical swamps.

Special Limitation: None.

Holy Symbol and Grove: The jungle druid uses a tom-tom (jungle drum) as a holy symbol. Constructing a replacement takes two weeks. The grove is usually a circle of trees, often near a waterfall.

Mountain Druid

The mountain druid dwells in areas of rugged hills, alpine forests, and peaks and rocks above the tree line. Members of this branch, such as Dansil (illustrated on p. 19), wield over their environments a power gained from the element of earth and especially from stone. They also draw power from the weather, especially storms and clouds. Dansil and his fellows protect mountains and alpine flora and fauna from those who would exploit them. This role frequently brings them into conflict with miners, especially dwarves. Mountain druids often ally themselves with storm and stone giants, which further angers dwarves.

Minimum Ability Scores: Strength 9, Wisdom 12, Charisma 15.

Races Allowed: Human, half-elf.

Armor and Weapons Permitted: Leather armor, wooden shield; club, sickle, dart, spear, dagger, scimitar, sling, staff.

Weapon Proficiencies: *Recommended*—club, sling, spear.

Nonweapon Proficiencies: *Required*—(warrior) mountaineering, survival (mountain). *Recommended*—(general) animal training; (priest) healing, herbalism; (warrior) animal lore.

Spheres of Influence: All, Animal, Divination*, Elemental (earth, air), Elemental* (fire, water) Healing, Plant, Weather.

Granted Powers: The mountain druid has the following granted powers:

• Receives a +4 bonus to all saving throws vs. electrical attacks and to mountaineering proficiency checks.

• Gains a modifier of +3 to experience level when determining the effects of a spell from the Elemental (earth or air) or Weather spheres cast while in the mountains.

For instance, say Dansil, a 5th-level mountain druid, cast the Weather spell *obscurement* while in his mountain environs. That spell, which has effects normally lasting 20 rounds (four rounds per level), has an adjusted duration of 32 rounds, as though Dansil were 8th level. Modify its normal area of effect of 50 feet × 50 feet (10 feet × 10 feet per level) to 80 feet × 80 feet.

• Senses avalanches, volcanic eruptions, and rockfalls one turn before they happen when the player rolls 1 to 5 on 1d6. This ability also enables the druid to detect deadfall traps and falling blocks on a roll of 1 to 3 on 1d6.

• Learns the languages of mountain-dwelling sentient creatures (such as dwarves, red dragons, stone or storm giants, etc.), gaining one extra proficiency slot for this purpose every three levels (at 3rd, 6th, etc.).

• Identifies plants, animals, and pure water with perfect accuracy at 3rd level.

• Shapechanges into a normal, real-world reptile, bird, or mammal up to three times per day at 7th level, exactly as described in the *PH*. Each animal form (reptile, bird, or mammal, excluding giant forms) can be used only once per day.

Special Limitation: None.

Holy Symbol and Grove: The mountain druid uses an eagle feather as a holy symbol. The grove of a druid (such as Dansil) usually lies in the higher elevations, often a glade near a beautiful waterfall on a slope or an ancient circle of standing stones on a peak.

Plains Druid

The plains druid lives on open grasslands with few or no trees: temperate prairies and

pampas, hot veldts and savannas, cool steppes, and the like. Yalla is such a druid. (See illustration next page.) She often finds herself in the company of nomadic hunters and herders. Her powers and interests resemble those of a forest druid, but she has a closer interest in the weather and the health of great herds roaming her lands than in trees and crops. Second only to the forest branch, plains druids remain among the most common and best known of all druids.

Minimum Ability Scores: Wisdom 12, Charisma 15.

Races Allowed: Human, half-elf. *Optional* —centaur (14).

Armor and Weapons Permitted: Leather armor, wooden shield; club, sickle, dart, spear, dagger, scimitar, scythe, sling, staff.

Weapon Proficiencies: *Recommended*— club, sling, spear.

Nonweapon Proficiencies: *Required*— (general) riding (land-based), weather sense; (warrior) animal lore, tracking. *Recommended* —(general) animal handling, animal training; (priest) healing; (warrior) endurance, hunting, survival (plains/steppes).

Spheres of Influence: All, Animal, Divination*, Elemental (air, earth, fire), Elemental* (water), Healing, Plant, Weather.

Granted Powers: Yalla, a typical plains druid, possesses these granted powers:

• Receives a +2 bonus to all saving throws vs. fire and electrical attacks (due to this branch's need to fight such natural dangers as prairie fires, lightning strikes, etc.).

• Has a +4 bonus to any animal handling, animal lore, or animal training proficiency checks concerning plains-dwelling herd beasts or riding animals.

• Learns the languages of plains-dwelling sentient creatures (such as centaurs), gaining an extra proficiency slot for this purpose every three levels (at 3rd, 6th, etc.).

• Identifies plants, animals, and pure water with perfect accuracy at 3rd level.

• Speaks with any land animals that humans can ride, as well as plains-dwelling herd animals, at 3rd level as though she had cast a *speak with animals* spell.

• Shapechanges into a normal, real-world reptile, bird, or mammal common to the plains up to three times per day at 7th level, exactly as described in the *PH*. Yalla can use each animal form (reptile, bird, and mammal) only once per day and cannot assume giant forms.

Special Limitation: None.

Holy Symbol and Grove: Plains druids typically wear their holy symbol: a diadem or arm band woven from prairie grass under a full moon. They often choose as their grove a circle of standing stones on the open grass.

Swamp Druid

The swamp druid's role centers around guarding marshes, fens, bogs, wetlands, and swamps, as well as the abundant plant and animal life within them. Willoo, an average swamp druid (pictured next page), resembles a normal forest druid, but his particular habitat makes him less socially acceptable. He opposes anyone who would drain his swamp in the name of "progress," even if such land were needed for farming or urban construction. Swamp druids often live as hermits; the more sociable among them sometimes serve as priests for outlaws hiding in the swamps or for lizard men who lack their own shamans.

Minimum Ability Scores: Wisdom 12, Charisma 12.

Races Allowed: Human. *Optional*—saurial (9).

Armor and Weapons Permitted: Leather armor, wooden shield; club, dagger, dart, khopesh, scimitar, scythe, sickle, sling, spear, staff.

Weapon Proficiencies: *Recommended*—any two of the above.

Nonweapon Proficiencies: *Required*—(general) swimming; (priest) herbalism; (warrior) survival (swamp). *Recommended*— (general) seamanship (for small boats), weather sense; (priest) healing, local history; (warrior) animal lore.

Spheres of Influence: All, Animal, Divination*, Elemental (earth, water), Elemental* (air, fire), Healing, Plant, Weather.

Granted Powers: A swamp druid has the following granted powers:

• Has an immunity to insect-transmitted diseases common to swamps, such as malaria, and a +2 bonus on saving throws vs. any other diseases.

• Receives a +1 reaction adjustment from normal animals that live in swamps (such as crocodiles) and from monsters whose habitat is a swamp or marsh—for instance, black dragons, bullywugs, and lizard men.

• Learns the languages of intelligent humanoids and monsters that inhabit the swamp (black dragons, bullywugs, lizard men, shambling mounds, will o' wisps, etc.), gaining one extra proficiency slot for this purpose every three levels (at 3rd, 6th, etc.). (Note that to "speak" with a will o' wisp, a swamp druid needs a light source, such as a hooded lantern, to signal with.)

• Identifies plants, animals, and pure water with perfect accuracy at 3rd level.

• Passes through overgrown areas and mud at the full movement rate without leaving a trail at 3rd level. The swamp druid can use this power to cross quicksand without sinking.

• Uses the *animal friendship* spell (which usually affects only normal or giant animals) at 5th level to influence semi-intelligent swamp-dwelling monsters or those of animal Intelligence. The effects on such monsters,

Druid Characters • 19

including catoblepas, hydra, lernaean hydra, and pyrohydra, remain those of *animal friendship*. The druid has to want to befriend the monster, not use it as sword-fodder.

• Shapechanges into a normal reptile, bird, or mammal up to three times per day at 7th level. The druid can assume only the form of real-world creatures that live in swamps or wetlands (crocodile, frog, marsh bird, snake, etc.). The druid can adopt each animal form (reptile, bird, or mammal) once per day.

• Casts an *insect plague* (as the spell) once per day at 7th level. This power works only when the druid is within the boundaries of a swamp or marsh.

Special Limitation: Willoo's clothes, like those of most swamp druids, frequently look caked with mud and often drip with swamp water. He always has a faint odor of the swamp about him. His lack of cleanliness gives him a –1 penalty to reaction adjustment from most people and a –3 penalty regarding upper-class individuals, such as gentry or nobles.

Holy Symbol and Grove: The grove usually lies deep within a marsh or swamp—a stand of beautiful mangroves, weeping willows, swamp oak, or the like. Many groves are actually islands, sometimes guarded by natural traps such as quicksand. A swamp druid uses as a holy symbol a vial of water from a sacred swamp grove.

Multi- and Dual-Class Druids

This section elaborates on the options for players who wish to role-play multi- or dual-class druids. The choices and descriptions are culled from a variety of sources, including the *PH* and *DMG*.

Multi-Class Druids

Only half-elves can be multi-class druids. Multi-class druids must abide by the weapon, shield, and armor restrictions of their branches. The *PH* (pgs. 22, 44) mentions the half-elf's options of druid/fighter, druid/ranger, druid/mage, and druid/fighter/mage. (Some earlier printings incorrectly cite only the druid/fighter combination on p. 44.)

Druid/Fighter. The core AD&D rules permit the druid/fighter.

Druid/Ranger. The core AD&D rules permit the druid/ranger. *The Complete Ranger's Handbook*, p. 79, gives guidelines for playing such characters: A Nature deity of good alignment must exist whose specialty priests are all druids. This priesthood must ally with a group of rangers. Any half-elf druid/ranger must obey the level limits for demihumans (*DMG*, p. 15), making it unlikely for the character to compete for high levels of druidic power. The druid/ranger's multiple interests antagonize conservative druids, and the character usually suffers from divided loyalties. (Create a similar character with fewer problems by giving a druid/fighter the Avenger or Beastfriend kit, described in the next chapter.)

Druid/Mage and Druid/Fighter/Mage. The core AD&D rules permit the druid/mage and druid/fighter/mage. While these combinations exist, they remain rare and require the DM's permission. They cannot wear armor or use shields, and must limit their weapons to those permitted to druids.

Dual-Class Druids

All normal rules for dual-class characters apply to druids. The druid's restriction to neutral alignment limits the options to bard/druid, fighter/druid, wizard/druid, and thief/druid. Some druids prefer to see the upper ranks of the Order filled by "pure" druids—those who have devoted their lives solely to the Order. Dual-class characters sometimes face prejudice from other druids.

Fighter/druids. Often acting as wandering guardians of Nature and country folk (much like neutral rangers), fighter/druids also can become hermit-knights, living away from society and defending a particular grove with their lives. Fighters who become druids often do so because they seek spiritual growth, because they have grown disgusted with the world of man, or occasionally as penance for a particular misdeed.

Druids who become fighters, on the other hand, want to take a more direct approach to defending the wilderness; others seek to attune themselves to Nature by mastering their own bodies using eastern-style fighting arts, often becoming rather enigmatic Zenlike warrior-mystics.

Wizard/druids. Looked upon with deep suspicion by most other druids, wizard/druids generally find themselves stereotyped as untrustworthy or scheming. Conservative elements within the druidic order often attempt to block wizard/druids from reaching 12th level. If they fail, they deliberately encourage rising druids to challenge the dual-class character to a duel in preference to other targets.

Wizards usually become druids for philosophical reasons: either a fear that unrestrained use of magical or divine forces threatens the cosmic balance, or a desire to learn the druidic arts to better understand the workings of Nature. Druids who study wizardry most often see this magic as another part of Nature to study and master.

Thief/druids. Such combinations appear rarely, since the city serves as the optimum home base for the thief. As with wizard/druids, people tend to distrust thief/druids. A druid who becomes a thief usually does so after becoming disillusioned with the druidic order. A thief becomes a druid usually as the result of highly unusual circumstances—an outlaw flees to the wilderness to escape pursuit only to befriend a local druid, come to love Nature, and decide to adopt a new way of life.

High-level Dual-Class Druids. A dual-class character who achieved a high level as a fighter or wizard before becoming a druid has an edge in the challenge a druid faces to advance beyond 11th level. For fairness, the Order generally bans such player characters from initiating challenges; they can gain experience levels above 11th only to fill a vacancy.

DMs with a taste for political intrigue may permit an exception if the character receives special dispensation from the druidic order. This means a dual-class druid must have a sponsor: in theory, a higher-level druid who attests to the character's fairness and commitment to the Order. In practice, the sponsor is often a druid who wants a dangerous rival removed and believes the dual-class character has a good chance of doing so! In the case of wizard/druids, however, the Order often (but not always) forbids wizard spells during the challenge.

A peculiar situation can occur if a character has achieved 12th to 15th level as a druid, then adopts another class. In effect, such characters have "dropped out" of the Order. Although inactive as druids, they retain their former Hit Dice and hit points. When they wish to use their druidic powers again (after achieving one level more in the new class than their druid level), they must challenge an incumbent for the high-level druidic position they once held.

A dual-class character who loses the challenge must drop a level, as usual—but then may face another challenge and another, until the player character eventually wins a position or falls to 11th level. As a result of this danger, dual-class player characters usually prefer to switch classes before reaching 12th level or after exceeding 15th level.

Agriculture: Expanded Rules

The DM may use this expansion of the agriculture proficiency when druid characters assist a small village facing tough times or if a PC takes up farming. These rules can figure the prosperity of an entire village if the DM groups area farms together and uses the proficiency rating of the village leader or druid with Tables 1 and 2. Before applying the following rules, the DM must decide how many people the farm in question is designed to support.

A medieval farm needs a manager with the agriculture proficiency. At optimum level, a farm has one worker per every two people it supports. A farm with more workers may produce a slight surplus; if it has fewer workers, it will yield less, since the crew would have more chores than hands. Children between ages 7 and 11 count as half a worker each, and those 12 and older each count as another full worker.

How Did the Farm Perform?

To quickly determine the success of a farm (or garden or village) for the year, the DM looks at the number of people it can support. For instance, a family farm might produce enough to support six people. If the family has five members, the farm shows a profit. With six, the farm merely scrapes by. A family of seven is starting to get hungry.

Figuring Farm Profitability

DMs wanting more precise details about a farm's performance can follow these steps:

1. Determine Proficiency Base. Every year the DM rolls 1d6 and adds the result to the farmer's Intelligence score. Then, the DM locates the farmer's adjusted agriculture proficiency rating (base score) on Table 1.

TABLE 1: **Farm Rating**

Base Score	Farm Profitability
1–5	Disastrous year
6–10	Poor yield
11–16	Average harvest
17 and up	Bumper crop

2. Apply the Worker Modifier. The number of farm workers modifies the base proficiency score. For each 10% by which the farm crew falls below its optimum number of workers, the DM applies a –1 penalty to the base score in Table 1. If the farm has 20% more workers than optimum, the DM adds a +1 bonus to the base score in Table 1. (Having more workers gives no extra bonus.)

3. Figure the Random Events Modifier. As any farmer would tell you, what makes the farming life interesting is Nature's eternal cussedness: random events. The DM should

roll on Table 2 to see what's in store for the farm, then apply the random events modifier to the adjusted base score.

Table 2: Farm Random Events

d20	Event	Check Modifier
1	Ruinous weather	–6
2–3	Bad weather	–4
4–6	Animal disease	–2
7–8	Building damaged	–2
9	Predators	–1
10	Poachers or bandits	–1
11–14	No bad news	0
15–17	Used good seed	+1
18–19	Good weather	+2
20	Special	DM

Note that often the actions of the farmers (or PCs helping them) and available priestly or druidic spells can reduce the penalty from random events. See the descriptions below:

• Ruinous weather may include flooding or a long drought. A successful weather sense proficiency check by the farmer halves the penalty. (The farmer had advance warning and prepared for the weather.) If the farmer knows a druid to use the *control weather* spell, the DM can negate the penalty.

• Bad weather might mean an early frost, a slight drought, or excessive rain. The weather sense proficiency and *control weather* work as in "ruinous weather," above.

• A disease breaks out among the farm's domestic creatures. A successful healing proficiency check (one try) by the farmer halves the penalty; the *cure disease* spell negates this penalty.

• Building damage may result from a severe storm, fire, or other disaster. The penalty applies only if the farmer cannot afford to fix things, and continues to apply every year until repairs are made. Paying 10 gp for every person the farm supports "repairs" each penalty point.

• Predators, poachers, or bandits repeatedly steal food or animals. If PCs negotiate with, drive off, or destroy the menace(s), the penalty does not apply.

• A special roll means something unusual occurs. Perhaps a wizard war or a dragon devastates the farm—apply –10 to all checks this year! If a god's avatar stops by and blesses the crops, apply +5 to farm rolls.

Note: A *plant growth* spell can add 20% to 50% to a farm's annual yield (*PH*, p. 212).

4. Find the Farm's Profitability. After applying the worker and random events modifiers to the base proficiency score, the DM determines profitability using Table 1. A disastrous year means the farm produces 50% less than it should. A poor harvest yields 20% less than normal. An average year means the farm produces at capacity. Finally, a bumper crop comes to 20% above normal yield. (Normal yield is the amount required to feed those the farm supports.)

The Harvest's Cash Value

DMs also can measure farm productivity in cash terms. The value of the harvest equals the number of people the farm can support times 36 gp (the minimum annual cost of living for a person in squalid conditions—*DMG*, p. 34). The DM subtracts the yearly cost of living of the farmer and workers from the harvest value, leaving the farm's profit. With this information, the DM can see if any families are starving and how much aid would get them back on their feet.

Determining a farm's profitability can provide role-playing opportunities for druids in a party. The guidelines of many branches and kits require druids to offer aid to farms and villages in need. In the course of helping, the druid can stumble on a number of adventure hooks. DMs can even design whole campaigns around a party's effort to get a farming village back on its feet.

CHAPTER 2

Druid Kits

A *kit* is a collection of proficiencies, restrictions, hindrances, and benefits intended to make a druid more colorful. A kit helps you, the player, create a detailed personality and background for your PC, which makes the character fit easily into the DM's campaign.

Using Kits

A druid kit works with the basic *PH* druid or with any of the branches described in the previous chapter. Thus, a desert druid could be a Savage (coming from a primitive desert tribe), a Wanderer (traveling the desert wastes), a Guardian (protecting a certain oasis), or some other kit.

Branch and Kit

When building your druid character, choose the branch first, as it has specific ability score requirements. After that, pick from any of the applicable kits. However, make sure you have enough proficiency slots to take the weapon and nonweapon proficiencies required by both the branch and the kit—although in many cases branch/kit proficiency requirements overlap.

DM Restrictions

Prior to letting players select kits, the DM should examine each kit and decide whether it fits the overall campaign. The DM might want to restrict some kits to NPCs or prohibit others altogether.

The DM also may wish to make changes or add material to some kits, to better match the conditions of a particular campaign. Take the Savage druid, for instance. If the campaign already features a primitive tribe of, say, pearl divers, the DM might adjust the Savage kit to fit established details of that tribe's cultural background—for instance, the DM might make swimming a required or bonus proficiency.

Reaction Bonuses and Penalties

Druid kits occasionally receive reaction bonuses or penalties as part of their special benefits and hindrances. A reaction adjustment due to either the druid kit's requirements or an extreme Charisma score (*PH*, p. 18) is expressed as a bonus (+1, +2, etc.) or a penalty (–1, –2, etc.).

When rolling 2d10 for encounter reactions (Table 59, *DMG*, p. 103), the DM must *subtract* the bonus or *add* the penalty—not the other way around. For instance, the druid Snapdragon has a combined +7 reaction adjustment bonus for her high Charisma and her druid kit. The DM then subtracts 7 from the 2d10 encounter reaction roll to reflect the bonus, due to the way Table 59 in the *DMG* is designed.

Kits and the Character Record Sheet

To record a druid kit on your character record sheet (pgs. 125–127), take the following steps:

• Add the name of the druid kit following the druid's branch. For instance, a druid with the Hivemaster kit and the plains druid branch would be written as: plains druid (Hivemaster).

• When recording the character's proficiencies, put an asterisk next to those the character received free through the druid kit. This will help you and your DM remember how many proficiencies the character is due.

• Where you have space (on the back of your character sheet or on a separate piece of paper), write down the kit's special benefits, hindrances, and any other features you wish to recall quickly. You also can use the space provided on a copy of the druid character sheets.

A Look at Druid Kits

This section provides a short explanation of the structure of kit entries. The entries themselves follow in alphabetical order.

Kit Structure

Each kit entry begins with a description discussing the nature of the kit and listing any special requirements a character needs to take it. (For instance, to live as a Savage druid, the character must have been born into—or adopted by—a primitive tribe.) This description introduces an archetype character designed to demonstrate general attributes of the kit, *not* to serve as a character you, the player, have to role-play in a campaign. A character of either gender can take any kit.

The kit entries also include the following sections:

Role. Role-playing suggestions are offered, as druids of varying kits can play widely different roles in a campaign.

Branch Restrictions. If a member of a specific druidic branch cannot take this kit, that restriction is noted.

Weapon Proficiencies. A druid with the kit in question should take *recommended* proficiencies but must take *required* ones.

Secondary Skills. If your DM uses the rules for secondary skills, you may choose from Table 36 (*PH*, p. 53) or select one of the choices listed here, in addition to those skills appropriate to the character's druidic branch.

Nonweapon Proficiencies. A given druid kit usually *requires* the character to choose certain nonweapon proficiencies. Sometimes a proficiency merely is *recommended*—the character doesn't have to take it. Often kits offer a *bonus* proficiency, which does not use up a proficiency slot. Druids can take both priest and warrior proficiencies at normal cost (*PH*, pgs. 54–55).

Equipment. A few druid kits limit the type

and amount of equipment the character can start with, acquire, or use.

Special Benefits. This paragraph details additional abilities of druids with this kit.

Special Hindrances. This section discusses any kit's restrictions, limitations, or disadvantages.

Wealth Options. Usually the character starts with the priest's standard 3d6×10 gp.

Adviser

As a druid, your character can act as (or work to become) counselor to a ruler—perhaps a local knight or a high king. Think of Merlin, whom older tales cast as a druid.

An Adviser like the druid Elam (pictured above) tries to make himself indispensable to his lord. The class's well-known neutrality makes a ruler perceive his advice as nonpartisan, while the druid's high Charisma almost

guarantees that the lord listens to his counsel. Elam can use his "eyes in the wilderness" (described in Chapter 4: Role-playing Druids) to provide his master with timely and vital information.

At the same time, the druid subtly manipulates his master to serve his own ends. For example, Elam might encourage his lord to hunt in a beautiful forest the druid wishes to protect. Why? Because Elam knows the lord is a jealous man. Once he sees the beautiful forest and its fine animals, the lord will pass a law making the forest a royal game preserve. As a result, the lord's foresters will keep poachers away and prevent peasants from cutting the trees down. The ruler and his courtiers will hunt there only once or twice a year—not enough to threaten the animals seriously.

For similar reasons, a druidic Adviser like Elam might take over part of the education of the lord's children, ostensibly to teach them herb lore, history, survival, and similar skills. Actually, he uses the opportunity to instill in them a respect for Nature and the neutral world view—and perhaps encourage them to become druids when they grow up.

Role: As an Adviser, Elam is a man of subtlety and mystery. He rarely speaks unless he has something important to say, and he always thinks carefully before he says it. While not a fixture at his lord's court, he keeps an eye on things from a distance, often using animals to observe the ruler. He tends to pop up when most needed or least expected, stay a day or a month, then vanish into the wilds.

Always hungry for information, Elam often roams the land disguised as a common traveler (or, at high level, in animal form), listening to the gossip of peasants, traders, and innkeepers to better serve his own interests and those of his lord. As a PC, he carefully considers the purpose and long-term ramifications of each adventure and insists on careful preparation and information gathering before taking action.

Branch Restrictions: None.

Weapon Proficiencies: *Recommended*—staff.

Secondary Skills: Scribe.

Nonweapon Proficiencies: *Bonus*—etiquette. *Recommended*—(general) heraldry, weather sense; (priest) healing, local history, spellcraft; (rogue, double slot) reading lips; (rogue, one slot, per "Special Benefits") disguise.

Equipment: The Adviser need not spend all starting money on equipment, but can retain any leftover coinage.

Special Benefits: As an Adviser, Elam can purchase the rogue's disguise proficiency at normal rather than double cost. He stays free at the ruler's stronghold (no cost of living), and has the ear of the ruler.

The DM should establish an NPC ruler for the druid to advise. Help the DM develop a reason why the ruler trusts the PC, beyond his druidic background. Perhaps Elam is a relative (a cousin and younger son who failed to inherit and so joined the druidic order), or the apprentice of a (recently deceased) older druid who used to tutor the lord. For play balance, the DM should place a 1st-level player character as only one of several counselors to a lord of a small domain—perhaps a knightly manor or a barony. (If you, the player, really want to role-play an Adviser to a king, make it an exiled king trying to regain his crown.) It's up to the PC to increase the lord's influence.

Special Hindrances: People of the lord's domain (and immediate neighbors) easily recognize Elam as the court druid. If the lord favors him or if the populace knows him to give good advice, many will ask him to intercede for them with the lord. In addition, he may become a target for his lord's enemies or jealous rival courtiers.

On the other hand, if Elam fails to please his master, he will find himself in disfavor at court: He suffers a minimum –2 reaction penalty from the lord and court—possibly from all in the region (if his bad advice led to a spectacular failure, like defeat on the battlefield). Depending on the lord's temper, an Adviser who has fallen into disfavor may face exile or worse until he makes amends.

Wealth Options: 3d6×10 gp.

Avenger

The Avenger druid has seen Nature suffer great wrongs. Take the case of the druid Torrens. (See illustration.) He had hoped to live as a Guardian or Village Druid (listed later in this chapter). However, during his training, forces defiled the area under his protection and slew his mentor. Maybe he feels he was too gentle, too weak. It doesn't matter. He won't let it happen again.

Torrens the Avenger no longer holds the defensive. Instead, he roams the world seeking wrongs to right and foes to fight. And whether his opponent is a brutal king cutting down an ancient forest to build a fleet of war galleys, or an evil vampire menacing a peaceful halfling village, the Avenger acts to stop him. Permanently.

Role: This druid is a grim, strong, and silent warrior of the wilds. Torrens has little time for anything but his mission, although he's as patient as a spider when it serves his plans. A loner, he avoids love or friendship, fearing either could compromise his mission; if he associates with a party of adventurers, he treats them as allies, but not as friends.

The Avenger rarely speaks more than absolutely necessary to humans and most demihumans (although he may talk to animals or sylvan races like wood elves). He doesn't bother to explain or justify his actions. The Avenger dislikes remaining in one place, and frequently moves on after finishing a particular job.

Branch Restrictions: None.

Weapon Proficiencies: *Recommended*—scimitar, spear.

Secondary Skills: Hunting, weaponsmith.

Nonweapon Proficiencies: *Bonus*— tracking. *Recommended*—(general) animal training; (priest) herbalism; (warrior) animal lore, endurance, set snares, survival.

Equipment: The druid should spend his initial allotment of gold pieces entirely on equipment, for he loses any unspent starting money in excess of 1 gp.

Special Benefits: The Avenger receives an additional *free* weapon proficiency slot to use for any proficiency his branch allows.

Special Hindrances: The druid's grim and silent demeanor gives the character a –1 penalty to reaction adjustment from people in encounters. Torrens, like all Avengers, cannot have henchmen, hirelings, mercenaries, or servants until he reaches 13th level. He can have any amount of treasure, but cannot own

more treasure and equipment than he can carry on his back—any excess must go to a worthy cause.

Wealth Options: 3d6×10 gp.

Beastfriend

A deep—perhaps instinctive— knowledge of the habits, actions, and behavior of animals comes naturally to a Beastfriend. Lasell, a typical Beastfriend character (pictured on the next page) feels quite protective of animals and fiercely punishes those who inflict unnecessary harm upon them. She has nothing against people hunting for food (which, after all, animals also do) but considers hunting for sport repugnant and the use of animals in gladiatorial games a horrible crime.

Role: A Beastfriend like Lasell spends most of her time in the company of animals. In fact, she lives so much of her life around animals that sometimes she lacks social graces among humans. Many Beastfriends are gruff and hostile, preferring the company of honest natural creatures to deceitful humans, demihumans, and humanoids; others like people, but feel shy or tongue-tied around them and sometimes behave with poor manners. Lasell, like most with her kit, usually travels with one or more animal companions to whom she feels especially devoted.

Branch Restrictions: None.

Weapon Proficiencies: *Recommended*—staff.

Secondary Skills: Groom, hunter.

Nonweapon Proficiencies: *Bonus*— animal lore. *Recommended*—(general) animal handling, animal training, riding (land-based), riding (airborne); (priest) healing.

Equipment: The druid should spend her initial allotment of gold pieces entirely on equipment, as she loses any unspent starting money in excess of 1 gp.

Special Benefits: If Lasell, as a Beastfriend, carefully but fearlessly approaches a tamed or untamed animal, she can try to modify the beast's reaction. The druid can affect only natural animals—that is, those found in the real world (bears, wolves, snakes, etc.), as well as giant or magically enlarged versions of normal animals. When dealing with a nonhostile or domestic animal, the druid can approach and befriend it automatically. Wild beasts or animals trained to fight (like attack dogs or war horses) get a saving throw vs. rods to resist the druid at a minimum penalty of –1. An additional –1 penalty applies for every four full levels the druid has achieved: –2 at 4th level, –3 at 8th, etc. (The druid's power is not magical, though.) If the animal fails to save, the druid may choose to shift its reaction one category either direction on Table 56 (*DMG*, p. 103).

The Beastfriend receives a +4 bonus on animal lore, animal training, and animal handling proficiency checks. If she does not have the actual proficiency, she can function as if she did, without the +4 bonus.

If Lasell, as a Beastfriend, casts an Animal sphere spell on an animal, the subject saves against it at a –2 penalty.

Thanks to her knowledge of animals, a Beastfriend can recognize a lycanthrope (whether in human or animal form) on a successful animal lore check. The Beastfriend notes subtle differences in the behavior of a lycanthrope in animal form compared to a normal animal; she also notices subliminal clues in the movement and behavior of a lycanthrope in human form that point to its animal nature. The Beastfriend may make her one check only after she has been in the lycanthrope's presence for a round.

Special Hindrances: A Beastfriend does everything she can to help and treat a hurt animal or free an abused one and will kill an animal only to put a dying beast out of its misery. A Beastfriend who has come to know an animal may not harm it, allow others to hurt it, or send it suicidally into harm's way.

In general, the Beastfriend does not recruit animals specifically as bodyguards; rather, she accumulates friends and pets, who may choose to do favors for her, such as scouting or defending her. In return, the druid feeds and shelters them, heals their injuries, and rescues them from captivity.

As with all Beastfriends, Lasell's lack of social grace prevents her from learning the etiquette proficiency and gives her a –1 penalty to encounter reactions with those of her own race (except another with her kit).

Wealth Options: 3d6×8 gp. Beastfriends have little interest in civilized matters such as money, and seldom venture into towns.

Guardian

Some druids establish themselves as the guardians of a particular place—the habitat of an endangered species, a stand of ancient trees, the lair of a dryad, or a sacred grove. Often the druid watches over a sacred grove with magical powers that others try to exploit for selfish or evil purposes.

The DM should decide the extent of the Guardian's responsibility—usually one druid protects no more than a few acres of wilderness—and establish why the area needs special druidic attention. For instance, a mountaintop might serve as the nesting place of a rare breed of hawks prized by nobles as hunting falcons, forcing the druid to continually guard against those who want to steal the chicks or eggs.

A druid with the Guardian kit may act as the protector of several places in a lifetime. Say the druidic order places Wazir, a low-level Guardian druid, in charge of a nonmagical grove. If he fulfills his charge (and rises to at least 3rd level), the Order may grant him the responsibility of a magical grove, while a lower-level druid takes over his old position.

In order to abandon this kit, a Guardian like Wazir has to find someone else (usually a druid of similar level) to take over his guardianship. He must abandon the kit involuntarily if someone destroys or irreparably desecrates his grove. In this case, the Guardian might become a Lost Druid or devote his life to revenge as an Avenger.

Role: A Guardian lives deep in the wilderness, away from humanity. Like most Guardians, Wazir normally feels wary of strangers, suspecting that they come to exploit or threaten the site he defends.

Some Guardians can become fiercely protective: If Wazir were to witness the near-extinction of a particular species of plant or animal, the last few examples of which now live only in his grove, he could grow into an angry and ruthless protector. Such druids may strike out without warning to frighten off or kill intruders or even may make pacts with local monsters to protect the grove.

Other Guardians are simply shy hermits who welcome good-intentioned visitors. Perhaps Wazir lives as a lonely, dedicated sentinel; he misses human contact, but his strong sense of duty prevents him from leaving his post undefended.

Frequently, a Guardian goes years without seeing another human; Wazir may have as his only friends just the animal or nonhuman residents of his protectorate. As a result, he may seem eccentric or awkward relating to humans —even other druids.

Branch Restrictions: None.

Weapon Proficiencies: *Recommended*—staff.

Secondary Skills: Hunter.

Nonweapon Proficiencies: *Bonus*—local history (of his guardianship). *Recommended*—(priest) herbalism, ancient history, religion; (warrior) animal lore, set snares.

Equipment: The druid should spend his initial allotment of gold pieces entirely on equipment, as he loses any unspent starting money in excess of 1 gp.

Special Benefits: The druid receives a +1

bonus on saving throws and attack rolls when fighting to protect his guardianship. Enemies suffer a –2 penalty to saving throws while they remain in this protectorate.

As a Guardian, Wazir receives the respect of other druids (+1 reaction adjustment) in his circle. (See Chapter 3: The Druidic Order for more on circles.)

Although not all Guardians serve as warders of sacred or magical groves, some receive this responsibility. (For details on these special sites, see Chapter 6: Sacred Groves.) A low-level druid character should watch over a grove with no more than one lesser power. In addition, the DM must come up with a good reason why a magical grove falls into the hands of a low-level druid; perhaps the original Guardian, the PC's mentor, met with an unexpected fate while still grooming the character to take over.

Whenever a grove has any special abilities, the DM always should take care to limit the power they give the druid. For instance, a grove containing a magical pear tree with unique golden-hued fruit that gives the eater the effect of a *treasure finding* potion could unbalance a campaign. Perhaps the tree produces only one such magical pear a year—the remaining fruit is normal, although exceptionally succulent. When the special fruit ripens, the druid must turn it over to a messenger from the great druid.

Special Hindrances: The druid needs to guard a site containing something others eventually will want. The DM should encourage the player to have the character devote some time to defending the place, setting up magical or normal traps, checking with animal spies, and so on.

If the druid, such as Wazir, fails in his guardianship, he becomes seriously depressed. He suffers a –1 penalty on all attack rolls, saving throws, and ability and proficiency checks until he recovers from his loss. He also loses standing in the Order (–2 reaction penalty from other druids in the region, instead of the previous +1 bonus). Wazir cannot recover from this depression until 1d4+1 years pass *and* he performs some action to atone for his failure.

For instance, if a dragon destroyed the ancient stand of elder trees Wazir guarded, he must either defeat the dragon or find a way to restore the forest to life.

Wealth Options: 3d6×10 gp.

Hivemaster

The Hivemaster druid lives to foster insectoid and arachnid life wherever it exists. Most low-level Hivemasters, such as Cagua (pictured on the next page) work as beekeepers or the like.

Role: Hivemasters appear somewhat enigmatic. Many attempt to instill insectoid virtues in their followers, such as patience, hard work, and close cooperation. Some higher-level Hivemasters even attempt to influence human societies to adopt a communal pattern modeled on that of hive insects. Others—often styling themselves Webmasters—take on the patient, deadly personas of predator arachnids or insects such as dragonflies or spiders, ruthlessly hunting down (or lying in wait to trap) the enemies of the druidic order. A Hivemaster's grove usually centers around the dwelling place of the creature for which the druid has the greatest affinity—a forest covered with spider webs, a field with beehives, etc.

Branch Restrictions: None.
Weapon Proficiencies: *Recommended*—scimitar, staff.
Secondary Skills: Farmer, woodworker/carpenter.
Nonweapon Proficiencies: *Recommended*—(general) agriculture; (warrior) animal lore, endurance, set snares.
Equipment: The druid should spend her initial allotment of gold pieces entirely on

equipment, as she loses any unspent starting money in excess of 1 gp.

Special Benefits: A Hivemaster receives a +4 bonus to saving throws against stings or bites of poisonous insects or arachnids, including giant versions.

The druid also gains a +4 bonus on agriculture, animal training, and animal lore proficiency checks concerning insects or arachnids, and can apply the animal training proficiency to giant insects and arachnids.

A Hivemaster like Cagua may pass harmlessly through spider webs of all sorts, including webs created by the *web* spell. When she casts a *summon insects, giant insect, creeping doom,* or *insect plague* spell, the player increases her effective level by three.

Upon reaching 7th level, the druid gains the ability to shapechange into a giant insect or arachnid type *once* per day. She can take the form of a nonpoisonous giant ant, giant centipede, giant spider, or giant wasp. The Hivemaster may assume this insectoid form instead of one of her other shapechanging choices (bird, mammal, or reptile). For example, Cagua may choose to avoid the bird form today in favor of the insectoid form, but tomorrow she may decide not to shapechange into reptile form. The druid still can assume only three forms per day, just like the normal druidic shapechanging ability. Note: Gray druids with the Hivemaster kit may assume the insectoid form instead of any one of their usual shapechanging choices: mammal, reptile, or nonpoisonous giant spider.

Special Hindrances: The Hivemaster's *animal friendship, speak with animals,* and *summon animals* spells allow her to summon or communicate with only insects, giant insects, or arachnids. Hivemasters receive a –3 penalty when using animal proficiencies (animal lore, animal training, etc.) on creatures that are not insects or arachnids.

Wealth Options: 3d6×10 gp.

Lost Druid

The strangest members of the druidic order, Lost Druids find that many other druids no longer consider them kin. The Lost Druids come from lands that have been maliciously destroyed—forests burned to the ground, swamps drained, mountains ruined by mining, and so on. Rather than try to rebuild or move on, a Lost Druid such as Struma (pictured next page) allows his heart to darken from brooding on the devastation and embraces strange magic to seek revenge.

Under extreme stress (and the DM's discretion), a druid may renounce a particular kit forever and become a Lost Druid. Druids of 2nd or higher level lose one level as a result of the change but suffer no other penalties. Note that this is an exception to the rule on abandoning kits (p. 42), so the DM may wish to restrict it to NPCs.

Role: Lost Druids always feel bitter. Sometimes they go insane, their hearts filled with an insatiable, often impossible, desire for vengeance against those who destroyed their land. For instance, say Struma became a Lost Druid when he found his forest destroyed by orcs. He may attempt to plot the downfall of the entire orcish race and the death of every last orc. Most Lost Druids live solitary existences, but sometimes they group together, often within the sinister Shadow Circle. (See Chapter 3: The Druidic Order.)

Branch Restrictions: None.

Weapon Proficiencies: *Recommended*—scimitar, staff.

Secondary Skills: Hunter, weaponsmith.

Nonweapon Proficiencies: *Recommended*—(priest) herbalism, spellcraft; (warrior) animal lore, endurance, set snares, survival.

Equipment: A Lost Druid such as Struma should spend his initial allotment of gold pieces entirely on equipment, as he loses any unspent starting money in excess of 1 gp.

Special Benefits: The druid gains minor access to the Necromancy spell sphere. Upon reaching 6th level, he gains an additional power, the ability to animate dead animals. Treat this power as the priest spell *animate dead*; however, the druid may use it only once per day, and it affects 1 HD of normal (real-world) animals per level of the druid.

Special Hindrances: The Lost Druid cast only the *reversed* versions of *heal* or *cure* spells.

As a Lost Druid, Struma may never attain Grand Druid status, and thus may not progress past it to hierophant rank. A character of Grand Druid or hierophant rank may not become a Lost Druid.

All rangers and druids with other kits react to Lost Druids at a –4 penalty, usually with a mixture of pity and fear. (Other Lost Druids have only a –2 penalty to encounter reactions.) Most druids consider Lost Druids enemies and attempt to hunt, slay, or imprison them.

Wealth Options: 3d6×10 gp.

Natural Philosopher

From youth, the unbridled curiosity of Natural Philosophers has lent them a fascination about everything from the characteristics of plants and animals to the workings of natural forces like lightning and weather, in addition to the ancient history of the druidic order. Besides the usual ability score requirements, a druid needs at least Intelligence 15 for this kit.

Role: Xenia, a typical Natural Philosopher, delights in the study of new plants and animals. She thinks nothing of venturing into a haunted forest to observe a rare circle of toadstools or visiting a dragon's den to observe firsthand the miracle of a hatching. She rarely interferes with her subject of study, preferring to observe and sketch rather than bring home specimens.

Natural Philosophers often undertake adventures out of sheer curiosity. This

Druid Kits • 33

becomes a good role for an NPC druid: Xenia (as either a doddering old sage or a brash young student) hires a party to accompany her on a dangerous scientific expedition to visit a living island spotted in a sahuagin-controlled ocean. A party also might accompany her to study the ecology of the salamander on the Elemental Plane of Fire or to check out a rumor that a previously extinct species of giant owl now lives in the woods by a lich's castle.

Branch Restrictions: Arctic and jungle druids cannot take this kit, as their harsh home terrain forces them to devote their time to mere survival, not scientific pursuits.

Weapon Proficiencies: *Recommended*—staff.

Secondary Skills: Hunter, navigator, scribe.

Nonweapon Proficiencies: *Bonus*—ancient history. *Recommended*—(general) artistic ability, languages (modern), weather sense; (priest) herbalism, languages (ancient), reading/writing; (warrior) animal lore.

Equipment: The druid should spend her initial allotment of gold pieces entirely on equipment, as she loses any unspent starting money in excess of 1 gp.

Special Benefits: The Natural Philosopher may use weapon proficiency slots for nonweapon proficiencies. This allows Xenia to devote multiple slots to a single proficiency (such as animal lore, herbalism, or weather sense), making her an expert in zoology, botany, or meteorology.

Special Hindrances: Remember to reflect in your role-playing the Natural Philosopher's insatiable curiosity. For instance, Xenia would rather study a new monster than kill it or run away. She finds puzzles and riddles irresistible and risks even her life to find the answers.

Wealth Options: 3d6×10 gp.

Outlaw

In a region where evil forces have triumphed and hold a position of authority, good people who resist have turned outlaw. From their exile in the wilderness, these folk conduct guerrilla warfare against the cruel victors in the fashion of Robin Hood and his Merry Men. Since the balance has swung so far to the side of evil, the druid may freely act as a military commander in the struggle to overthrow the oppressors. In some situations, the druidic order itself may be outlawed; then the Outlaw druid faces threats like widespread persecution of druid followers and burning of sacred groves.

Role: Because an outlaw band often fights in the wilderness (ambushing enemies along forest roads or defending against patrols), the druid's powers and skills naturally come to the forefront. One such Outlaw druid is Mackay. (See illustration on this page.) Out-

34 • Chapter Two

side combat, he proves excellent at gathering information and using his priestly curative powers. Depending on the nature and alignment of those in the group, you can role-play the Outlaw druid as just another party member or as the band's spiritual (or actual) leader.

Weapon Proficiencies: *Recommended*—scimitar, sling, staff.

Secondary Skills: Farmer, forester, hunter, weaponsmith.

Nonweapon Proficiencies: *Bonus*—set snares. *Recommended*—(general) animal training, brewing, rope use, singing, weather sense; (priest) healing, herbalism, local history, religion; (rogue, double slot) disguise; (warrior) animal lore, tracking.

Equipment: The druid should spend his initial allotment of gold pieces entirely on equipment, as he loses any unspent starting money in excess of 1 gp.

Special Benefits: None.

Special Hindrances: Local authorities are always hunting for Outlaws like Mackay. Capture means imprisonment—or worse.

Wealth Options: 3d6×10 gp.

Pacifist

The Pacifist druid believes in the sanctity of all life, but especially that of creatures with animal Intelligence or higher.

Role: The restrictions on the druid's actions (below) make this a challenging role to play, and one that works best within a party of good-aligned adventurers. To give the player of a Pacifist druid a chance to shine, the DM should design adventures in which the character can help negotiate a diplomatic settlement of a crisis between neighboring lords or where party members sometimes can win over opponents by negotiation or moral persuasion.

For example, suppose a tribe of goblins menaces human lands. The DM alone knows

that the goblins actually were displaced from their old caverns by an evil vampire and would return home if someone destroyed the vampire. A scenario like this gives a clever Pacifist druid, such as Lark (above) a chance to talk to the goblins, discover why they intruded into human land, then convince the party to ally with them against the vampire.

Branch Restrictions: None.

Weapon Proficiencies: *Recommended*—staff.

Secondary Skills: Farmer, groom.

Nonweapon Proficiencies: *Bonus*— healing. *Recommended*—(general) brewing, cooking; (priest) herbalism, religion, spellcraft; (warrior) animal lore, survival.

Equipment: A Pacifist like Lark can purchase no weapons except darts or a staff. She should spend her entire initial allotment of gold pieces on equipment, as she loses unspent starting money in excess of 1 gp.

Druid Kits • 35

Special Benefits: The Pacifist druid can use some or all of her weapon proficiency slots to buy nonweapon proficiencies.

Pacifists such as Lark have the ability to speak soothing words to ease tempers and calm savage beasts. This power can remove the effects of a *fear* spell, calm an enraged animal, or pacify a hostile crowd. Lark can use this power a number of times per day equal to her experience level. Using soothing words accomplishes one of the following:

• Negates one *fear* spell (or similar monster ability) on a single victim;

• Halts a single creature's berserker rage; or

• Temporarily calms down a number of animals, characters, or monsters (whose combined levels or Hit Dice total no more than twice the druid's level). A calmed group usually remains calm for 1d4+1 rounds, as long as others refrain from hostile action against them, their allies, or their property. During this time, the druid or others can attempt to escape or to negotiate a resolution to the situation.

Special Hindrances: You, the player, must role-play this druid as a strict pacifist. A character like Lark does not totally oppose others who do harm when necessary—after all, animals kill for food. However, she never injures a person or animal herself. In addition, she encourages her companions to use the minimum required force during encounters: to ask foes to surrender before attacking them, let retreating enemies flee if she thinks they won't be a menace again, and so on.

Use of herbal brews or magic that does not permanently harm enemies is perfectly appropriate. For instance, Lark can *entangle* foes, turn them into trees, use sleeping poison, etc. However, she absolutely refuses to let harm come to captives or innocents under her care; in fact, she uses her powers and risks her life to protect them.

The Pacifist druid's code against violence does not extend to evil undead. These creatures are already dead but need help finding their rest; in other words, the druid will destroy them.

Like all Pacifists, Lark eats only vegetarian meals. (You, the player, decide whether your Pacifist character eats fish.) She won't prevent others from eating meat, but usually expresses disapproval.

High-level Pacifists find themselves disadvantaged when attempting to advance a level, as winning a druidic challenge usually requires violent behavior. However, if Lark wanted to even up her chances in the challenge, she either could get her opponent to agree to a nonviolent contest, or she could win using harmless tricks or magic.

Finally, the player cannot roll or choose the following secondary skills: armorer, hunter, trapper/furrier, or weaponsmith.

Wealth Options: 3d6×10 gp.

Savage

This druid lives in primitive Stone Age tribe, usually in a rain forest. Haro, a typical Savage druid (pictured on the next page), differs from a savage priest, shaman, or witch doctor in that he belongs to the worldwide druidic order and, of course, to a druidic branch. Some Savage druids work and live among primitive tribes as missionaries from more civilized cultures.

Role: Rather than associate with a particular tribe—as do most shamans or witch doctors—the Savage druid adopts a neutral position, mediating intertribal feuds and handling relations between human tribes and neighboring humanoids, demihumans, or intelligent monsters. Most Savages live as hermits in the wild, although if Haro gains high rank, he could control a coalition of tribespeople, nonhumans, and animals.

If Haro joins a party in more civilized lands, he occupies the role of outsider and observer. The Savage character should act puzzled by some aspects of more advanced civilization, impressed, amused, or disgusted by others. The Savage druid's reaction to big cities is unlikely to be favorable!

Branch Restrictions: None.

Weapon Proficiencies: Savage druids are restricted to a choice of blowgun, club, dagger, harpoon, knife, spear, or staff. After adventuring in civilized lands (advancing at least one level doing so), they can learn other weapon proficiencies.

Secondary Skills: Hunter.

Nonweapon Proficiencies: *Bonus*—firebuilding, survival. *Recommended*—(general) direction sense, fishing, swimming, weather sense; (priest) healing, herbalism, local history, musical instrument; (warrior) animal lore, endurance, mountaineering, running, set snares, tracking.

Equipment: The Savage druid can buy no armor (though he may acquire a wooden shield) and can buy only those weapons listed above under "Weapon Proficiencies." He should spend his entire initial allotment of gold pieces on equipment, as he loses any unspent starting money in excess of 1 gp.

Special Benefits: The Savage druid's body is covered with ceremonial scars and tattoos. These eliminate the need to use the holy symbol of Haro's branch when casting spells—his tattoos and other markings are as effective as holy symbols other druids use.

Special Hindrances: Haro, like most Savage druids, has an unusual and imposing appearance. While he could alter his primitive dress easily, his strange accent, weathered appearance, tattoos, and scars mark him as a foreigner when he travels in civilized lands. These alien features give him a –2 reaction penalty among civilized NPCs; players can decide how their PCs react.

Wealth Options: 3d6×5 gp. Savage druids begin adventuring unfamiliar with money; all their starting wealth is actually an equivalent value in goods.

Shapeshifter

Shapeshifter druids master their shapechanging powers at a lower experience level than other druids. This ability takes a special gift (perhaps a taint of lycanthropic or silver dragon blood in the druid's family tree) and intense training. But, those who persevere, such as Rimi (pictured on the next page) gain unusual metamorphic powers.

Role: Shapeshifters have mercurial personalities. Although by no means chaotic, they are quick to anger, and easily moved to joy or tears. Rimi, like many Shapeshifter druids, makes an excellent spy or messenger and stands a good chance of being picked as a servant to a high-level druid, an archdruid, or a great druid.

Branch Restrictions: Only forest, plains, and mountain druids can take this kit, as druids in other branches have limits on their shapechanging powers.

Weapon Proficiencies: *Recommended*—staff.

Secondary Skills: Hunter, groom.

Nonweapon Proficiencies: *Bonus*— animal lore. *Recommended*—(priest) spellcraft; (warrior) endurance, survival, tracking.

Equipment: The druid should spend her initial allotment of gold pieces entirely on equipment, as she loses any unspent starting money in excess of 1 gp.

Special Benefits: As a Shapeshifter, Rimi gains her branch's shapechanging power at 1st level rather than at 7th level. However, until she reaches 7th level, the druid can assume only the form of natural creatures whose Hit Dice total no greater than half her level. (A 1st-level Shapeshifter only assumes the form of a creature with ½ HD or less.) Rimi can shapechange *twice as often* as her branch normally allows, which doubles the number of changes she can make daily. (Forest Shapeshifters, then, can change to animal, reptile, and bird form, each twice per day.) However, using this power more than the normal three times per day may have dangerous consequences. (See "Special Hindrances.")

At 7th level, Rimi the Shapeshifter can transform a portion of her body. Instead of turning into a reptile, she can give herself a snake's fangs, which she can use in an attack to cause 1d2 bite damage plus poison. Rather than turning into a bird, she can transform her arms into a bird's wings and fly at a movement rate of 21. Short of transforming into a bear (or other mammal), she can sprout a bear's claws from her fingers and make two attacks causing 1d3 points of damage each, plus Strength bonus. Each of these actions counts as one change for the day.

Special Hindrances: A Shapeshifter regains hit points only when resuming her human form, and then recovers only 1d4 hp. If the druid has 0 hp or fewer, she regains none with her human shape.

If Rimi uses her Shapeshifter power more than three times per day, she must make a saving throw vs. spell after each extra use. A failure locks her into her current form until the next day, when she can attempt a new saving throw. However, for each failed save, the druid's next one bears a –1 penalty. If Rimi fails three saving throws in succession, she keeps her current animal form permanently, as if she had been reincarnated as that creature. Only a *polymorph any object*, *limited wish*, or *wish* can turn her back to human or another form.

Wealth Options: 3d6×5 gp. Shapeshifters spend too much time in animal form to concern themselves with money.

Totemic Druid

The Totemic Druid closely identifies with a particular species of mammal, reptile, or bird. While Vanier, a typical Totemic Druid, stops short of worshiping his totem animal, he believes that particular animal represents his spirit. The Totemic Druid picks a normal (real-world) wild mammal, reptile, or bird as his totem. This creature cannot be larger than a bear or smaller than a mouse. Some common choices include the black bear, bobcat, eagle, owl, wolf, rattlesnake, and beaver. In addition, Vanier's totem animal must correspond to his branch; if Vanier belongs to the desert druid branch, he can select as his totem only an animal that normally lives in the desert.

Role: Totemic Druids tend to adopt characteristics associated with their totem animal. They feel especially protective of their totem animal in the wild and want to befriend the creatures. As a Totemic Druid, Vanier acts to promote the interests of the totem species and its individual members.

Even if his totem is traditional prey (a deer, for example), Vanier never hunts the animal himself, nor does he eat its meat. While he usually does not try to ban hunting of his totem (except in the case of endangered species), he opposes cruel or wasteful hunting practices.

Branch Restrictions: None.

Weapon Proficiencies: *Recommended*—staff.

Secondary Skills: Groom, hunter.

Nonweapon Proficiencies: *Bonus*—tracking. *Recommended*—(general) animal handling, animal training; (priest) healing, herbalism; (warrior) animal lore, survival.

Note that Totemic Druids have a reduced number of proficiency slots. (See "Special Hindrances.")

Equipment: The druid should spend his initial allotment of gold pieces entirely on equipment, as he loses any unspent starting money in excess of 1 gp.

Special Benefits: A Totemic Druid like Vanier can shapechange into the form of his totem animal a number of times per day equal to his experience level divided by three (rounded down), plus one. So, a 3rd- to 5th-level Totemic Druid can change twice per day, a 6th- to 8th-level druid can change three times per day, and so on. This ability functions as normal druidic shapechanging, except that the druid does not regain hit points when shapechanging into or out of the totem form; the druid's spirit remains so closely bound with the totem that he fully experiences any damage the animal form took. The Totemic Druid can use this shapechanging ability *in addition* to his shapechanging granted powers.

A Totemic Druid can communicate freely with normal or giant examples of the totem animal species (as with the *speak with animals* spell). He receives a +4 bonus to any healing, animal training, animal lore, or animal handling proficiency checks related to the totem. A druid who doesn't have one of these proficiencies may behave as though he did when dealing with his totem animal, but does not apply the +4 bonus.

Special Hindrances: A Totemic Druid has one fewer nonweapon proficiency slot than normal, as a result of spending so much time in animal form. So, Vanier would start with three slots rather than four.

Wealth Options: 3d6×5 gp. Totemic Druids, like Shapeshifters, have a less pressing need for money due to the amount of time they spend in animal form.

Village Druid

Kabil the Village Druid (next page) associates himself closely with a single rustic village or hamlet. As he gains experience, his influence can extend to cover a shire, barony, or entire region. However, his focus remains rural. A Village Druid always hopes to see ordinary folk live in harmony with Nature.

As a Village Druid, Kabil's aim is twofold: to keep people from exploiting Nature (by short-sighted agricultural practices, etc.) and to defend and protect villagers who follow the proper druidic path. Thus, although he will not stand idly by to see the wilderness threatened, his more vital interest lies with the local crops, domestic animals, and his own followers. Kabil uses his skills and magic to protect all living things within his village from foes, disease, drought, forest fires, or natural disasters.

Role: A Village Druid normally replaces a conventional priest or cleric in villages where most inhabitants subscribe to the druidic ethos. As well as offering protection and guidance, the druid leads the citizenry in ceremonies to observe births (of humans and animals), deaths, marriages, harvests, the changing of the seasons, and so on. (See Chapter 4: Role-playing Druids for details.)

This kit suits PCs when the DM decides to set the campaign in a rural area under a threat or perhaps near unexplored ruins.

Branch Restrictions: None.

Weapon Proficiencies: *Required*—sickle or scythe. *Recommended*—staff.

Secondary Skills: Farmer, forester, groom.

Nonweapon Proficiencies: *Bonus*— agriculture. *Recommended*—(general) animal training, brewing, rope use, weather sense; (priest) healing, herbalism, local history, religion.

Equipment: The druid should spend his initial allotment of gold pieces entirely upon equipment, as he loses all unspent starting money in excess of 1 gp.

Special Benefits: With the DM, decide which village a druid like Kabil protects; the druid lives in or near this village.

Locals respect Kabil highly and provide him with information about happenings in the area. He receives a +2 reaction bonus from people and domestic animals in the village— as long as he remains diligent about his duties. In addition, the villagers support Kabil at a middle-class lifestyle (*DMG*, p. 34). This hospitality, rather than tithes, represents the generosity of a grateful people willing to provide their Village Druid with the best of everything he needs to live in their midst.

Special Hindrances: As a Village Druid, Kabil doesn't have a lot of free time. Locals ask him for help with all their problems, ranging from bandit raids to a child lost in the woods. In addition, the druid must spend at least one day each week attending to village matters: listening to grievances, mediating disputes, finding lost livestock, tending animals, offering advice on crops, curing diseases, delivering babies, etc. If he misses a week, his reaction bonus drops by 1 point (minimum 0) and his income declines a step (from middle class to poor to squalid) as people become less hospitable. The druid can avoid these penalties if he arranges with someone else (another druid or a ranger) to look after the village in his absence.

Kabil's villagers also expect him to protect them from serious harm. If he fails—or if no one sees him at least making an honest effort—the DM may reduce or eliminate his reaction bonus and benefits for as long as the villagers likely would feel resentful. Roleplaying can win back a Village Druid's lost respect; Kabil can regain his lost reaction bonus and benefits quickly by doing a great deed to benefit the village, or slowly by simply completing his duties diligently for several months.

Wealth Options: 3d6×10 gp.

Wanderer

While most druids eventually settle in a specific locale, Wanderers travel widely, delighting in Nature's infinite variety of life. They typically have a better idea of the "big picture" in the world than other druids and usually remain on good terms with local bards and rangers. Druidic leaders often use Wanderers as messengers or missionaries.

Role: Wanderers like Fife (right), more gregarious than most druids, enjoy meeting and talking with people—especially rural folk. Although Fife acts carefree, this genial nature masks a keen mind and a strong interest in everything going on around her. Many Wanderers have animal companions.

Branch Restrictions: None.

Weapon Proficiencies: *Recommended*—staff, one other weapon.

Secondary Skills: Hunter, navigator.

Nonweapon Proficiencies: *Bonus*—direction sense. *Recommended*—(general) animal training, singing, weather sense; (priest) healing, herbalism, religion; (warrior) mountaineering, running, survival, tracking.

Equipment: The druid should spend her initial allotment of gold pieces entirely on equipment, as she loses all unspent starting money in excess of 1 gp.

Special Benefits: A Wanderer like Fife receives a +1 reaction adjustment bonus from bards, rangers and traveling folk such as tinkers and Gypsies.

When traveling over long distances, Fife covers ground at a one-third faster rate than a normal traveler would—that is, if a normal person can walk 24 miles in a day without force-marching, the druid can walk 32 miles with the same exertion. Fife, like all Wanderers, simply feels more accustomed to walking long distances than most—plus, she knows short cuts and secret trails. (This heightened speed is cumulative with the ability of many druids 3rd level and higher to travel through overgrowth or other difficult terrain without penalty.)

With a Wanderer guide, a party can increase travel time by one-sixth; thus, an unencumbered party led by a Wanderer would travel 28 miles in a day, not 24.

Special Hindrances: Constantly on the move, a Wanderer never allows herself to be burdened. Fife cannot have retainers, hirelings, mercenaries, or even servants until she reaches 12th level (but animal companions can travel with her). The druid cannot possess more treasure than she can carry; she either converts the excess into a portable form (gems, etc.) or donates it to a worthy cause, such as the druidic order.

Wealth Options: 3d6×10 gp.

Abandoning Kits

A character who started with a druid kit later may desire to abandon it. There should be a good campaign reason for this decision. For example, an Adviser whose lord has died or whose schemes have been thwarted repeatedly might decide to give up politics in favor of more personal involvement with Nature. Or, an Outlaw who has won a pardon has no reason to remain an Outlaw.

Discuss the question of abandoning the current kit with your DM. If this decision hinges on a specific event that happened to the *character,* change the druid's kit as soon as it's convenient. If, on the other hand, you have simply grown tired of *playing* a certain kit, the DM should come up with a scenario whose story line presents the character with a good reason for abandoning the kit.

Suppose, for instance, that you have been role-playing an Avenger—a druid who became an Avenger because orcs destroyed his forest. It can become boring to play a character whose sole goal is vengeance. Here are some possibilities for retiring the kit:

• The DM arranges a scenario in which the Avenger destroys the orc leader, then realizes he has sated his thirst for revenge.

• The DM sets up an adventure in which the Avenger chances upon a village threatened by marauding monsters. After saving the villagers, he decides to devote his time to continuing to protect them, rather than hunting down his one-time foes.

• The DM designs a story in which the Avenger, in his obsessive thirst for vengeance, comes close to harming innocent people or wildlife. As a result, the Avenger decides to alter his approach to life.

The player whose druid character abandons a kit must role-play the decision and any consequences that arise from it. The druid gives up all the kit's benefits and hindrances. The PC does not lose any bonus proficiencies (marked with asterisks), but they are no longer bonuses. The former Avenger in the above example must pay for them as soon as possible by spending the next proficiency slots he gains on them.

Modifying and Creating Kits

You and your DM may change the kits to customize them for your own campaign world, or even restrict the availability of some kits to NPCs. Similarly, feel free to create totally new kits. For guidelines on doing so, refer to the kit creation rules in *The Complete Fighter's Handbook* (*PH*, pgs. 37–38). However, make sure that no kit is more powerful than any in this book.

CHAPTER 3

The Druidic Order

The druidic order—often simply called the Order—can be thought of as a federation of regional priesthoods that form a loosely organized worldwide faith, all of whose members worship Nature and follow a similar ethical philosophy.

Druids divide up their world into regions, here called *domains.* A domain is a well-defined geographic area bounded by mountain ranges, rivers, seas, or deserts— druids normally divide a good-sized continent into three or four domains. Druidic regions do not rely on national borders, or on racial or ethnic groups; a domain can encompass several countries, races, and peoples.

For example, in a fantasy world based on our Earth, one European domain might include England, Ireland, Scotland, Wales, and the Channel Islands; a second could consist of Western Europe (west of the Rhine and north of the Alps and Pyrenees, bounded by the North Sea and the English Channel to the north and the Bay of Biscay to the west); a third might contain Southern Europe (south of the Alps and bounded by the Mediterranean Sea and Danube River); another would include the Iberian peninsula.

North America could be divided into an Atlantic domain (east of the Mississippi River and south of the St. Lawrence River and Great Lakes), a Pacific domain (west of the Rocky Mountains), a Central domain (between the two domains above, roughly south of the Missouri River), a Caribbean domain, a Southern domain (south of the Rio Grande and east of the Rockies), and a Northern domain (all of North America roughly north of the Missouri and Ohio rivers and east of the Rocky Mountains).

The Circles

All druids dwelling within the bounds of a domain are organized into a *circle.* Circles typically are named for the geographic area their domain occupies, but sometimes they bear other names, harking back to their founders or the gods the druids worship (if they worship deities rather than Nature itself). For instance, druids might have formed "The Dragon Isles Circle" or "The Circle of Danu."

The members of a circle hold themselves responsible for the well-being of the wilderness and the continuation of the orderly cycles of Nature within their domain. This doesn't mean a circle remains unconcerned about what occurs in other domains—forming circles is just the druidic order's way of recognizing that those druids who live in a particular region can best serve to protect it, and should therefore hold formal responsibility for the domain.

Circles operate within a very loose structure. They use no large temples or abbeys, for rarely do more than a few druids live together. When they do, their dwelling places are usually less than ostentatious: small cottages or huts of the style of local hunters or farmers. All druids within the circle acknowledge a single great druid as their leader and recognize this figure's moral authority. The great druid gives the circle's members great freedom compared to most other religious leaders. The druids adhere to a rather informal hierarchical structure and require their initiates to hold true to the basic ethos of the druidic order and respect higher-ranking druids.

A few traditions described in this chapter have grown up to govern the harmonious workings of a circle: initiations, the challenge, the ban, the moot, and selection of acolytes. All druids, from the humblest initiate to the great druid, may freely follow their own interpretation of druidic beliefs and act however they believe best serves Nature.

Druidic Demographics

A typical domain (one that has seen no persecution of druids but includes other priestly faiths as well) contains, on average, one druid for every 10 square miles of rural farmland or 400 square miles of lightly inhabited wilderness or steppe. Druids dwelling in rural areas usually are initiates (1st to 8th level, generally). Those in the wilderness usually have reached higher experience levels, frequently 7th to 11th level. A circle may include a maximum of nine 12th-level druids, three 13th-level druids, and one 14th-level druid. Often circles have no higher-level druids at all.

Below 12th level, the number of druids of a given experience level stands at about double the population of the next level up. So, a typical circle may include 18 initiates of 11th level, 36 initiates of 10th level, etc., all the way down to some 18,000 1st-level initiates. The entire circle thus consists of more than 36,000 druids. A domain might feature one druid per 500 to 1,000 citizens, although this statistic gives a distorted picture, since druids are concentrated in some locales and rare in others.

Circles and Branches

Chapter 1: Druid Characters examined the different branches of the Order: forest druids, desert druids, and so on. A given circle normally covers a domain vast enough to include members from several, but usually not all, branches. A domain with a temperate climate might contain a circle composed of forest, swamp, and mountain druids. In contrast, a circle in a tropical domain with flat terrain would consist of jungle, plains, desert, and swamp druids.

All druids should possess an equivalent number of advantages and disadvantages regardless of branch. However, equality is never guaranteed. In most fantasy worlds, the forest druids exercise the most influence. Due to the resources of the woodlands and humanity's desire to clear them for use as farms, forest druids often consider their problems the most pressing. The Order's priorities frequently reflect this stance; circles dominated by forest druids try to make sure that a member of that branch ends up as Grand Druid, the leader of the druidic order. As jungle druids and swamp druids share many of the forest druids' concerns, they often become allies.

A well-balanced druid sees each branch as part of a single tree, all equally important. Unfortunately, though, not all druids have this vision. Members of the informal forest-plains-swamp-jungle coalition sometimes look down upon desert and arctic druids due to the relative infertility of their habitats. Sometimes druids fall too deeply in love with their own particular part of the world—forest druids who see trees as the be-all and end-all of Nature may hold arctic, desert, and gray druids to be inferior. The victims of such prejudice, in turn, can come to resent the forest branch. Great druids from the few circles dominated by arctic or desert druids often ally to try to keep a forest druid from becoming Grand Druid— although more often than not, they fail.

Initiates

Initiates constitute the 1st- to 11th-level druids within a circle. Their experience level determines their role in the circle.

A typical 1st- or 2nd-level initiate (an NPC) often works part time as a Village Druid. This initiate keeps up a rural occupation (beekeeper, farmer, herder, etc.) while studying under a higher-level druid mentor. The exceptions to this stereotype are rare individuals (PCs). An average person finds it tough to recognize beginning druids, since most seem just like other peasants.

Initiates between 3rd and 6th level have achieved most of their granted powers, with the exception of shapechanging. The cornerstones of the druidic order, they frequently devote their full time to their faith. They normally live in stone, wood, or mud-brick cottages and act as the protectors of a small tract of wilderness—a wood or river valley—or of a village or group of hamlets. Most druids of this status have the Village Druid or Guardian kit, and those who choose to protect a village usually have become respected community leaders.

Initiates between 7th and 11th level have received all their branch's granted powers. Such druids live simply but have widened their areas of influence, perhaps becoming the guardians of entire forests or mountains, or of all the villages in a barony. These druids often dwell near a sacred grove surrounded by a few acres of virgin wilderness—a sanctuary for rare and magical plants, animals, and supernatural creatures. This natural setting may be magically defended as well. Temporal rulers of the area respect (or fear) druids of such level.

High-level Druids

Only a limited number of druids in a given circle can reach the *inner circle*—nine of druid rank, three archdruids, and a single great druid. A character cannot replace one of these druids without having sufficient experience. In addition, a vacancy must open up, or the rising druid must defeat one of the current higher-level characters the druidic challenge to assume a new rank.

Some tension exists between druids of the inner circle, since they remain constantly aware that a subordinate may be preparing a challenge. Unlike clerics, who normally settle down by this point, high-level druids continue adventuring as part of their duties and to stay in shape to fend off challengers.

Druids

Upon reaching 12th level, a character receives the official title *druid*, of which a circle never has more than nine. (Lower-level characters, though called "druids" by most, are technically "initiates.") A druid's role in the circle resembles that of a 7th- to 11th-level initiate, with some exceptions.

At 12th level, a druid has gained access to the *commune with nature* spell and should use it along with other druidic resources to aggressively root out emergent threats to the wilderness within a domain. Druids attend the High Council of the Moot (described later this chapter) and always act based on the needs of the circle as a whole. The circle's great druid at times asks 12th-level druids for advice and sends them on missions for the good of the circle.

But the life of a druid involves more than just adventuring—serving as a mentor takes up much of a druid's time, too. Selecting young people to train as druidic candidates constitutes a major responsibility of those who reach druid rank. Each year druids (and other inner circle members) pick the single most worthy of their advanced students to initiate into the Order as 1st-level druids. (For more on initiations, see Chapter 4: Role-playing Druids.)

Archdruids

A 13th-level druid is called an *archdruid*. Each circle can have only three archdruids and, as with the druid rank, advancement requires either filling a vacancy or winning a challenge against a seated archdruid.

An archdruid's role resembles that of a druid, with two differences. Archdruids concern themselves more with maintaining the balance of Nature, making sure no one alignment or ethos comes to utterly dominate the domain. Also, archdruids spend time training to step into the role of the great druid. To accomplish both these goals, they devote much time to travel, ensuring their familiarity with the geography—human, natural, and

The Druidic Order • 45

magical—throughout the domain.

The Moot. The three archdruids share the druid's responsibility for initiating newcomers to the Order. In addition, they each have the right to summon a moot: a gathering of the entire circle, traditionally held at the solstices and equinoxes. By ancient custom, moots are called four times a year at these set dates, once by each archdruid and once (usually in spring) by the great druid. A moot on a nontraditional date means the summoner sees something so deeply amiss in the domain that the entire circle must discuss it as soon as possible.

These gatherings enable the circle to celebrate the changing of the seasons, to gossip and socialize, to exchange information on the state of the domain, and to fight druidic challenges before an audience. Druids at a moot perform ceremonies to celebrate Nature, honor their dead, marry a couple within the Order, and initiate new 1st-level druids. Along with these ceremonial duties, small groups at moots disappear together into the wilds to talk quietly while searching for herbs or mistletoe.

The climax of any such gathering is the High Council of the Moot; the circle's nine druids, three archdruids, and great druid meet in a secret location to discuss the state of the domain and make plans to rally the circle against a particular problem, if necessary. Sometimes an ambassador from a neighboring circle (usually a character of at least druid rank) or an emissary of the Grand Druid attends a council. These personages bring news and greetings—and sometimes requests for help. After the High Council, the great druid (or an archdruid) addresses the entire moot, answers questions, and takes advice.

To call a moot, an archdruid (or the great druid) sends messengers out across the domain to spread the word to druids of all branches. All members of the circle above 7th level must attend or explain the absence. Members of 3rd to 6th level may come, but usually do so only if their journeys bring them to the vicinity or if they have business with others there. Those of 1st or 2nd level may attend a moot only with the permission of a member of the inner circle.

The moot is scheduled to begin two weeks after the summoner dispatches the announcements, giving all druids in the circle enough time to settle their business and arrive. Such a gathering generally takes place at a sacred grove under the stewardship of the summoner. Though most moots last about four days, the meeting cannot end until the summoning archdruid or the great druid dissolves it.

Bards, elves, rangers, swanmays, and other sylvan folk often are invited to a moot, but its location remains a secret to others. In troubled times, elves, rangers, friendly beasts, or forest creatures may patrol the moot and take trespassers prisoner.

If the domain's circle is on good terms with the land's rangers, a spring or autumnal moot may take place in conjunction with a rangers' forgathering. (See Chapter 10: Forgatherings in *The Complete Ranger's Handbook*.) However, like rangers, druids prefer to keep their gatherings to themselves, and such cooperation usually results from personal friendships between the great druid and notable rangers —or signals a desperate alliance against a greater foe.

Great Druids

As stated earlier, the *great druid* leads a circle. Like other inner circle members, the great druid usually has won the position through the challenge and has to maintain the ascendancy by defeating other challengers. However, some great druids become so respected (or feared!) that subordinate archdruids forgo challenging them, instead preferring to enter the service of the Grand Druid or wait until the great druid advances in level.

All druids within a circle know the name of their great druid—even if they have never met in person—because this figure wields a certain amount of power over their lives. The DM should decide how strongly the great druid influences the members of the circle. For instance, a great druid who is loved, respected, or feared holds more sway over NPC druids than would a weak or unpopular leader. While PCs remain free to pursue their own goals, opposing the policy of a strong great druid means a character has little chance of receiving support from superior druids. Supporting the leader's policy, on the other hand, can win lesser druids praise and aid from the top.

Turmoil can erupt within a circle governed by a weak or unpopular great druid, as the ranking archdruids vie for the head post or ignore the leader's advice to follow their own paths. Player characters may get occasional assistance from inner circle druids in this scenario, but for the most part, individuals all go their own way.

The great druid has the same power to initiate druidic candidates and summon a moot as archdruids. In addition, this figure has the job of maintaining harmonious relations among all the druids of the circle—preventing factional battles and infighting, other than what is allowed through the challenge. To do so, the great druid has one special tool: the ban.

The Ban. The great druid can impose a strong, nonviolent sanction upon those who have offended the circle. All must shun someone placed under the ban; no druid in the circle will aid, speak to, or associate with the target of the ban. When an entire town or village suffers the ban, no druid may enter that area or speak to or aid any resident. Some druidic allies volunteer to follow the custom of the ban as well. For instance, a clan of sprites or centaurs on good terms with a circle may receive word of a ban and choose to honor it.

The great druid has the right to pronounce a ban on any druid in the circle. A ban also can cover nondruids, whole communities, or druids visiting from other domains (except the Grand Druid and personal servants), to demonstrate the circle's displeasure.

To pronounce the ban, the great druid stands up during a moot and announces to the group the reasons to impose the ban. Then the subject of the ban—if present— answers the accusations before the assembly. Finally, the High Council of the Moot votes on the matter openly, usually at sunset. If a majority of the council votes in favor of the ban, it passes. If not, the great druid should start keeping an eye on the circle's archdruids—the opposition to the ban likely reflects an impending challenge.

A ban punishes a druid for violating the tenets of the druidic order or reprimands a character whose actions, while within the bounds of the druidic ethos, nevertheless were contrary to the Order's interests. For instance, suppose an angry druid massacred the inhabitants of a human hamlet because they would not turn over two hunters who slew a stag in the druid's sacred grove. The druid acted within the bounds of the druidic ethos, but the great druid might call the character's indiscriminate vengeance out of proportion to the crime, adding that the slaughter has threatened to make local commoners hate and fear all druids in the circle. So, the great druid imposes the ban, both as a punishment and as incentive for the character to change.

Nondruid individuals are less likely to fall victim to a ban—usually the great druid finds that direct action against the offender proves more effective. However, if the people of an area depend on druids rather than other priests for healing and religious ceremonies, a ban sends them a message of disapproval. And sometimes a ban can serve as a symbolic gesture against a subject too powerful or influential to confront directly—a baron or king, for instance.

A ban generally lasts 10 summers. However, the inner circle can vote to lift a ban early or (once the time is up) to extend it. The shunning does not extend outside the domain, so banned druids usually choose to go into exile—the result the great druid probably intended in the first place.

The Challenge. The traditions of the Order prohibit an inner circle from including more than nine druids, three archdruids, and one great druid. If a character gains enough experience to achieve official druid level but finds no vacancy in the inner circle, the only way to advance involves ceremonial combat: the druidic challenge.

The challenge remains one of the oldest druidic traditions. It purges the weak and complacent, ensuring that the highest ranks of the druidic order remain filled with strong and cunning individuals. The masters of the druidic order are not politicians, but men and women of action. They believe that the challenge, by bringing ambition into the open, allows them to by-pass some of the worst excesses of hypocrisy and behind-the-scenes power plays found in other religions.

A circle's great druid expects at any time to face a challenge from one of the archdruids, while the archdruids keep an eye on rising druids. Those of druid rank, in turn, look out for ambitious 11th-level initiates. This system puts a constant strain on the Order's upper ranks: It's hard to stay on good terms with folk who want your job and eventually will challenge you to a battle to gain it. As a result, most friendships and alliances form among druids of equal level or among characters several levels apart.

All inner circle druids do their best to appear strong, to avoid looking like easy targets. Many actively adventure to enhance their reputations and gain power through acquiring magical items and experience. Others simply try to remain popular among the other members of the Order. If an inner circle member takes an unpopular or controversial stance, fellow druids may decide to encourage the ambitious to aim for that particular target; the replacement would likely prove more cordial.

The challenge operates under prearranged rules: Characters who violate the letter of the rules will fail to advance in level, just as if they had suffered defeat. Always a one-on-one battle, the challenge does not allow even servants or animal companions of the combatants to participate.

First, the two parties must agree upon the time of the duel—if they can't agree, it will take place at the next moot. Druids consider it impolite to set a challenge outside of a moot, although it's still done.

Second, the challenge needs a witness—a druid whose level equals or exceeds the challenger's. Hierophant druids (described later in this chapter) work well as witnesses, as do druids or archdruids visiting from different circles or from the Grand Druid's entourage. This individual must witness the terms of the challenge and make sure the combatants obey the rules. The great druid of the circle always names the witness, even if the challenge involves that very leader.

Third, the terms by which the battle will be fought are set out by mutual agreement. Once agreed upon and witnessed, the terms may not change. If neither side can agree on the terms, the witness selects them and proclaims the duel an all-out battle until one druid surrenders or becomes incapacitated.

The Druidic Order • 49

Terms to discuss include:

• The size of the battlefield. Until the duel ends, leaving the bounds of the area means conceding defeat. Usually the space is no more than a dozen yards across, to ensure the battle does not take too long.

• Whether to allow weapons, magical items, granted powers, and spells. (Note: Nondruidic spells *cannot* be used.) Most contests involve full use of weapons and spells, although many commonly disallow magical items. Some memorable duels have permitted *only* granted powers—no spells or weapons. The combatants used only the claws and fangs of their different animal forms. A few challenges have forbidden all weapons and magic—they became simple wrestling matches.

• Whether to alter the normal battle-oriented conditions of the duel. Although rare, methods less stringent than actual combat have been honored, especially between two friendly rivals. Such unorthodox formats include a race, a scavenger hunt, a competition to defeat a particular monster, a drinking contest (the first druid to fail three Constitution rolls loses), or even a game of hide and seek.

The challenge begins with the witness's invocation, asking Nature (or a druidic deity) to watch over the duel. This means that challengers who defeat foes through cheating will find themselves unable to gain a level after all, and incumbents who cheat automatically lose the level. Once the witness concludes the invocation, the druids enter the battlefield from opposite ends, and the contest begins.

Appointment of Acolytes. Great druids, archdruids, and druids have the traditional right to select initiates as their servants. The number and level of these retainers depends on the level and position of the inner circle member. (See the *PH*, p. 37, for details.) The chosen initiates are called *acolytes*.

Acolytes, chosen from the high-ranking druid's own circle, are restricted to serving only certain inner circle members (again, based on their experience level). The appointing druid must determine which eligible initiates will serve him.

An inner circle druid usually approaches a favored initiate quietly and offers an acolyte position. The initiate then decides whether to accept the post. While serving as an acolyte holds honor, it also entails a loss of freedom. Therefore, the decision depends on factors such as the reputation of the inner circle member.

An acolyte swears an oath of service: to be loyal and obedient, to listen and learn, to keep no secrets from one's master, but to guard the master's secrets. An acolyte who breaks this oath faces the wrath of the high-ranking druid. In addition, unless the acolyte can prove the master's commands violated the spirit of the druidic ethos, the servant usually becomes subjected to the ban.

The advantage of serving as an acolyte is that the character wins the patronage, and perhaps the friendship, of a powerful druid. The position enhances the initiate's prestige in the eyes of the entire circle. Furthermore, acolytes injured or wronged by an enemy can expect assistance from their master.

The disadvantage? The character—always at the beck and call of a master—loses personal freedom. An acolyte fulfills all the normal duties of a loyal retainer but, most importantly, acts as an emissary and representative of the inner circle druid. As high-level druids cannot be everywhere at once, acolytes often go on long journeys to do their master's bidding. Whether the mission involves finding a reclusive swamp-dwelling initiate to notify of the next moot's date and location or delivering a stinging ultimatum to a dwarven king to shut down his mines or face the circle's wrath, acolytes can expect to visit a lot of interesting—though sometimes unpleasant—places.

An acolyte's term of service lasts until the master's experience level changes or until the acolyte advances a level. In the latter case, the acolyte leaves service, and the inner circle member must select a replacement.

The Grand Druid

Above all others within the Order stands the figure of the *Grand Druid*, the highest-ranking (although not the highest-level) druid in the world. The Grand Druid, a 15th-level character, attains this position through a selection process rather than by the challenge. Since only one person can hold the title of Grand Druid, each world can have only one 15th-level druid at a time.

Duties of the Grand Druid. First and foremost, the Grand Druid acts as a politician, responsible for keeping harmony between the great druids of each domain and between the various druidic branches.

The Grand Druid also rallies the circles against the rare global threat to Nature or the cosmic balance. This always proves a difficult task, as many circles fiercely cherish their autonomy, believing each one should remain self-sufficient and not meddle in other domains' affairs. Few circles willingly send contingents off to aid other circles unless they feel absolutely certain that the threat will menace their own domain as well. To make matters worse, the inflated pride of many circles prevents them from accepting help from "foreign" druids. As a result, often only one thing can convince the Order a threat warrants a combined effort: the destruction of an entire circle. Fortunately, such occurrences are few and far between.

The Grand Druid and entourage (detailed below) spend most of their time visiting different regions and speaking to the great druids, archdruids, druids, and, rarely, lowly initiates. In particular, this leader serves as a diplomat and peacemaker, who mediates disputes between druids of neighboring circles and struggles involving members of the mysterious Shadow Circle (described later in this chapter).

Normally the circles act with autonomy. However, if a circle appears in great disarray—for instance, an enemy has killed most of its members or forced them into hiding—the Grand Druid may try to rally the circle or recruit aid from other domains. If a circle has been effectively destroyed, the Grand Druid might decide to rebuild it from scratch. After selecting a rising archdruid from a neighboring circle to step in as the new great druid, the Grand Druid helps recruit volunteers from nearby domains to replenish the circle. Often this assignment proves difficult and dangerous; whatever destroyed the previous circle probably still lurks nearby, ready to pounce on the new circle that, while wary, will remain understrength for some time.

Servants of the Grand Druid. Like other inner circle druids, the Grand Druid has personal servants: an entourage of nine druids of various levels. These druids no longer owe allegiance to their original circles but are subject only to the Grand Druid. All druids consider it a high honor to serve the leader of the Order, an honor that bears great responsibility but gives a druid prestige and influence far beyond others of similar level. Assuming a vacancy arises—and service involves enough danger that openings occur reasonably often—a druid of any level can seek out the Grand Druid and petition to become a retainer. This relationship lasts as long as both sides wish—often many years—and can end by mutual agreement at any time.

Three archdruids, often called the Emissaries, always serve the head of the Order. They act as the Grand Druid's personal agents—their leader's eyes, hands, and voice. To aid them in their duty, they receive four additional spell levels (one 4th-level spell, two 2nd-level spells, etc.), usable as they see fit. To keep the Grand Druid informed on the operations of the circles in every land, they roam the world, visiting the various circles as well as other places of interest to their master. The arrival of an Emissary often coincides with the ascendance of a new great druid. While conveying the respects of the head of the Order, the archdruid takes the new leader's measure and reports back to the Grand Druid. These servants also visit a circle in response to a great druid's request for aid.

Traveling Emissaries normally find themselves welcomed, for their visits give circles a chance to learn news from far-off lands. An Emissary also may offer counsel about a menace or carry a request for help to the Grand Druid or neighboring circles.

But Emissaries also must remain on the alert for problems within a circle that the great druid has failed to adequately handle—such as widespread conflicts between druids or corruption in the ranks. In such cases, it is the Emissary's solemn duty to take action to remedy the problem or, lacking sufficient power, to report it the Grand Druid. For this reason, some circles— particularly those secretly dominated by the ruthless Shadow Circle— regard the arrival of an Emissary with deep suspicion. In their role as agents of the Grand Druid, these archdruids sometimes resemble spies. More than one Emissary has met a mysterious end while visiting a supposedly friendly circle.

Besides the Emissaries, a Grand Druid has six other servants. These druids, usually of 7th to 11th level, come from a variety of branches but have all proven their dedication to the Order. Many Grand Druids have been known to take on the occasional lower-level druid, either because they feel the need for a fresher viewpoint or because they sense a special worthiness in a particular individual. These six druids of mixed level act as servants, counselors, bodyguards, and useful agents.

Selection of the Grand Druid. One of the duties each Grand Druid must perform is appointing a successor, always an acting great druid. After serving usually a minimum of four years, a Grand Druid steps down to allow the chosen successor to assume the mantle of leadership.

In theory, selecting a new Grand Druid is solely up to the last Grand Druid. In practice, druidic order politics plays a major role. For instance, if the forest druids have held the position of Grand Druid for several generations, they may come to consider it "their right" to do so. However, in the name of fairness and harmony, druids from other branches may lobby to convince the current Grand Druid to pick a successor from a different branch. On the other hand, choosing a Grand Druid from a minority branch could alienate large segments of the druidic order's membership, even with an extremely competent Grand Druid.

As a result, when a Grand Druid begins getting on in years, the impending choice of successor becomes the subject of much gossip, speculation, lobbying, and intrigue by archdruids, great druids, and hierophant druids. For instance, a great druid afraid of being passed over for the position in favor of a rival may encourage a powerful, ambitious archdruid to challenge that rival, hoping to put the favorite out of the running before the Grand Druid can finalize the succession.

Hierophant Druids

The *hierophants* make up a unique part of the druidic order. Some even go so far as to say they *are* the Order, and that the other ranks represent mere practice for hierophant status. Check p. 38 of the *PH* for details on achieving the rank of hierophant (pictured on the next page) and the powers that go with it.

Hierophant druids live as free agents. They are encouraged to respect the Grand Druid, but need not obey the druidic leader's mandates nor operate within the borders of any circle. Although a few settle down in particular groves, many become famous wanderers, some even visiting other planes or (by spelljamming) distant worlds. They often travel about in disguise, using their appearance-alteration powers. Wherever they go and whatever they do, they always aim to promote the ethos and values of the druidic order.

Unlike lesser druids, hierophants typically have a global perspective and agenda. They concern themselves with the rise and fall of empires, the migrations of peoples, the growth or extinction of species, and the role of each race in the destiny of the world. Some devote their lives to a particular cause, such as reclaiming the forests of a continent infected by evil, or acting as the personal nemesis of a being whose actions threaten the world's balance.

Hierophants are notorious behind-the-scenes manipulators. They use their long life spans to weave subtle schemes with far-reaching plots that might take decades to hatch, but which—they believe—ultimately will benefit their cause. The 17th-level druidic ability to hibernate enables most of them to appear effectively immortal: some hierophants will hatch the initial elements of a scheme, go into hibernation, then awaken decades later, unaged, to bring the next stage into play. Such druids might become patrons of gifted families of adventurers, recruiting the latest generation when they need heroes.

The existence of hierophant druids tends to make great druids and Grand Druids very nervous, for they represent a power beyond their control—and sometimes beyond their ken. Whether any hierophant druids belong to the Shadow Circle is not known.

The Shadow Circle

The druidic order tolerates a wide range of philosophies under the umbrella of its loosely organized structure. The variety of different branches demonstrates this scope. So does the existence of the Shadow Circle.

A secret society of druids within the larger druidic order, the Shadow Circle accepts members who see Nature as a hostile, cleansing force that ensures the survival of the fittest. According to their philosophy, civilization—especially the building of towns and cities—has weakened humankind and many demihuman races.

Methods

The Shadow Circle sees barbarian humans and more primitive races as inherently more vital than civilized peoples. Thus, the Shadow Circle often allies itself with barbarian tribes or hostile humanoids such as orcs, giants, and goblins, especially those who choose to live in forests or mountains in the wilds.

They deliberately encourage people to abandon civilization's "decadence" and return to the more natural existence of hunting and gathering.

But while their intentions are neutral, the methods of Shadow Circle members tend to promote chaos and evil. They behave as they do not due to an evil nature—their enemies include powerful evil empires as well as good kingdoms. Rather, they feel their cruel activities work toward the best interests of evolution and of Nature itself. For instance, the Shadow Circle may provide magical assistance to barbarian hordes trying to sack a city or lead humanoid tribes in raids against human or dwarven towns.

Sometimes the Shadow Circle even assists the cause of good. For instance, members would consider an evil city-state based around slavery a fair target, and they would feel as eager as any lawful good paladin to support a slave revolt in the hopes of toppling the city. The difference? The Shadow Circle would encourage the slaves in revolt to burn the city to the ground and then settle down as farmers, hunters, or outlaws in the countryside.

Lower-ranking members of the Shadow Circle often wage campaigns of terror against small settlements, usually working behind the scenes. Their favorite puppets are intelligent monsters like evil lycanthropes.

Membership

The members of the Shadow Circle keep their allegiance secret from other druids while maintaining their parallel "circle" rankings. An archdruid in the Shadow Circle is also an archdruid in a mainstream circle, for example. Shadow Circle druids of 11th level or higher follow the normal druidic practice of advancing in level through the challenge; in fact, Shadow Circle druids encourage each other to challenge nonmembers in mainstream circle hierarchy, thereby increasing their number among inner circle members. These duels almost invariably turn quite bloody.

An arc of the Shadow Circle exists in any domain where druids live, and its members may come from any druidic branch. Typically only one in five initiates—but as many as one in three 12th-level or higher druids—secretly belongs to the Shadow Circle. A great druid usually is not a member, but one never can tell for sure. In some troubled domains—particularly those in which druids face persecution and the wilderness displays signs of wanton destruction from human cities—*most* of the druids may join the Shadow Circle!

Shadow Circle druids adopt secret names to conceal their identities from each other. When they meet, they do so while shapechanged or wearing masks carved to represent predators native to the domain. This secrecy is important. Although the Shadow Circle ethos corresponds to that of the Order, most druids disdain the group's methods—and therefore, its members.

A known Shadow Circle initiate faces the enmity of other druids—and possibly the ban, for refusing to recant—as well as the ire of local authorities. Lower-level druids constantly challenge exposed Shadow Circle druids 12th level and higher, seeking to depose—and possibly destroy—offenders.

In turn, the Shadow Circle often tries to cause trouble within the druidic order. For instance, in order to recruit disaffected druids into their midst, group members covertly encourage rivalry between druidic branches (such as the jealousy between the dominant forest druids and the members of less influential branches). Characters may learn of the Shadow Circle when they discover a plot to ferment such trouble between druids from rival branches.

Note that these are the methods of a group of extremist druids, not evil ones. Their anti-civilization feelings do not alter their neutral alignment.

Shadowmaster. The highest-level druid in the Shadow Circle—usually an archdruid or druid—takes command of the group as the Shadowmaster. If two or more druids of equal level seek the post, they generally duel to the death, though one combatant—usually the younger—could agree to serve under the other. Unlike the semiautonomous mainstream circles, the Shadow Circle maintains strict discipline over its various far-flung arcs. The Shadowmaster exercises absolute authority over the membership.

Inner Circle. Under the Shadowmaster are the members of the inner circle, which consists of all the druidic order's Shadow Circle druids (12th level) and archdruids (13th level). (The Shadowmaster remains apart from the inner circle.) Together, the Shadowmaster and the inner circle make policy and direct the initiates. Only the Shadowmaster knows the real names of members of the inner circle—the identities of even these high-ranking members remain unknown to each other.

The 1st- through 10th-level initiates within this secret society, unlike the more independent initiates of mainstream circles, are expected to obey all orders from inner circle members and the Shadowmaster. Failure means punishment—death.

Shadowed Ones. Initiates who have reached 11th level have special status in the Shadow Circle. These initiates are known as "Shadowed Ones," the Shadowmaster's special tools. In particular, they act as enforcers and assassins for the secret group, hunting those who have disobeyed their fearsome leader or have been expelled from the mysterious society. The Shadowmaster sometimes encourages Shadowed Ones to serve as ambassadors to arcs of the Shadow Circle operating in other domains. Shadowed Ones automatically advance to the inner circle in this secret group when they achieve 12th level in their mainstream circle.

Shadowclave

Members of the Shadow Circle work in secret, pretending to be mainstream druids. For example, they attend all druidic moots. But every season each arc of the Shadow Circle also holds its own secret meeting—the Shadowclave—in the dark of the moon. The meeting lasts three nights, during which the membership celebrates its own version of traditional druidic ceremonies and receives new orders from the Shadowmaster and inner circle. Prisoners the Shadow Circle has taken throughout the season—along with disloyal or disobedient members—are kept alive until the Shadowclave. There, the inner circle tortures and publicly executes them, to remind the membership of what happens to traitors and enemies of the Shadow Circle.

Recruitment

The Shadow Circle does not take volunteers—it finds new members on its own. Recruitment, by invitation only, is in the hands of the Shadowmaster and the inner circle, always on the lookout for druids who seem ready to embrace the ruthless Shadow Circle philosophy.

For example, if a druid massacres a party of travelers who ventured into a sacred grove, the Shadow Circle soon comes looking for this prospective candidate. Another good possibility is a character who has destroyed a village whose peasants dared to clear a wood for use as farmland.

A Shadowed One spies on the potential member for a few weeks or months, often using animal spies as additional eyes. If the druid's deeds and words seem in sympathy with the Shadow Circle's goals, the character receives a visit from this Shadowed One (or a pair for a candidate 11th level or higher) before the next Shadowclave. The Shadowed One explains the group's purposes, inviting the newcomer to join. Of course, druids who refuse—or even waver—coincidentally turn up dead shortly thereafter.

Candidates who agree to join are blindfolded, given a mask, and taken to the Shadowclave. There the Shadowmaster gives each a secret name. After receiving their sworn allegiance, the Shadowmaster formally welcomes the new members into the Shadow Circle and commands them to perform some symbolic but dangerous task to prove their ruthlessness and dedication. (The difficulty of the assignment depends on the character's experience level.)

This kind of mission usually involves assassinating a specific enemy of the Shadow Circle, such as a noble or priest in a city the group has targeted for destruction. However, the task might be physically much simpler—say, poisoning a town well. The Shadowed One who recruited the druid will follow along (secretly), ready to slay a newcomer who shows weakness, risks capture, or tries to betray the group. Those who succeed, the Shadow Circle embraces as full members.

Creating a Druidic History

The druidic order and hierarchy presented here are designed to work as a default or base system. Many circles of druids have their own customs, and on many worlds the druidic order has its own unique history that shapes its structure.

The DM always should understand the history of the druidic order before beginning a campaign involving druids. A typical Order, like the one this chapter has detailed, is an ancient organization whose origin has become lost in the dim reaches of the past.

But that doesn't have to be the case. Instead, the druidic order may have an origin alive in history or myth. This background should explain where the first druids came from, why they worship Nature (or a specific Nature deity), why they protect the wild, and their purpose in standing at the crossroads between good and evil. The druidic origins might reflect true history, a legend whose truth remains uncertain, or a mixture of both. In any case, the origin tale must have a profound effect on how druids see themselves in the campaign.

As an example of how the druidic order springs from a more detailed history, three very different possible beginnings for the druidic order are sketched out below.

The Exiles

The secret founders of the druids were the crew of a spelljamming vessel, long-ago exiles from a world that would not accept their neutrality following the final triumph of evil—or good. (Exile was preferable to the fate of the members of the vanquished alignment, however.) The present druidic order traces its legacy to these ancient castaways.

As victims of an unbalanced world, the exiles and their descendants and followers vowed to preserve the volatile relationship between good and evil in their adopted home. They can see this balance best illustrated by the forces of Nature. In addition to their normal druidic duties, the members of the Order remain on guard against invasion from their ancestors' home world.

The New Faith

The druids belong to a relatively new faith, founded less than twenty years ago by a charismatic Nature priest. This amazing leader also preached that the older gods constitute only one small aspect of great Nature.

Active missionary work, the charisma of this founder, and the simplicity of the Order's beliefs draws more and more converts to druidism every day from the old, tired, polytheistic religions. But the largest rival religion considers druidism a threat; its priests have convinced the region's rulers to begin persecution of the "godless, troublemaking" druids.

The Myth of the Great War

Almost two thousand years ago a terrible war broke out between the two mighty guilds of wizards—one good and one evil—that controlled great empires. Wizards on both sides vowed to fight until they were utterly triumphant, seeking to purge their rivals from the earth. With fearsome magic and dragon armies they battled for centuries, neither side winning final victory.

In the process of their warfare, the wizards wrought vast devastation on the world—forests blazed up, islands sank into the sea, entire races became extinct. Eventually, the great goddess of Nature awakened from her sleep to witness the savage conflict. Shocked by the destruction, the Goddess sent a vision to a single human: the woman who would become the first Grand Druid.

Through the vision, this chosen figure saw that she must found a druidic order to preserve the fragile remains of her world's ecology. With the guidance of her goddess, the Order grew in strength until finally it had the power to intervene in the wizard war. The force of young druids pooled their powers and together vanquished the members of both battling guilds, transforming the combatants into innocent wild beasts. Once the former wizards—now unable to fathom the concept of good versus evil—slithered, bounded, loped, and crawled off into their ruined habitats, the Order began to heal the world.

Since then, the druidic order continually works to prevent such destruction from ever occurring again. Druids pledge to make sure the wars of good and evil no longer mar the precious earth. But, the Order also has bitter enemies in the ancient remnants of the guilds of warring wizards—those good and evil mages who luckily escaped the fate of their fellows. Each guild claims it had been on the verge of victory and would have won, had druids not interfered.

Each of these backgrounds—or one that you, the player might create with your DM—provides the druids of a world with a history, a purpose, and some idea of who their enemies might be. Add more details to these options as desired, to explain the Order's triumphs and failures, the history of its relation to other faiths, and perhaps the attempts of factions within the druidic order to deviate from its original purpose.

CHAPTER 4

Role-playing Druids

So, now that you have learned about the druidic order and selected your branch and kit, you think you're ready to assume the challenge of role-playing this colorful class? Well, there's still a lot more to know about druids. For example:

• What is a druid's world view like?
• How can a druid fit into a normal adventure?
• How does one role-play the neutral alignment?
• How do members of the Order relate to others?
• What are some typical druidic duties?
• Can druids become the center of entire campaigns?
• What strategies do druids follow as champions of Nature and the balance?
• How can a player make a specific druid stand out?

This chapter gives you, the player, hints for making your character really come alive.

Druidic Faith

Druids fit into the hierarchy of a worldwide Order that espouses a well-defined ethos yet grants each member considerable freedom of action. This liberty makes druids much more diverse than many other priest classes—reflected in the different druidic branches and kits—as they pursue their shared goals in their own ways.

Druids serve the force of Nature and its inherent natural cycles, such as that of birth, growth, death, and rebirth (*PH*, p. 37). Though some druids do choose to worship Nature embodied in a particular god, Nature, as a force, has no specific form or personality. (*The Complete Priest's Handbook*, on p. 11, defines a force as a process, natural or unnatural, that influences the world.)

The processes of Nature generate magical power its worshipers can tap. Failure to perform the ceremonies and follow the tenets of druidism leads a druid to fall out of touch with Nature and lose spell access, just as other unfaithful priests do.

Druids Who Worship Gods

Not all druids worship Nature as a force. Some see it personified by a great deity of Nature, often either formless or possessing many forms.

The most common manifestation of a druidic Nature deity is that of the Great Goddess—Chauntea and the Earthmother in the FORGOTTEN REALMS® setting or Beory in the WORLD OF GREYHAWK® setting, for example. The Great Goddess embodies Nature through multiple avatars that represent her different aspects: a virgin warrior-huntress, an adult mother, and an ancient crone.

The Great Goddess sometimes has a Consort (often appearing as an antlered huntsman), the subordinate lord of the hunt, death, and animals. Followers frequently worship both Goddess and Consort as a single power rather than as two deities.

Life after Death

Since they see the universe as a cycle or series of cycles, druids tend to believe the life force of a person (especially one who follows the druidic faith) is reborn again and again. A being's reincarnation will not remember a former life but may possess a similar personality.

All druids believe a person's soul may be reincarnated into an animal instead of a sentient being—yet another reason they revere all the world's creatures.

Are the druids correct? That depends on the nature of the DM's universe.

Nature and the Gods

Druids differ in their attitudes toward non-Nature gods. Before beginning a new campaign, it's important for you and your DM to establish a circle's position toward other gods. Some possible beliefs include:

Nature as Supreme. These druids consider Nature a force beyond mere gods. Other faiths do exist, but they are mere aspects of the greater whole. To worship one of them means celebrating just a fragment of Nature (like the thunder, the ocean or death) rather than the whole, as druids do.

Most druids in AD&D game worlds use this approach. They believe their own faith is somewhat superior, but do not actively oppose other faiths and may ally themselves with the worshipers of natural, agricultural, or elemental deities.

Nature as Progenitor. Followers of this philosophy see Nature as an integral part of a pantheon of gods. In this case, druids identify the other gods as "children of Nature," perhaps born in some mythic way. For instance, the druids may teach that, in the time before the world, first came formless chaos, and out of it emerged Nature. From Nature was born the Great Goddess, who married the Sky and gave birth to many children: all the other gods.

Nature by Another Name. Druids may identify Nature as one aspect of an existing god—usually a powerful and primal earth or natural deity. For instance, if the DM wants druids in a fantasy world involving the gods of Greek myth, Nature may be worshiped as the great earth goddess Gaia without causing other changes in druidic behavior. This belief pattern enables the druids to participate directly in a pantheon of deities.

Nature is All. Other gods do not exist! Druids who hold this belief see other priests either as deluded or worshiping Nature under a different name. Unless the druids are right, (in which case, no other class of priest would function in the campaign!) this philosophy leads them to have a rather close-minded and inflexible faith. Druids may live apart from mainstream society as hermits or work as missionaries to recruit people to the "one true faith." Quite possibly, believers in other faiths would take a dim view of such druids, as no one likes to hear their beliefs called lies!

The Gods Threaten Nature. Other gods are acknowledged as powerful entities, but the druids consider them *unnatural*— interlopers from the outer planes or beings and philosophies created by the belief of foolish mortals. Followers of aggressive, proselytizing religions that actively seek converts and start religious wars become dangers to the natural order. Druids with this belief tend to act hostile to those of most other faiths, considering them instruments of "outside influences" that threaten the balance of Nature!

Nature as Equal with Other Forces. These druids believe that other primal forces exist on the same level as Nature, such as Magic or Entropy. The priests of these forces may become either rivals or allies to druids.

The Neutral Alignment

True neutral, the most misunderstood of all alignments, often causes problems for players. One common mistake is for neutral characters, such as druids, to seek a balance by deliberately acting chaotic evil one day and lawful good the next. Such behavior makes characters unpredictable, and the cumulative effect promotes chaos more than anything else.

Druids consider each alignment equally valid in a cosmic sense. They try to remain nonjudgmental and uncommitted to any specific moral, legal, or philosophical system beyond the basic tenets of the druidic order. Because a druid's main charges—plants, animals, and the health of the planetary ecology—essentially lack alignment or ethos, the character feels free to use almost any means necessary to protect them.

Chapter 4 of the *Player's Handbook* discusses alignments in a general sense; the druidic order works to maintain the natural balance among these alignments. (See "Keeper of the Balance" later in this chapter.) However, druids do realize that most individuals' actions—including their own—will not prove significant to the cosmic balance. The druid sees the friction between alignments as the driving force in the world. Although most druids personally may *prefer* to live among good people, they recognize that the existence of evil keeps intelligent beings from stagnating.

Despite their neutral status, druids don't resent being pulled into the struggle between alignments. Neutral individuals do *not* lack interest, ambition, or passion—they value their own well-being and that of friends and loved ones. They may struggle passionately on behalf of themselves and others, as well as feel a compassion blanketing everything that makes up the Nature they swear to protect. Never doubt that druids will act for their own goals and the Order's.

For example, the druid Rebecca has no philosophical objection to helping a group of lawful good paladins and clerics defeat an evil dragon—if they can demonstrate a good reason. She won't agree to kill the dragon merely "because it is evil." But, she might help if the dragon had harmed or threatened her friends or a forest or village under her protection. She might also offer assistance simply because she realizes the danger of living near a powerful and unpredictably evil creature inclined to wreak havoc upon the natural surroundings. Finally, she might join the party in return for a pledge that the members aid her in protecting a wilderness area from those who would exploit it—or in order to get treasure and magical items to do the job on her own.

Clearly, playing a druid true to alignment is no easy task. The character must consider carefully all the variables in a situation before acting. Remember that, when faced with a tough decision, a druid usually stands behind the solution that best serves Nature *in the long run.* So, Rebecca could have an equally valid reason to join a band of evil adventurers hunting a lawful good dragon as she has to join a good party hunting an evil dragon. Although a gold or silver dragon is unlikely to threaten Rebecca or her sacred grove, she might wish to use its treasure to purchase equipment to fight a greater threat or win the trust of an evil party she can use for her own ends.

Of course, druids understand that others may not take so pragmatic a view. Rebecca knows a party of adventurers wouldn't be pleased to find she has stymied its efforts. Alignment struggles constitute just another aspect of Nature, so Rebecca would never seek to stop the members of a party from continuing the struggle unless she deems it harmful to her own interests or those of the force she worships and safeguards.

A druid allied with a party of adventurers usually goes along with the party's actions unless they threaten trees, crops, wild plants, and other things the druid holds sacred. At the same time, the character needs a reason for joining a party—often something as simple as a desire to gain the experience and power needed to become a more effective guardian of Nature.

Druids tend to react nonjudgmentally toward other races. With the possible exception of undead, they feel that every race and species has its place in the world. For instance, a druid recognizes most orcs as evil and cruel. The character might not enjoy the company of orcs, but doesn't consider this feeling an excuse to exterminate the entire race. Conflict between orcs and humans is the way of the world, some druids say. They point out that orcs live a harsher existence than humans, often dwelling in the deadly subterranean world. And, while the average human may be less cruel than the average orc, mankind is capable of greater evil through superior organization and civilization.

60 • Chapter Four

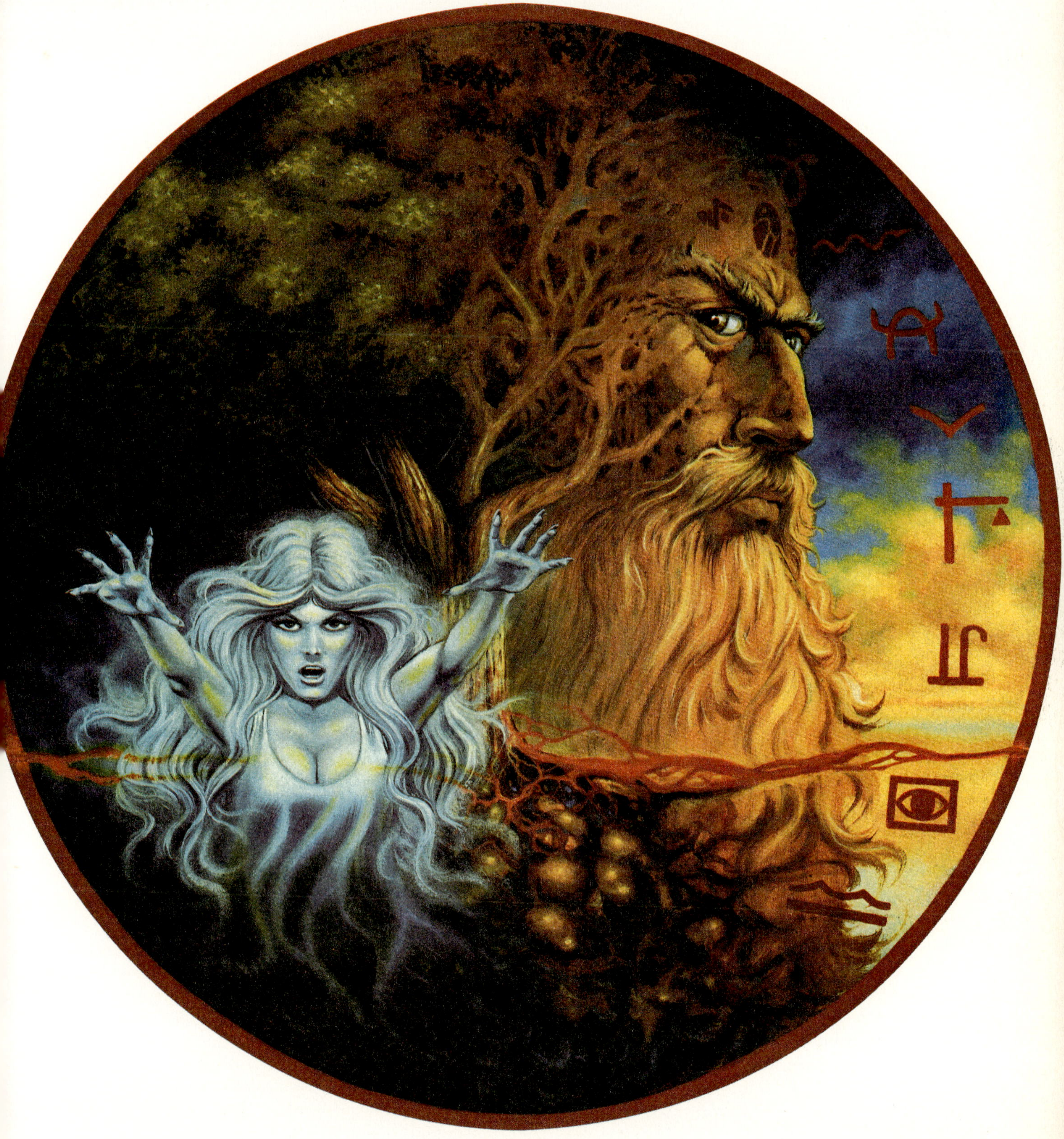

Druids who stray from their alignment or cease to follow the tenets of the Order lose major sphere spell access and granted powers until they make atonement. In addition, the circle's great druid may place any subordinate druid under the ban as a temporal punishment for such violations.

A Druid's Responsibilities

The beliefs and ethics of druids cover two main areas: keeping the balance between the alignments and serving as guardians of Nature. When role-playing a druid character, keep in mind that the character's behavior should reflect the importance of these duties.

Keeper of the Balance

Druids have seen that a balance between the forces of good and evil, law and chaos, best fosters the continuance of life from one generation to the next. This druidic duty is not so much a personal matter as the ethical responsibility of the entire Order.

Only an event or threat of considerable magnitude can cause the balance to tilt toward one alignment or another—a matter that could affect the destiny of nations. Deciding that a menace of this degree exists and how best to handle it is traditionally left to those of archdruid or higher rank, or the High Council of the Moot. However, lesser druid PCs may decide they know better and take action on their own!

Remember, keeping a balance doesn't spell stagnation. Druids view a slight shift in the balance—like the ascendancy of one alignment—to be as natural as a change in the weather. An individual druid may prefer a period of good (or of law) just as one might prefer a warm summer day. But autumn and winter remain just as necessary—in a world of eternal summer, the autumn harvest never comes.

But druids also believe in free will, and with free will comes the danger that the balance will tilt too far in one direction. Many druids believe—rightly or wrongly— that powerful beings (gods and extraplanar entities) manipulate mortals for just such an end: to see their own alignment or faith permanently triumphant.

When druids perceive the balance tilting too far in any direction, the Order becomes concerned. Some individual members may profess that the balance will swing back by itself, regardless of the actions of mankind. Such druids contentedly sit back and let events pass without taking action. A druid with this belief would not make an interesting PC, although such a mindset gives the DM a good excuse to have senior druids refuse to aid the player character!

But most druids do not share this belief. The majority see human and demihuman races in general and the druidic order in particular as pivotal to maintaining the cosmic balance. They look at the cycles of the world as driven by the actions and machinations of mankind (and other intelligent races) and believe that, as individuals play their part in the great cycle, they can also upset it.

This means that, when the cosmic balance is obviously in danger of being tilted in favor of one alignment or faith, druids will ally themselves (openly or covertly) with the opposing side. Normally an archdruid or great druid makes this decision and devotes all energies to rallying the circle against the threat. Sometimes a circle of druids becomes divided about the situation: Is it serious enough to warrant intervention? The circle leaves it up to individual druids to decide whether to offer assistance. However, keep in mind that druids who frequently refuse to aid their circle's cause will find themselves unable to attract help from senior druids when they need it.

Although the balance could swing too far

in any direction, DMs should set their campaigns at times when *evil* has grown alarmingly in strength, for such periods allow druid PCs to become heroes. With the balance threatened by the power of evil, most druids find themselves in the position to serve the cause of good willingly. This motivation is good for the game, as it provides plenty of adventure for good-aligned PCs while giving druids a chance to fight by their sides.

Similarly, in a game featuring the PCs as rebels or outlaws against authority, the balance may have swung in favor of inflexible law. In such a case, druids may side with the forces of chaos—good, neutral, and maybe even evil—in the struggle of liberty against oppression.

Defense of the Wilderness

The second major responsibility of druid characters is to defend the wilderness and its wildlife. Players sometimes feel uncertain as to the limits of a druid's concern for Nature, especially in regard to how druids treat those who make a living hunting or farming.

Since all druids are charged with protecting natural wilderness, trees, wild plants, wild animals, and crops, they also protect the people who follow druidic beliefs, such as peasants and hunters living in harmony with Nature. (See the Guardian and Village Druid kits, Chapter 2.)

Druids realize all creatures have basic needs for food, shelter, and self-defense. Humans must hunt animals for food and must clear trees to farm and build houses. These actions constitute a necessary part of the natural cycle. But druids do not tolerate unnecessary destruction or exploitation of Nature. Sensing violations, a druid investigates the motives of the people involved, weighing them against the risk to the land. Then the druid decides whether to take action.

Protecting Animals. Only a very few druids (like those with the Pacifist kit) oppose hunting or raising animals for food, skins, or fur. In fact, many druids hunt animals for food and clothing themselves. They do frown upon killing animals simply for sport, over-hunting (or over-trapping) a region, and treating animals with excessive cruelty. And most druids do not even take this feeling to extremes. They know that feudal nobles, for instance, enjoy the hunt; few such hunters are cruel killers, and their game ends up on the lord's tables.

Druids oppose trapping or hunting beasts to use their fur or other body parts for frivolous reasons. A hunter may kill a single wolf and take its pelt to make a wolfskin cloak, according to druidic philosophy. If the hunter kills a couple wolves every year and sells their pelts, a druid may or may not be upset, depending on the prevalence of wolves in the area. But if a hunter regularly traps dozens of wolves and makes a fortune selling their pelts to local merchants, a druid will become angry and take action.

Even more than trapping for food or fur, druids hate to see animals captured for use in events like bear baiting, bullfighting, or other such "sports." Druids always try to stop these spectacles and free the animals. They may wreak terrible vengeance on those who capture wild beasts for sport or operate the arenas where animals are forced to fight.

Protecting Trees and Woodlands. Druids have nothing against most forms of farming, even if it means clearing woodlands or draining swamps to create new fields. Although druids feel a special reverence for trees, crops are plants too, and civilized races have a right to practice agriculture.

The druid may object to destroying a wilderness area for a farm extension that is strictly for profit. For instance, clearing a forest for a large plantation to grow cash crops—especially ones intended for pleasure, such as tobacco—would raise a druid's ire.

Role-playing Druids • 63

A druid also will oppose farming that requires the destruction of ancient wilderness areas, large spreads of land, or any region that serves as a sanctuary for rare, endangered, or magical plants and animals. Most importantly, no druid ever tolerates the destruction of a sacred grove! Druids also discourage farming practices that harm the soil and selfish irrigation schemes (dams, aqueducts, etc.) intended to parch one region to slake another's thirst.

Druids sometimes tolerate logging or clearing land to mine useful minerals like salt, copper, tin, and iron. After all, they use manufactured items themselves. Whether to accept such land use depends on the motives and need of those involved and the nature of the region in question, just as with farming.

Cutting down a forest to build houses is one thing—especially if the builder makes some effort at replanting. Using the wood to build a fleet of warships to satisfy the ambitions of a tyrant is much less likely to find sympathy with the druid. On the other hand, if the proposed fleet will oppose the invasion force of a king whose conquests threaten to tip the balance of good and evil, some druids may justify the forest's loss.

Cleansing Nature. Some acts defile the very essence of Nature and require immediate opposition. For instance, the magical forced transformation of a large forest into a bizarre, otherplanar landscape instantly draws the enmity of the circle. If a sacred grove falls under a curse, druids will work to lift it and reclaim the land.

A more common perversion of Nature is the undead. The fact that no druidic branch has the power to turn or control undead does *not* mean druids tolerate them. Rather, the druid's lack of power over the living dead reflects the absolute aversion this class has toward them. Things exist in a natural cycle: birth, growth, death, rebirth. The undead break this cycle—worse, they are the enemies of life. Therefore, most druids see the undead as abominations to stamp out to restore the proper workings of Nature.

Yet, druids do not actively hunt undead. This is primarily because undead rarely directly invade a druid's sphere of interest. However, if a vampire starts menacing a peaceful village, a banshee begins stalking the moors, or a lich introduces a reign of terror to the wilderness, a druid may intervene. Because druids lack the key powers necessary to fight undead (although their elemental magic can prove useful), they will ally with a good-aligned party also interested in wiping out the undead.

Defending Croplands and Farmers. A druid feels an obligation to protect farmers who worship Nature and to safeguard fields and livestock. For details, see the Village Druid kit (Chapter 2) and the "Festivals" section in this chapter.

Eyes in the Wilderness

Defending an entire tract of wilderness and safeguarding the balance of forces within it spells a *lot* of work for one druid. (In addition, sometimes druids are asked to give reports on their section of the domain at moots.) Clearly, to do a good job, the druid needs reliable sources of information and early knowledge of possible threats.

Druids' own powers do go a long way in keeping them aware of the goings-on in and near their area. The ability to pass without a trace and blend into the woods allows druids to maintain watch on anyone entering the wild. Even better is their shapechange power. Druids risk detection when using it, but very few people—unless they know they have a druidic enemy—ever would suspect that a spy lurks in the form of the mangy hound munching a bone under the lord's table or the cat hiding under the bed. To infiltrate a foe's stronghold, druids often assume the shape of a domestic animal, allowing themselves to be bought at market or given as a gift—although those shapechanging into an edible animal should take care to avoid the stew pot!

At high levels, the ability to cast *speak with plants* or *stone tell* proves very useful. If the druid is looking for general information, good recipients for such a spell include trees or standing stones at crossroads, at wells, or near town or castle gates.

Animal Aides. Still, druids can be in only one place at a time. In addition to their own powers, they also use animal resources. *Speak with animals* gives druids an ability enemies always regret underestimating.

Druids rely on animals mostly in the wild: a spread of furry, feathered, and scaly "spies" all over the land to keep watch on the movements of friends and enemies alike. Normally, small, inconspicuous animals work best—especially birds, with their excellent mobility, aerial vantage point, and good eyesight. Rodents, from squirrels to mice, rarely get noticed. Domestic animals constitute another good choice due to their intelligence. They have the added bonus of being able to tell the druid about the activities inside a building.

To this end, a druid who can speak with animals should use every opportunity to insinuate these aides into important areas, such as the lord's stronghold—perhaps a character can even covertly cast *animal friendship* (or better, *charm person or mammal*) on a foe's animals. Some individuals may protect their servants from charm, but few think to check domestic animals.

One problem with using animals kept inside a building involves the difficulty of staying in touch with them. Animal helpers should have an opportunity to slip out to meet the druid (like a cat that is put out at night) or should remain in magical contact with the druid. (See the *animal spy* spell in Chapter 5: Druidic Magic.) With this logistical problem solved, domestic animal spies can prove exceedingly effective. People may search high and low to discover a traitor, never dreaming that traitor is actually a falcon, pet dog, or war horse!

Animals have a limitation, though: They often don't understand what they see and hear and sometimes can't determine what is worth reporting. A dog can recognize certain people and usually has a general idea what its owners are doing, but it cannot understand speech. A mouse or bat probably cannot tell one person from another. Animals can tell druids of unusual events, like the passage of a large body of men. They can warn druids when people have entered or left buildings or mention when a new monster appears. But, for detailed and reliable intelligence, the druid needs just that: intelligent spies. To this end, all druids should make use of the eyes and ears of other inhabitants of the wilderness.

Human and Demihuman Assets. Druids who have lived in an area for a long time should cultivate friendly contacts among the surrounding manors and villages. If the people openly follow druidism, they generally inform the druid of unusual happenings as a matter of course. Otherwise, druids try to place one "agent" in each village or castle in their area; low-ranking servants often have reason to go into the wilds every now and then (chopping firewood, grazing the animals, etc.), giving them an excuse to secretly meet the druid. Some druids befriend children for this purpose, since no one will miss them when they go out to play, nor will most people suspect children of passing information.

Druids try to keep in touch with a friend at every roadside and village inn within their territory. This source isn't necessarily the innkeeper: Someone less obvious, like a servant or stablekeeper, works better. Since adventurers and other interesting travelers usually stop at inns, the source can update druids on newcomers.

The druid must contact these aides regularly

to advise them of the sort of information they should look for and receive their news. Just as important as having agents is having a means of collecting updates from them, after all. The 2nd-level *messenger* spell suits this purpose ideally. Innkeepers and the like tend to stay terribly busy, so providing them with a trained messenger animal (often a bird) can ensure periodic reports. If the agent (or druid) cannot read or write, the pair can arrange a simple code: a red ribbon on the bird's foot means, "Come immediately," a blue ribbon means, "Interesting strangers staying at the inn."

A druid's agents almost never work professionally as spies, and few know much about the druid's doings (helpful, if an enemy questions them). Most are just ordinary (0-level) men and women. Druids don't have to reveal their identity to these contacts—they just use their natural charm (Charisma of 15 or better) to appear as romantic, mysterious figures who will pay well if kept informed of local gossip. Just as often, druids recruit from among those who are in their debt. For instance, a druid who used magic to save a child from disease might recruit the grateful mother as another set of eyes. Also, druids utilize members of families that have followed the druidic faith for generations (often in secret). Finally, druids do not hesitate to use *charm person or mammal* to create excellent involuntary spies when necessary!

Besides these local folk, druids should also strive to be on good terms with travelers like tinkers, Gypsies, bards, merchants, entertainers, and rangers. These people, often the first to bear news from the next county, always know what the neighbors are talking about. Being on "good terms" usually requires making friends with a few prominent members of these groups and offering magical assistance at times.

Sylvan Creatures. Elves, satyrs, dryads, treants, sylphs, and similar native creatures represent a priceless resource every druid should cultivate to the utmost. Their special powers and ability to blend into the wilderness make them excellent scouts. In addition, their goals usually parallel those of the druid—the protection of the woodlands and wilderness—so their information likely will prove timely and reliable. A character tends to receive a more regular flow of gossip by befriending *particular* sylvan beings—make friends with Shaylara the Pixie rather than just staying on good terms with a "band of pixies." To foster this comradeship, the druid should often visit the dwellings of local pixies, sprites, elves, and the like, and always stand ready to offer help, such as magical *cures* or protection from adventurers or monsters.

Humanoids and Evil Monsters. Druid characters should not forget that their neutral alignment enables them to make use of all sorts of information sources. Those who live near a monster and stay on speaking terms with it sometimes receive a messenger with information from the creature—which undoubtedly hopes for a favor or bribe. This relationship generally requires that the druid first win the monster's trust: by providing food in a harsh winter, using magic to heal injuries, etc.

However, druids must use the stick along with the carrot—most evil creatures prove truly helpful only after the character demonstrates the fury of druidic wrath! Even so, humanoids and monsters usually feel happy to alert the druid if something mysterious is making them uneasy—or if *good* forces are infiltrating the wilderness.

Remember, evil creatures are notorious liars: They will tell the druid only what suits them. A tribe of forest-dwelling goblins attacked and routed by two high-level rangers and a paladin might warn the druid of these intruders—after changing some details of their encounter with ". . . dozens of human warriors! We got many, but they were too much powerful. We see them chop down tree . . ." *Caveat emptor.*

Druidic Ceremonies

Besides protecting the wilderness and maintaining the cosmic balance, druidic responsibilities include worshiping Nature through the appropriate ceremonies. This duty also involves casting spells and presiding over rites, many of which involve the use of the druids' secret language. (See Chapter 1.) Other ceremonies benefit the druid's flock—those rural folk who worship Nature (or a Nature deity) and follow the druidic ethos. The exact rituals vary from circle to circle and branch to branch, but all druids practice the common ones, including:

Prayers. Druids almost always pray in the form of poems or songs celebrating the beauty and power of Nature and the druid's role in it. These poems are valued as much for the beauty of their language and imagery as for their ritual value; dual-class bard/druids created some of the most memorable ones. A druid should create new prayers after personal inspiration. Many prayers celebrate a specific aspect of Nature, such as the beginning of spring, and are sung, chanted, or spoken only certain days.

Wild Dancing. The ceremonies of druids—especially younger initiates—often involve dancing. The movements, rarely formal or ritualized, are wild, impulsive, individual, and ecstatic—a spontaneous celebration of Nature's energy. Druids may dance while praying to regain spells; although in motion, the druid remains in deep communion with the powers of Nature during the dance, as oblivious to the rest of the world as if deep in study.

Holy Days. Like other priests, druids offer brief prayers one or more times a day, but they also have holidays in which they devote the entire day (or night) to sacred ceremonies. Druids typically spend two full days every month observing the holy days of their particular branch and of the Order as a whole. Minor celebrations usually take place in accordance with the lunar calendar; on the highly important first days of the full moon and new moon, most druids hold daylong or nightlong rites, either on their own or in the company of other druids.

Even more important are those ceremonies held four times a year to celebrate the changing of the seasons. At such times, an archdruid or the great druid summons most druids in the circle together for a great moot. Initiations and challenges often, but not always, occur at these times.

Festivals. Festivals are holy days celebrated not just by druids but by the entire community. If a village or tribe openly follows the druidic philosophy, some or all the seasonal rites include a joyous public festival. Druids praise Nature and bless the village, livestock, and crops. Then, with the locals, they sing, dance, and make merry for the rest of the day around a tree or Maypole in the village green.

Following the day of celebration, the assemblage builds bonfires on the hills to ward off evil, enjoys performances by visiting bards, and watches locals dressed as animals dance to ensure good hunting. Springtime rites, the most important, end with the casting of *plant growth* on the fields to guarantee their fertility come harvest time.

Private rites involving only the druids usually follow a festival—often late at night.

Appeasement. Druids, while they do not always object to replacing wilderness with cropland, insist on performing a ceremony before any land is cleared. These rites, designed to appease, comfort, and lay to rest the spirits of the trees and plants about to be cut down, normally require a druid's presence for half a day per acre of wilderness slated for clearing. In some cases, a druid high enough in level casts a *commune with nature* spell to determine if permitting the destruction is the right thing to do.

A druid unable to perform the rites before the clearing of the land begins will become very upset. At the DM's discretion, this lack of appeasement also may lead to the appearance of creatures such as treants, who seek to avenge the destruction.

Rites of Passage. A young person coming of age usually undergoes a rite of passage into adulthood. A druid living among the local folk administers this usually secret rite, which may involve anything from a spiritual revelation to a painful ordeal, depending on the culture.

For example, the druid, after invoking a blessing, might lead the candidate into the deep woods, then leave the adolescent to find the way home. Along the way, the druid may appear in shapechanged forms to act as a guide. Candidates who make it out of the woods (very likely, unless they ignore or mistreat their animal guides) are considered adults from that day forward. If they guess that the druid had been watching over them in animal form, they may find their destiny lies in a druidic career.

Marriages. Druids perform marriage ceremonies for locals under their spiritual care, usually simple affairs in a druid's grove or village green. There, the man and woman share vows to love, respect, and protect one another, with the druid serving as witness. Following the vows comes an exchange of tokens, prayers for the couple's health and fertility, and finally a party and feast.

Druids themselves, rarely celibate, usually choose to marry and raise children. Some circles prefer their druids to limit their choice to "suitable" mates: druids or bards, and perhaps elves, dryads, or sylphs. Independent rural folk like tinkers, rangers, Gypsies, or foresters also constitute good choices. Love can be blind, but a druid generally prefers a mate of neutral alignment, from a rural background, who follows the druidic faith.

Funerals. Most druids bury their dead (although some prefer cremation), returning the body of a loved one to the earth near a sacred grove. Mourners celebrate the deceased through poems and prayers, and a hired bard may offer additional memorials in song. Finally, the presiding druid blesses the departed spirit and—since most druids believe in reincarnation—prays for its safe rebirth. Friends and family then hold a wake to remember the departed person through song, dance, and merrymaking.

Initiations. Worthy aspirants seeking to enter the druidic order must be initiated by an inner circle member. The initiation takes place at a moot or in a sacred grove on a holy day. The candidate, after being purified with holy water, takes the druidic oath: a promise to preserve the balance of the world, to follow the druidic ethos, to respect the freedom of other druids in and beyond the circle, to act as a guardian of Nature (or the deity that personifies Nature to the Order), and to live true to the druidic order and keep its secrets safe.

Character Strategy

Exactly *how* do druids go about fulfilling the responsibilities discussed above? In role-playing terms, there are some interesting strategies you, the player, can use to make the most of your druid character's potential.

Suppose the druid Dannay wished to preserve an old wood, but the local baron and his peasants want it cut down, claiming they need the land to plant crops to keep from going hungry. What does the druid do?

Find the Root of the Problem

First, Dannay must determine the truth of the situation—what lies behind the decision to chop down the wood? Are the peasants really in need or just greedy? Is their lord simply attempting to increase his own income? Why are the peasants likely to starve? Is there any other land to plant?

After investigating, Dannay decides the peasants do have a legitimate need to develop the old wood. Next, he considers the threatened trees themselves. Is the woodland ancient? (Druids prefer to preserve the eldest trees.) Does it harbor species of rare animals or plants? Will its destruction displace sylvan races? Is this forest one of the few unspoiled areas left in the region? Does a sacred grove lie within the forest? All these, particularly the last, constitute good reasons for a druid to take a stand opposing the destruction of the wood.

Assume that, for one of these reasons, Dannay finds this wood of ancient oak worth preserving. In most cases he first seeks a peaceful compromise.

Negotiate a Solution

For instance, if the area possesses no other available land, Dannay might show the peasants that expansion isn't necessary. Say the peasants' problem is that their current crops don't yield enough to feed them and cover their tithes. Dannay might offer his services as an adviser if the lord agrees to lower the peasants' taxes. If the baron refuses—or already levies merely reasonable taxes—the druid could try to help directly.

How should Dannay help? As an expert in agriculture, he can suggest techniques to increase the yield of the peasants' current crops so they don't require expansion. Or he might make a bargain: In exchange for the peasants agreeing not to encroach on the wood, he will use druidic magic to cure (or prevent) disease among their animals, or heal sick villagers and livestock. High-level druids could promise to control the weather to extend the growing season or to prevent droughts or floods. Most useful of all, a druid with access to the 3rd-level spell *plant growth* can increase the prosperity of any farm dramatically.

But suppose the idea of a compromise does not meet with favor. Maybe the peasants have a priest of their own who already provides this sort of magical aid. Perhaps they follow a religion that distrusts druids. Maybe the baron has determined to expand his land at all costs—or perhaps he just doesn't like a druid telling him what to do! In any event, Dannay may have to turn to harsher measures. Exactly what he does depends on his assessment of the strength and character of the opposition and the importance of the wilds in question.

Several options make themselves available when negotiation fails. Many call for the druid, short of destroying an enemy, to break that enemy's morale instead.

Ultimatum

Dannay could simply announce to the peasants and lord, "Violate my wood, and you will regret it." This threat may work for prestigious druids; it also may prove successful if backed up with a flashy demonstration, like a *wall of thorns* around a portion of the threatened wood or a *call lightning* spell in the midst of the speech.

The DM should judge the effect of the ultimatum depending on the alignment of the NPCs involved, how desperately they want the land, and the reputation and actions of the druid. Most likely the lord and peasants will not be so easily cowed, and Dannay will have to turn to direct action.

Harassment

The druid could choose to use passive, nonviolent resistance to prevent the leveling of the wood. Suppose a party of lumberjacks enters to begin work. Dannay could have enchanted plants entangle or snare them, order chipmunks and squirrels to steal their food, cast *summon insects* to harass them, make them lose their way using *obscurement*, summon rain and wind down on them, and so on.

Strong, determined loggers may succeed in clearing a few acres despite Nature's torment. But, what will they do when, upon waking the next day, they see all their work undone thanks to a *hallucinatory forest* spell? If they are wise, they'll turn around and head for home!

Fear

Alternately, Dannay might try to convince the locals that the wood is haunted; he wants them to stay out just for their own safety. Even if the wood was previously safe, the druid may convince the peasants that their intentions to cut it down have awakened ancient wood spirits ready to rise against any intruders.

Careful use of spells like *faerie fire* and *dust devil* can simulate ghosts; *obscurement* makes mysterious mists; *control temperature, 10' radius* creates eerie chills; and druids also can call up packs of howling wolves or flocks of bats. Props like an erected gallows with a human skull or two lying around in the wood strike terror into the hearts of peasants and common soldiers alike.

Naturally, some people will suspect Dannay is behind this, especially if he tried negotiating with the locals and lord earlier. So, some druids simply use fear tactics *before* attempting a compromise!

Hit-and-Run

A ruthless druid facing a determined foe may combine fear with violent actions, such as killing intruders and leaving their bodies for others to find—or just allowing the victims to vanish without a trace. This technique can prove very effective, especially when the deaths are mysterious and not directly traceable to the druid's magic. But Dannay should be wary of doing the job too well: Misleading the natives into believing that murderous undead roam the wood, for instance, may lead them to call upon outsider paladins or clerics to purge the area.

Defense

Dannay may decide merely to defend his land aggressively, attacking anyone who enters the wood. Druids frequently resort to a defensive stance when fear or harassment fail. The character aims to convince intruders exploitation is too costly to be worthwhile. The druid's tactics resemble a more violent form of harassment. In particular, Dannay would mobilize native creatures (using *animal friendship* and sometimes *animal growth* spells) to attack intruders and—if he has time— would set lethal traps, such as pits and deadfalls. The druid also may recruit allies, perhaps other druids or monsters who could lose their lairs to the axe.

Like many good generals, Dannay himself often stays back from the fighting, instead setting up magical traps and sending animals and plants into battle. Normally a druid would risk himself to save an animal, but in this case he is battling not just for one creature, but for an entire habitat. Dannay knows he must spare his own life so he can continue to preserve the lives of others.

War

Usually as a last resort, the druid may choose to carry the fight to the enemy's castle

Role-playing Druids • 71

or village. Typically, only a high-level druid has the ability to do this. And remember, Dannay has no obligation to use "honorable" tactics. If he has chosen to fight, it is because he believes his opponents have failed to compromise.

A druid's actions in war may range from subtle tricks, like stealing some or all the local plow animals and war horses, to something direct but nonviolent, like shapechanging into a bird, sneaking into the offending lord's bedchamber, and taking his first-born hostage for his good behavior. Or, Dannay could use spells like *call lightning, conjure fire elemental, creeping doom,* or *earthquake* to wreak destruction. Even low-level spells like *produce flame* can easily set fire to a peasant's cottage or a field of grain.

Please note that Dannay will direct his every action solely against those who cause the problem. If a greedy baron represents the threat to the wood, the druid targets the baron. If the problem lies with the peasants, he tries to intimidate them or drive them away. A druid never engages in wanton violence for its own sake.

When a PC druid uses any of these strategies, the DM should work out the response of the factions opposing the druid's interests. For instance, perhaps the baron sends up to three village work parties daily into the wood, each of which can clear one acre of forest if allowed to work unimpeded. If the druid decides to harass them or frighten them off, the DM should refer to the rules for morale and NPC reactions (*DMG*, pgs. 69-72, 114-115) and make morale checks any time the druid succeeds with an action the DM deems would frustrate, impede, or frighten them. If a work party fails enough checks, the workers either get nothing done that day or return home, too scared to come back. Perhaps soldiers or the lord's mage escort the next work parties. If Dannay succeeds in dealing with this new threat, the DM may wish to check the *baron's* morale. Failing this check, the baron may negotiate.

Revenge

A druid who has failed to stop the defilement of Nature often seeks vengeance, for one of three reasons. First, the druid removes his foe to make sure the defilement doesn't happen again. Second, a druid's act of revenge sends a message to others. And third, as most druids are human, they can succumb to anger and feelings of injustice as easily as anyone else.

Vengeful druids must consider this question carefully: Who is the intended object of revenge? For example, a druid may immediately target as foes trappers massacring winter wolf cubs for their fur. But, upon investigation, the druid discovers that the trappers are merely poor yeomen or peasants simply trying to earn money to support their families. The real enemies become the gentleman furriers who grow rich off the sale of the pelts, and the lords and ladies who demand winter wolf fur as this year's high fashion. The druid should take revenge on these people.

A character seeking vengeance will wait patiently and make careful plans. This behavior sometimes makes them seem cold-blooded, but the druid has a long memory—a foe who appears too strong today may prove weaker tomorrow.

Druids prefer subtle forms of vengeance. If a wicked sheriff were responsible for the destruction of a druid's grove, the druid might try to frame the sheriff for treason against his lord rather than risk a direct attack. For the sheriff to be executed as a traitor would be a fitting revenge!

Some druids enjoy irony. Suppose a noble cleared an ancient forest to set up a vineyard. After the first pressing, a druid might sneak into the wine cellar and spoil the vintage.

A druid carefully considers the consequences of an act of vengeance and works them into the overall plan. For instance, if a king's sheriff were the druid's enemy, the druid would not try to destroy the sheriff without knowing what would happen afterward. In particular, the druid would not try to destroy an enemy who might be replaced with an even worse foe. Instead, the druid might take vengeance in a different form—perhaps by kidnaping the sheriff's infant to raise as a druid who one day would prove a foe to the sheriff.

Relations with Others

Here's how relations often stand between druids and the people and monsters that live in or near the wild.

Woodcutters and Hunters

Druids act much as game wardens do, letting woodcutters know which trees they may cut and which they must leave standing, and telling hunters which species they may hunt and which are protected.

Sometimes these folk resent or even disobey such orders, but most druids temper their restrictions with reason and balance punishment with reward. People who live or work in the wild and follow a druid's laws remain under druidic protection. Druids use their spells when necessary to cure injury or sickness in hunters' families, prevent starvation among woodcutters in harsh times, and so on. Those who don't follow druidic rules cannot expect help, even in cases of dire need.

Local Animals

Druids try to get to know most wild animals within a few miles of home, learning their daily habits, the locations of their lairs, and so on. A druid makes a point of keeping

Role-playing Druids • 73

track of animals that are pregnant, weak, or sick, and usually aids (or puts down) diseased, mad, or injured local creatures. However, a druid does not interfere with normal cycles of predators and prey. Think of this attitude as that of forest rangers or game wardens: Protecting species holds greater importance than safeguarding individuals. Still, druids often befriend a few local animals, whom they respect and protect as they would human companions. Animals frequently serve as a busy druid's eyes and ears.

Sylvan and Faerie Creatures

Druids respect certain creatures as sentient embodiments of the "spirit" of Nature. Forest druids, in particular, would risk their lives to protect sylvan or faerie beings and would oppose other humans to protect the wilderness where they live. In return, these creatures often give druids official standing in their communities, perhaps as ambassadors to human realms. A druid might receive an invitation to speak at a sylvan or faerie council to offer a "human viewpoint," although only rarely would humans extend the same courtesy.

Outlaws, Fugitives, and Bandits

Folk living away from society sometimes find themselves operating in the same wilderness areas as druids. As druids know their woods intimately, they can become vital allies—and bitter enemies, for they know exactly where outlaws hide and can lead pursuers to them if they choose. Thus, any outlaws exist on the druids' sufferance.

Druids usually prefer to avoid becoming involved with criminals. They sometimes shelter individual fugitives and, rarely, offer assistance to entire bands of outlaws whose activities further druidic goals and show proper respect toward Nature. Druids' actions generally depend on the situation.

For instance, a character wishing to discourage farmers or loggers from making inroads into a forest might consider an alliance with bandits, while one on good terms with neighboring villagers and nobility would seek to drive them away or reveal their location to the law. But most often, the druid remains uninvolved, acting only to protect the wilderness from threats.

Local Monsters

Druids usually stay on good or neutral terms with local monsters, opposing them only if they threaten the entire area or the druid personally. For instance, a beholder that uses a woodland cave as its sanctuary makes a fine neighbor for a druid; one that tries to enslave large numbers of sylvan folk to conquer a nearby elven kingdom means trouble and should be eliminated before it engulfs the forest in a devastating war.

In general, the druid will act more favorably to creatures that "belong" in an area. A green dragon, a native of woodlands just as much as an elf or bear, finds it only natural to prey on elves and men. A druid has no argument with this tendency. After all, the humans and elves can always send a knight to slay the dragon.

Most druids make an effort to stay on speaking terms with intelligent monsters, good, evil, or neutral. The druid may do occasional favors for a creature on a *quid pro quo* basis. For example, the druid might volunteer to heal a sick or injured monster; the druid wants something in return, like a promise that the beast will refrain from attacking a certain village, will free its captives, or will aid the druid in battle.

Evil Humanoids

The druid knows these evil humanoid races make up a natural part of the world and have a right to struggle for existence. As a result, druids will not act against orcs, goblins, or the like simply because of their race or "evil" nature. In fact, in the eyes of the druids, these races represent less of a threat to the wilderness than do humans or dwarves: Few humanoids organize beyond the tribal level, they rarely build big cities above ground, and they prefer hunting and gathering to extensive farming.

A few druids—especially Shadow Circle members—ally with native humanoids to protect the wilderness against encroachment or to aid weaker tribes being persecuted for no good reason. However, they make these agreements with care and in utmost secrecy, for they realize the humanoids' evil nature makes them treacherous comrades. Moreover, if word of such an alliance got out, it could damage the druidic order's reputation among humans and elves.

Evil humanoids hold the druids in fairly high regard—some tribes always release druid captives. While these races couldn't care less for the sanctity of Nature or the welfare of animals, most humanoids respect Nature's mighty power and its servants.

Rangers and Elves

The ranger class and the elven race resemble each other in that both consist of good aligned beings dwelling in the wild, protecting it from evil forces. Elves and rangers sometimes argue with druids over how best to guide the sylvan peoples and maintain the guardianship of the forests, but this is usually a friendly disagreement. If an area has a particularly effective ranger presence, druids may agree to divide up responsibility for its guardianship: Rangers handle human and demihuman affairs, while druids take care of sylvan creatures and the problems of native animals and plants. Such informal arrangements, however, often prove subject to swift change.

Druids consider it a courtesy for a ranger of equivalent or lower level to ask permission to operate in an area they occupy and usually resent those who neglect this courtesy. If a ranger does ask permission, a druid generally feels pleased to cooperate.

Occasionally druids find elven or ranger actions one-sided, impetuous, or insufficiently ruthless to the job at hand. On the other hand, some elven council chambers and ranger gatherings ring with the accusation that druids would give as much credence to the word of an orc or a green dragon as they do an elf or a treant. Those outside the Order fear the overly cunning druidic stratagems do not have the best interests of the elven nations at heart. But despite the occasional suspicion, many friendships grow up between druids and rangers or elves, and each group respects the other as protectors of the wild.

Gnomes and Halflings

Druids generally get along with the small folk and help them when the need arises. In turn, a majority of gnomes and halflings (even those that do not follow the druidic religion) respect druid characters.

Most gnomes and halflings follow an ethos compatible with druidic beliefs: Live in harmony with the environment and rarely take from it more than needed. Moreover, druids see them as practical people who, though inclined toward good, rarely develop the fanatical opposition to "evil" the druids have seen in some humans, elves, and dwarves.

Dwarves

The dwarven affinity with the earth primarily extends to unliving stone and metal, while the druids prize living trees and animals. As a result, druids and dwarves have very different philosophical outlooks.

It doesn't help relations when dwarves cut

down forests and dig ugly mine shafts in green mountainsides in their quest for the coal and firewood needed to feed their hungry forges. Nor do dwarves enjoy seeing druids favor elves and advocate a "live and let live" policy with the dwarves' arch-foes, the goblin races. The result? Druids and dwarves remain on poor terms and have harsh words for each other when they meet.

Personality Types

You've now read how typical druids act in a variety of situations. But every druid—just like every other PC or significant NPC—should be different, with unique habits and personality traits. Chapter 2: Druid Kits illustrated the "role" of each kit and how a druid with a certain kit usually behaves. But not every druid of the same branch and kit acts the same way. To expand on this idea, a half-dozen common personality archetypes for druids follow.

Please note that using these personality types is totally optional—feel free to make up your own! This section, while intended for use primarily by novice role-players, can prove quite useful for experienced players who feel temporarily stumped for role-playing ideas or for DMs wanting a quick personality for an NPC druid.

Diplomat

The diplomat serves Nature best by resolving conflicts between intelligent beings through negotiation; wars must be avoided, as fields and forests burn regardless of which side wins. The fabled druidic neutrality makes these characters the clear choice for settling disputes, especially between human and nonhuman races.

For instance, if a heated dispute between wood elves and sylvan centaurs threatened to flare into war, the character might step in as a peacemaker, discover the root of the conflict, and arrange a just compromise. Or, the druid could act as an ambassador for a kingdom of sylvan folk, representing them in a human court.

In role-playing, the diplomat behaves with fairness and empathy. He always tries to see someone else's point of view, whether that someone else is an angry green dragon or a frivolous pixie, a proud knight or a hard-working farmer. But this fairness often masks an adamantine core of ruthless pragmatism. The character prefers solutions that benefit an entire region—including animals and plants —rather than a single faction. The diplomat isn't necessarily a pacifist—he may fight if talking fails or to enforce a peace he's brokered—but he prefers that a velvet glove mask the iron fist. Even so, the character generally takes the long view and values the harmony of the whole over the good of the individual.

This personality type works especially well with the Adviser, Pacifist, and Wanderer druid kits. It doesn't fit the Avenger or Guardian, but it can work with any other druid kits. The diplomat is best suited to an all-druid campaign, since other classes prefer fighting to talking. However, a peacemaking role can lead to adventure and intrigue (providing roles for bards, thieves, illusionists, and other characters skilled in subtlety), especially if—as often happens—a third party or warlike faction secretly works to foment wars or quarrels. And trying to mediate a dispute between an angry green dragon and a human baron can prove both exciting and dangerous!

Gardener

The gardener views the world as a garden: It needs loving care and someone to cut down the weeds. The character remains very much aware of her responsibilities as a druid. A deep love for the land—with all its animals and people—drives her to take decisive action to nurture and protect it.

A gardener believes a druid should actively intervene to promote the goals of the druidic order. She won't isolate herself in a grove in the wilderness. On the other hand, she usually stays in a particular region or country, feeling a close kinship to her own land, and knowing that she cannot take responsibility for the entire world.

The gardener sees combat as a job that sometimes has to be done: Avoid the unnecessary battles, but win the necessary ones. She uses her head when she fights, trying whatever tricks and tactics might give her an edge. However, she does not believe the ends justify the means and will not resort to strategies that go against the druidic ethos or her own conscience.

The character will see other people's points of view. Nevertheless, she lives devoted to the druidic ethos and actively carries the fight against anyone who threatens the land she holds dear.

The gardener personality is common among druids. It suits the Adviser, Savage, Wanderer, and Village Druid kits, but avoid using it with the Guardian kit—a gardener doesn't limit her attention to just one area.

Idealist

An idealist character—usually a young initiate—feels convinced that Nature needs saving, and he's the one to do it. Always optimistic, he sometimes bites off more than he can chew. He prefers to seek simple solutions to complex problems.

The idealist is usually pure of heart, meaning he doesn't lie or cheat and has few vices. While he seems fond of saying "Nature doesn't lie," he has yet to learn that many people do. Perhaps for that reason, people find it relatively easy to trick this character. However, if he realizes he's been manipulated or if he discovers corruption in someone he considered honest, his temper will flare in a fierce fit of anger.

In combat, the idealist rarely uses sophisticated tactics. He prefers to wield flashy spells, but will fight with physical weapons if necessary.

A young idealist usually doesn't feel ready to settle down, so sedentary kits like the Guardian or Village Druid don't work for him. He does not possess the bitterness of an Avenger and lacks the discipline of a Natural Philosopher and the subtlety of a good Adviser. The best kits for him are Beastfriend, Shapeshifter, or Wanderer.

Mysterious Figure

The mysterious figure is a druid with an enigmatic nature. She tends to appear and disappear regularly—show up, take swift action, vanish suddenly, and appear again when least expected and most needed.

The mysterious figure normally has a personal mission to fulfill: a wrong to right, an archenemy to defeat, or a balance to redress. Often she has returned from exile, escaped death, or overcome some other personal tragedy, and uses her secretiveness to surprise and confound foes.

The mysterious figure travels regularly, often going about in disguise or in animal shape. She makes many friends in unlikely places, but reveals her real identity or purposes only to her closest companions. Her fondness for drama leads her to save her best spells for a grand entrance or for the crucial moment where she casts aside her disguise.

Some druids with this personality have a quirky sense of humor. For instance, the druid may shapeshift into an animal before joining a party, becoming "adopted" as a pet before revealing her true form (if she does reveal it). This mischief works best for an NPC among PCs, or vice versa.

But for all her showmanship, the mysterious figure remains a careful and cunning strategist. She always makes sure she has a few tricks up her sleeve that even her friends don't know about. If she has a flaw, it is an unwillingness to share with others the details of her plans.

The mysterious figure works well as an Adviser, Outlaw, Shapeshifter, or Wanderer. Avoid pairing this personality with the Guardian or Village Druid kits.

Nurturer

The nurturer always seeks to help those around him, whether the beneficiary is a plant, beast, or human; he feels especially drawn to the suffering of others. Unlike the gardener, the character concerns himself more with individuals than with communities or members of a particular alignment. The character may work as a professional healer, but also may take a more active role. For instance, he might go adventuring to seek and rescue captives and victims of oppression. Whatever his reason for joining a party, he cannot resist a genuine cry for help.

The character does well providing emotional support to others, and people frequently turn to him with their troubles. He often proves a tower of strength in a crisis, rarely losing his courage. In combat, the character prefers to take a defensive role, protecting others and healing the injured. The character, while not a pacifist, remains reluctant to engage in violence, except to defend those under his care.

The nurturer comes as close to a good alignment as any other druid personality archetype. However, he does provide care without regard to the victim's alignment. Also, unlike most good characters, this druid gives as high a priority to the suffering of beasts as to the plight of humans.

Rustic

This druid champions the common people. She prefers a roadside inn to a noble's castle and would rather visit a village fair than a knightly tournament. Depending on whether she likes to stay in one place or move around, she'll usually have either the Outlaw, Village Druid, Avenger, or Wanderer kits. She has no interest in wealth—what she earns or finds she either gives to the needy or devotes to projects aimed at improving people's lives.

The rustic won't take any actions she believes would endanger or exploit peasants; she always tries to suggest plans by which the party's actions might benefit the commoners. For instance, instead of rescuing a noble from a band of orcs, she'd prefer to take action against a robber baron who has been oppressing his tenants. Afterward, she'll try to make sure the peasants reclaim some of the treasure their greedy overlord took from them.

If the character witnesses any kind of oppression of the common people, she becomes angry and wants to do something about it. If possible, she'll try to fix the situation—overthrow the evil baron, free the slaves, etc. If she doesn't believe she can win, she'll usually try to make some gesture to help the victims, perhaps by giving agricultural advice, suggesting means of passive resistance, curing disease, donating money, or even helping a single family escape to a better life. Then she'll vow to come back and do more when she gains the power to help. In short, the rustic believes in treating all fairly, regardless of social class.

Traditionalist

The traditionalist takes pride in the old ways and opposes change for the sake of change. This mindset applies to alterations in land use, shifts in the structure of the druidic order, and fluctuations in the pattern of daily life in the character's region.

The traditionalist's philosophy means the druid vehemently opposes destroying the wilderness to replace it with crops, towns, or mines. Of course, he stands equally against radical druids like Shadow Circle members, who advocate the destruction of towns or cities. (However, some clever Shadow Circle members use a traditionalist facade.)

Traditionalist druids usually think things were better in the past and talk incessantly about how the present doesn't match ancient glories. They take pride in the history and accomplishments of the druidic order and usually have the ancient history nonweapon proficiency. A traditionalist believes unshakably in the basic tenets of druidism, such as protecting the wilderness and maintaining the balance of Nature, as well as protecting druidic customs, such as the challenge. Often the character takes an active interest in druidic politics to make sure that suitably tradition-minded druids find their way to high-ranking positions.

Almost any druid kit suits a traditionalist personality, provided the Order has an ancient history. On the other hand, say the DM decides that druids have developed the powers of the Shapeshifter kit only recently. In such a campaign, a traditionalist would avoid that kit.

Fanatic

A character with this personality has a drive to accomplish a particular self-appointed mission. All his personal efforts must go toward its fulfillment; he feels guilty if he has to devote time to other activities.

A fanatic believes the ends justify the means. Anyone and anything could become a sacrifice to the cause. One can inject fanaticism into any druid character by exaggerating the normal behavior of his branch or kit. Possible fanatics include the characters below:

• Druids with the Avenger kit may seek revenge for the defilement of a particular area of wilderness.

• Village Druids may act fanatically in defense of their villages, seeing all outsiders as potential threats and ruthlessly destroying anyone who harms "my people."

• Guardian druids can have a fanatical bent toward preserving the area under their protection. They have been heard to say things like, "You may travel through my forest, but if you cut even one living branch for firewood, damage one single leaf, or kill the smallest animal, you will regret it!"

• Druids with any kit may act like fanatics about duties to the Order, taking extreme actions against anyone who harms the wilderness. This kind of druid often adopts the viewpoint of the Shadow Circle.

The fanatic archetype does not normally suit a PC, but this personality can make an interesting NPC. In particular, fanatics make good rivals for more moderate druids, who work to rein in the excesses of extremists to maintain the Order's good name.

Misanthrope

The misanthrope doesn't like the company of people. Usually she considers mankind bad for Nature. A misanthrope may have had a particularly bad experience that soured her on mankind. Depending on her kit, she may prefer the company of animals or the solitude of the wilds.

In role-playing, the misanthrope generally assumes the worst of people. She may not act hostile, but it takes a lot of effort from the party to encourage friendliness. By her very nature, she tends toward dour, pessimistic behavior. She trusts no humans, and few demihumans or humanoids.

The misanthrope's unselfish love of Nature partially redeems her hostility; characters who display a similar affection for animals or the wild find her a true friend. Even so, deeds, not words, are the only things that can win her friendship.

The misanthrope has trouble verbalizing feelings—even if she likes or approves of someone, she won't say so. She'll simply offer her assistance. If she dislikes someone, or if something makes her angry, she's likely to turn her back and leave without a word.

In combat, she doesn't bluff and rarely utters a threat more than once. If she must use violence to protect herself or something she cares for, she'll strike without warning.

A misanthrope doesn't fit in with a party of human adventurers, but she makes a good NPC, especially if the party has a particular reason to seek her friendship.

This personality type works well with Beastfriends, Guardians, Shapeshifters, and Totemic Druids. It can fit Avengers, Natural Philosophers, and Wanderers, but does not suit Advisers, Savages, or Village Druids.

Druid Campaigns

So far this chapter has dealt with ways to role-play druid characters in normal AD&D campaigns. But it's quite possible to use this information to run an adventure focusing on druids alone. A DM could handle such a campaign one of several ways.

All or Mostly Druids?

The DM of a druid-centered campaign can choose to restrict players to druid characters only. This setup works best with fewer than four players. On the other hand, druid-centered campaigns involving many players can benefit from the presence of one or two appropriate nondruid characters. The DM may allow bards, rangers, and those clerics, mages, or fighters with Peasant or Outlaw kits. (See *The Complete Priest's Handbook, The Complete Wizard's Handbook,* and *The Complete Fighter's Handbook.*)

After DMs choose to run an all-druid campaign, they must next decide whether to have a party of druids from a variety of branches or from only one.

Single-Branch Campaigns. Some campaigns center around druids in a single circle and the doings of those native to the area. Most PCs will represent the same branch: that of the area's dominant terrain. For example, campaigns set in mountainous terrain feature mostly mountain druids; if the campaign were set in the Underdark, most of the characters would be gray druids.

This campaign gives the PCs a strong sense of identity and creates a united party, since all its members have similar goals. It also allows the DM to focus on interdruid politics (such as the rise of the Shadow Circle or the rivalry between various druidic branches). A single-branch campaign involving an unusual branch (like the arctic druids) gives the DM an opportunity to run a change-of-pace adventure set in a different environment. PCs can venture to remote locations, meet members of little-known cultures, and encounter monsters they otherwise would rarely happen upon.

On the down side, although players can distinguish the characters from each other by giving them each different kits, players still may wish for more variety within the party. Try making some of the characters druids from associated branches; for instance, if the adventure takes place near a forest on a mountainside, some of the characters resemble a mix of both the forest and mountain druid branches.

Multibranch Campaigns. In a campaign

involving only druids, the DM may encourage players to choose characters from different branches. The advantage of this arrangement? It provides a strong variety of characters—especially since they also may have different druid kits. However, a disadvantage is the difficulty of explaining why a jungle druid and an arctic druid want to adventure together in the first place.

One way to get around this problem requires bringing the PCs together for a reason. Perhaps the characters each represent their particular region in a quest the Grand Druid has launched to help fight a world-shaking problem. This scenario gives them the single-branch campaign's sense of shared mission, but more variety.

And, there could be any number of reasons why this special group of beginning characters was selected. Pick one of the following justifications:

• The Grand Druid chose them because they fit an ancient prophecy.

• The upper ranks of the druids are too conservative (or filled with untrustworthy agents of the Shadow Circle), and only these members of the younger generation see the true threat facing the world.

• There are few druids left—a growing evil wiped out most of the Order's upper ranks. (A very nasty situation indeed!)

A more serious problem in game balance for multibranch campaigns lies in the fact that each branch works best in a single terrain type: the desert druid operates best in the desert; the gray druid has optimal powers only in the underworld, and so on. As a result, a multibranch druid campaign needs to involve a fair bit of traveling; if the characters stay in the forest or the dungeon all the time, the player of an arctic or swamp druid will feel useless! Forcing the characters to travel widely, fighting an evil that recurs in several guises, can make for an exciting adventure involving all the characters.

For example, in a campaign with the goal of defeating the followers of a chaotic evil god corrupting Nature, the first adventure might take the party to a swamp that had been defiled into a place of horror. The druids would deal with toxic water, mutant giant insects, will o' wisps, black dragons, and other swamp monsters. A clue then can lead them to an adventure in the frozen arctic, where the PCs hear of a blizzard without end and the creatures that lurk within it. With this kind of approach, every branch of druid has a chance to shine.

Guardians of the Wild

In this campaign, the druids must defend a tract of wilderness from those who wish to exploit it. To make this story stronger, develop druid characters with a personal stake in the area. For example, the region could hold an ancient grove in which a PC was initiated into the druidic order. Or maybe it serves as home to a tribe of sylvan beings who have befriended a character.

An interesting problem develops if the druids discover that the individuals cutting down their wood or draining their swamp have a very good reason to do so. As a result, the druids—and players—find themselves faced with a more complex moral dilemma than simply, "Run those exploiters off the land." They must look behind the problem to get at its heart.

This campaign suits players who enjoy diplomacy and politics, and generally works best with relatively high-level druids. This scenario lets the characters explore a key element of the druid's ethos: the need to see everyone's point of view, then judge which path best serves druidic interests.

For instance, suppose the druids learn of a problem in the area when hundreds of migrant laborers—mostly poor folk with no farms of their own—descend like locusts on

Druid Mini-Adventures

Try these druid-centered adventures.

• The druid is approached by a female bard who loves a Shapeshifter druid. While she worked in town, he spent too long in the form of a bear and became trapped in that shape. Worse, hunters captured him and sold him to an arena, where handlers will force him to fight other animals (or humans) to the death. The games begin in a week. The bard beseeches the PC—the nearest druid—to help her free her love.

• A dryad heard that a group of pixies is tormenting a green dragon—playing tricks on it while invisible, stealing trinkets, and the like. The dragon can't find the ones responsible, and the dryad fears its rage will devastate the wood. Someone must tell the pixies to stop—and calm the dragon down.

• While hunting a stag in the forest, the king's youngest son was killed by a great wolf. The grief-maddened monarch has decreed that every wolf in the wood must die, enticing hunters with a bounty of 50 gp for each pelt. What should the druid do?

• A young elf and a human ranger love each other, but their parents do not approve. They run away to the woods, begging the druid to marry them. But the angry parents are not far behind. . . .

• A strange blight is afflicting the forest, turning leaves a luminous white. The druid must discover this disease's secrets before all greenery disappears from the forest.

• Someone has stolen a sylph's egg! She left it only an hour to visit her nymph friend. Now, heartbroken, she asks the local druid for help. Suspects or witnesses in this forest whodunit include a flighty pseudo-dragon, a pool of nixies, a jealous aerial servant, and a drunken satyr.

the characters' ancient forest, chopping down trees and bearing them away. Worse, several species of rare animals live near here, and the logging threatens to destroy their home.

Where did these laborers come from? The party learns they work for a nation of dwarves living nearby. These mountain dwarves, having exhausted their supply of coal, had to turn to wood to keep the forges burning. They pay the poor human laborers in gold for every log they bring in. Already the dwarves' own mountain stands denuded of trees. The druids' verdant preserve seems the only nearby source of firewood.

The migrant laborers have more immediate concerns than the dangers of exfoliation. A lean harvest this year has meant little work, and without the dwarves' bounty, the humans risk starvation. As long as the dwarves pay, they will be able to buy food for the winter. . . .

But what made the dwarves decide to expand their activities so much that they exhausted their coal resources?

War. The mountain dwarves are forging weapons for a small elven kingdom two day's journey away, struggling against an alliance of migrating bugbear and ogre tribes. Except for the royal guard, these elves—caught by surprise—lacked proper armor and weapons to withstand the onslaught. The dwarves didn't want to get involved, but agreed to forge the elves fine long swords, armor, and arrowheads in exchange for a share of the valuable emerald deposits located within the elven kingdom.

The DM could stop here and decide to call the bugbears and ogres the villains. But perhaps things are not quite that simple. What started the bugbear-ogre migration? Perhaps a powerful dragon drove them from their land; now they have become refugees themselves, wishing to settle in empty areas within the elven wood. However, the elves refused (not desiring such rude neighbors).

A campaign of this sort gives druids many

Role-playing Druids • 83

options. The characters could merely drive the woodcutters from the forest—but terrorizing them may spur the dwarves to hire adventurers to deal with the druids! The party could play it sneaky—help the elves win a quick victory by destroying the ogre-bugbear alliance. (The druids slay the bugbear chieftain, but make it look like a rival ogre chief did it.) Or, the solution could prove complex, if the druids decide to try negotiating a peace treaty between the elves and the bugbear-ogre alliance. If the DM works out the personalities and goals of the major figures, each of the druids' actions could carry its own set of consequences.

The Evil Woods

In the center of a once beautiful sylvan forest lies a place of power—a grove at one time sacred to the druids. Unfortunately, its defenders were not as strong as they thought and, in a weak moment, allowed a dreadful evil to creep into the land. These forces captured and defiled the sacred grove; now darkness has fallen over the ancient woods.

Nature itself has felt the corrupting power of this evil. Flocks of vampire bats, clusters of stirges, and clouds of stinging insects darken the skies. Bugbears and goblins roam the outskirts of the wood, but even they do not venture into the interior, which rumor calls home to horrors beyond imagining: flesh-eating treants, cannibal elves, undead animals, and dark unicorns with poisoned horns. All these creatures manifest the terrible cancer emanating from the once sacred grove, which now bears a terrible curse—a curse that is spreading. . . .

This campaign will prove a challenge for any druidic party. The evil forces include a mix of standard woodland monsters like bugbears and green dragons, and twisted, evil versions of normally good or neutral sylvan beings like dryads and elves. The druids—possibly allied with good-aligned adventurers—do not know exactly what evil corrupted the sacred grove, so they have to move carefully at first, scouting the forest. The cursed woods resembles a dungeon: The farther the characters penetrate, the more deadly it becomes, with the power that destroyed the original Guardians waiting, spiderlike, in the center of the sacred grove.

Against the Shadows

The Shadow Circle can spark adventures rife with intrigue, betrayal, and druid vs. druid conflict. Composing such an adventure requires a good understanding of the local druidic hierarchy. The DM should sketch out the personalities of the domain's NPC druids, then secretly decide which (if any) belong to the Shadow Circle. PCs can glean some information about the NPCs but will not know their secret allegiances.

Here are some adventure ideas:

The Horde. A rumor now circulating says druids from the Shadow Circle have set up a secret meeting with chieftains of nearby orc or barbarian tribes. Obviously they plan to mount an assault on one or more human towns or cities—but when, how, and where will they strike? As druids opposed to Shadow Circle policies, the PCs may try to find out what is going on so they can sound the alarm or nip the plan in the bud—but getting anyone to believe word of an impending invasion may prove difficult without concrete evidence, for few know the truth about the Shadow Circle.

If infiltrating the secret society seems like too great a challenge, the characters could kidnap an orc leader for questioning. And this step might be only the beginning; the PCs might learn that Shadow Circle druids have found a secret weapon—a dragon or a magical war machine. . . .

The Invitation. The DM can send a Shadowed One to recruit a PC druid who has been especially ruthless. This isn't good news for most PCs: Few want to become the obedient pawns of the faceless, secretive organization's inner circle. However, those who refuse must foil the dreaded Shadowed Ones intending to kill uncooperative druids.

The Traitor. One of the PCs—a druid loyal to the Order—learns that one of the three archdruids in the domain belongs to the Shadow Circle. This inner circle member has hired assassins to kill the circle's great druid next month, rather than have to face the leader in a duel. Unfortunately, the PC's informant mysteriously dies before revealing the traitorous archdruid's identity. Can the PC uncover the traitor in time to prevent the Shadow Circle's victory?

The characters may want to talk to those who know the three suspects and examine each archdruid's behavior for any hint of allegiance to the Shadow Circle. Of course, the real traitor may speed up the Shadow Circle's agenda if the PCs are discovered—or try to do away with the investigators!

The Defector. A druid defecting from the Shadow Circle has important information about the sinister organization's plans, but she will talk only to the Grand Druid, whom she knows stands outside the group. Her defection has not gone unnoticed—the dread Shadowed Ones plot her death—so the PCs must protect her on her way to an Emissary of the Grand Druid. They will face magical, monstrous, and personal attacks, as well as treachery from those they *thought* were allies.

CHAPTER 5

Druidic Magic

As detailed in Chapter 3 of the *Player's Handbook* (p. 35), druids have access to priest spells in certain spheres and can use a variety of enchanted weapons, armor, and other magical items. This chapter expands the magic available to player characters in the druid class, adding many spells and magical items along with the new field of herbal magic.

New Spells

Druids have major access to spells in the following spheres of influence: All, Animal, Elemental, Healing, Plant, Weather; they have minor access to the Divination sphere. (Note any sphere restrictions due to kit or branch.) As druids concern themselves with plants, animals, and natural phenomena more than most priests, they specialize in casting Nature-oriented spells.

Characters of any priest class have the potential to use these spells if they have access to the relevant spheres. However, DMs may make this magic available only to the druid class, on the grounds that these spells represent secret lore of the Order.

First-level Spells

Beastmask
(Illusion/Phantasm)

Sphere: Animal
Range: Touch
Components: V, S, M
Duration: 12 hours
Casting Time: 4
Area of Effect: 1 creature
Saving Throw: Neg.

Beastmask may affect any single person or animal, or characters may cast it on themselves. It allows the subject to take on the illusory form of a single animal species—but only that species of animal can perceive the illusion. The subject may not assume an animal form more than twice or less than one-quarter the character's size.

The almost perfect illusion the spell creates deceives the animal's sight, hearing, smell, and touch. For instance, once a character casts a "bear" illusion on a subject, bears believe that subject to be a bear, while to humans, other races, and other creatures, the subject remains the same.

Characters normally use *beastmask* to travel among or hunt a particular species. This spell lets a druid assume the guise of a caribou to move among a herd without causing them to panic. A character also could avoid being attacked by a pack of dire wolves by wearing a wolf's "mask."

Beastmask does not allow communication with the animal species, though it can be used with animal communication spells.

The material component is a miniature wooden mask carved to look like the animal.

Optional Sphere Expansions

Some existing Nature-related spells remain unavailable to druids due to sphere restrictions. To offer these spells to druids, DMs may expand the selection of spells accessible through certain spheres of magic:
• *Call woodland beings* becomes part of the Animal sphere.
• *Commune with nature* becomes part of both the Animal and Plant spheres.
• *Insect plague* becomes part of the Animal sphere.
• *Reincarnate* becomes part of the Animal sphere.

An expansion does not remove a spell from a sphere that already contains it, but merely makes the spell accessible from an additional sphere or spheres.

Puffball (Alteration)

Sphere: Plant
Range: Touch
Components: V, S, M
Duration: 2 rounds/level of caster
Casting Time: 4
Area of Effect: 1 mushroom, etc.
Saving Throw: Special

A character who casts *puffball* on a normal mushroom, truffle, or toadstool (up to 6 inches in diameter) transforms the fungus into a magical puffball, which the character may drop or throw. The DM should decide what type of roll, if any, is required to hit the target (Strength, Dexterity, etc.) See the *DMG*, pgs. 62-63, for rules on grenadelike missiles.

The puffball bursts upon landing, releasing a cloud of spores 10 feet in diameter. Those caught in the spore cloud must save vs. poison or suffer an attack of coughing and choking. Victims can make no attacks and lose all Dexterity bonuses to Armor Class and saving throws. The cloud dissipates in 1d3+1 rounds; residual effects still afflict characters one round after they escape the cloud or it fades.

The spell's effects do not affect undead or similar nonbreathing creatures. If no one throws (or drops) the missile by the time its duration expires, the enchantment is lost.

The caster sprinkles the material component—a pinch of ground puffball— over the fungus to be enchanted.

Whisperward (Alteration)

Sphere: Guardian, Weather
Range: Touch
Components: V, S, M
Duration: Permanent until triggered
Casting Time: 4
Area of Effect: 1 item
Saving Throw: None

Whisperward can be cast on any single item, portal, or closure (such as a book, door, or lid). It may ward up to a 30-foot radius.

The character keys the ward to become activated (like a *magic mouth* spell) under specific conditions—such as when a certain individual enters the area or opens the warded closure. When the ward is triggered, a soft whispering breeze blows across the caster's face. The caster must stay within 1 mile per experience level of the ward to receive the warning.

The material component is the priest's holy symbol.

Second-level Spells

Animal Spy (Divination)

Sphere: Animal
Range: 10 yards
Components: V, S
Duration: 1 turn/2 levels of caster
Casting Time: 5
Area of Effect: 1 animal
Saving Throw: Wizard familiars may save vs. spell to negate.

Only a normal (real-world) animal or a giant version of a normal animal species may become an animal spy. This spell enables the caster to share the animal's senses—see through the animal's eyes, hear with its ears, smell with its nose, and so on. The animal is completely unaware of the spell's effect, unless the druid warns the beast before casting. *Animal spy* grants no control over the creature. However, most casters will use it on a trained animal or one befriended via the *animal friendship* spell.

For the duration of the spell, the caster remains in a trance, unable to move or use human senses. This consequence can prove dangerous; for instance, characters attacked while using the spell cannot feel injuries to their bodies. However, at the start of any round, the caster may choose to return the animal's senses to the creature and resume control of the human body. This decision ends the spell immediately. The spell also ends if the animal travels more than 100 yards away per level of the caster.

Beastspite (Enchantment/Charm)

Sphere: Animal
Range: 10 yards
Components: V, S
Duration: 1 hour/level of caster
Casting Time: 5
Area of Effect: 1 person
Saving Throw: Neg.

Beastspite afflicts a single person with a magical aura that induces one species of animal to hate and fear the character. The character becomes loathed by any species of normal (real-world) animal. While this range excludes monsters, it includes giant animals of the same real-world species. (For example, if *beastspite* causes bats to hate the subject, giant bats will react similarly.)

When the character comes within 30 yards of an animal from the target species, the creature will make warning signals (barks, growls, etc.). Its further reaction depends on the animal's nature.

• Aggressive animals, including all predators and most trained guard animals, attack the spell recipient.

• Nonaggressive beasts shun the character, fleeing or attacking if approached.

• Owners can restrain their domesticated animals, but the beasts show obvious distress and may become very hostile if the character tries to touch them.

• If the subject was riding when the spell took effect, the mount tries to throw off the character. The subject must make a riding proficiency check each round to stay astride and to avoid a fall if thrown off.

• An animal extremely loyal to the subject, such as a pet dog, a creature influenced by an *animal friendship* spell, a wizard's familiar, or a paladin's war horse does not become utterly hostile to its owner. Instead it notices something "wrong" about the character and acts unusually nervous.

Fortifying Stew (Necromancy)

Sphere: Healing
Range: Touch
Components: V, S, M
Duration: Stew retains enchantment 1 turn
Casting Time: 5
Area of Effect: 1 bowl of stew, etc./level
Saving Throw: None

Any bowl of broth, porridge, or stew the priest has concocted can become subject to *fortifying stew*. A character can enchant one bowl of stew (about 8 ounces) per experience level. Someone must consume the enchanted meal within one turn of the casting.

Anyone partaking of an entire bowlful reaps magical benefits. First, the diner gains nourishment for an entire day from the single meal. In addition, for two hours plus one round per the caster's level, the character receives 1d4+1 temporary hit points. Any damage suffered comes off the extra hit points first. The effects of multiple helpings of *fortifying stew* are not cumulative.

For example, Snapdragon, a 7th-level druid, cooks a meaty broth, casts *fortifying stew* on it, and eats the bowlful. A roll of 2 gives her 3 extra hit points. When the spell's effects wear off just over three hours, she loses these extra points. If she suffers 5 points of damage in the meantime, she actually loses only 2 hp of her own, since 3 hp came off the extra hit points.

The material component is a vial of stock made of the first fruit of the harvest.

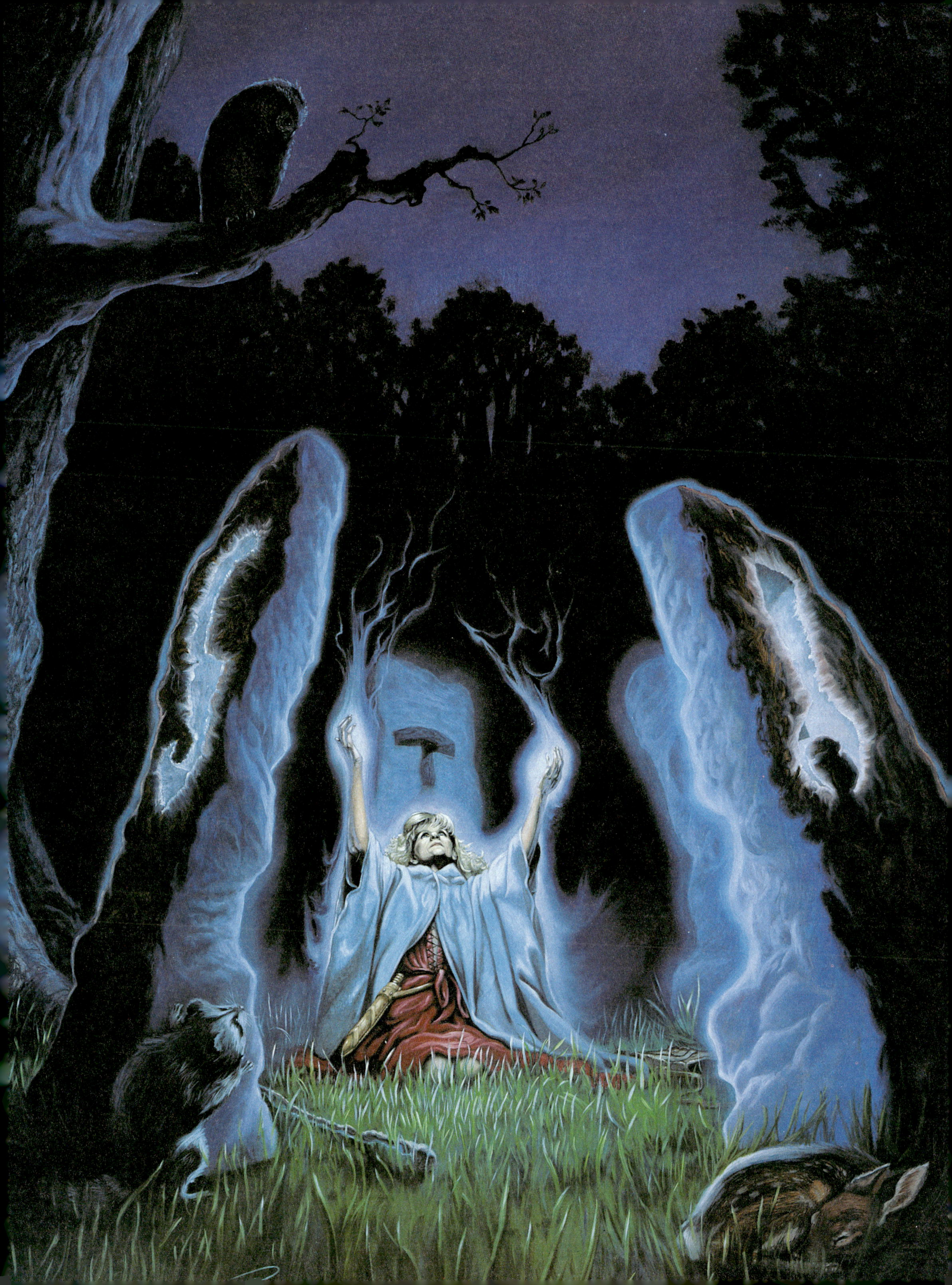

Gift of Speech (Enchantment/Charm)

Sphere: Animal
Range: 10 yards/level of caster
Components: V, S, M
Duration: 1 turn/level of caster
Casting Time: 5
Area of Effect: 1 animal
Saving Throw: None

The *gift of speech* spell grants a normal animal (or a giant version of a normal animal) the ability to speak any *one* of the languages the caster knows, whichever the caster chooses, along with the ability to understand words and simple concepts expressed in that language. The affected animal's reactions do not change, nor does its Intelligence increase. The spell has no effect if cast on a creature with an Intelligence score of less than 1.

The material component of this spell is the priest's holy symbol.

Third-level Spells

Pass Without Trace, 10' Radius (Enchantment/Charm)

Sphere: Plant
Range: 0
Components: V, S, M
Duration: 1 turn/level of caster
Casting Time: 1 round
Area of Effect: Radius 10 feet around caster
Saving Throw: None

Identical in function to *pass without trace*, *pass without trace, 10' radius* affects everyone within 10 feet of the caster. The effect moves with the caster, so creatures must stay within 10 feet of the caster to continue to avoid leaving tracks. A creature who leaves the area of effect can then be tracked normally. Creatures moving into the area of effect after casting are unaffected.

The material component is a sprig of pine burned to ash. Upon casting the spell, the character scatters the powder in a circle.

Shape Wood (Alteration)

Sphere: Plant
Range: Touch
Components: V, S, M
Duration: Permanent
Casting Time: 1 round
Area of Effect: 9 cubic feet+1 cubic foot/level
Saving Throw: None

By means of *shape wood*, the caster can re-form wood. For example, the character can cast it upon any appropriate-sized piece of wood to fashion a wooden weapon, make a rough door, or even create a crude figurine.

The spell also allows the caster to reshape an existing wooden door, perhaps to escape imprisonment. Again, the volume of the wooden object must be appropriate to the desired result and fit in the area of effect.

While a character might form a wooden coffer from a tree stump or a door from a wooden wall, the result does not bear high-quality detail. If a shaping has moving parts, there is a 30% chance they do not work.

The alteration endures permanently, at least until the wood rots or is physically destroyed. The caster blows the material component, a pinch of fine sawdust, over the wooden subject of the spell.

Fourth-level Spells

Detect Animal Attacker (Divination)

Sphere: Animal
Range: Touch
Components: V, S, M
Duration: Instantaneous
Casting Time: 1 turn
Area of Effect: 1 creature
Saving Throw: None

Depending on how it is cast, *detect animal attacker* gives the druid a visual image either of a creature that injured an animal or of an animal that attacked any victim.

While casting the spell upon any victim of an attack by a natural animal (a victim whose body still bears the marks of claws, fangs, or other natural weapons), the druid touches the victim's wound. This brief touch gives the caster a fleeting vision of the animal that caused the injuries as it looked at the time of the attack.

Likewise, a druid casting the spell upon an injured real-world animal can touch its wound and receive a vision of the person, monster, or animal that harmed it.

Even if the caster receives a vision of an unfamiliar attacker, the character usually can get an idea of its size, primary attack method, and alignment. (The druid senses good, evil, or neutrality.)

In addition, if the creature still lives and fails a saving throw vs. spell, the caster senses its current position, location, and direction of travel.

Detect animal attacker works only within one hour per level of the caster after the victim receives the injury in question. The spell is effective regardless of whether the attack proved fatal.

The material component is the priest's holy symbol.

Earthmaw (Alteration)

Sphere: Elemental (earth)
Range: 50 yards
Components: V, S, M
Duration: 1 round
Casting Time: 7
Area of Effect: 10-foot diameter circle
Saving Throw: Neg.

Earthmaw causes a patch of ground 10 feet in diameter to open and form a gigantic mouth with stalactite teeth. The mouth springs forth on a short serpentine neck, much like a water weird, and attacks once in a direction the caster dictates. Then it retracts into the earth and closes solidly. The site of an *earthmaw* spell appears as if the ground has been tilled recently.

The mouth can attack one large creature, two man-sized creatures, or four small-sized creatures within 10 feet of its outer edge. It can strike multiple creatures only if they remain clustered within a 10-foot diameter circle adjacent to the maw.

The earthmaw attacks as a monster with Hit Dice equal to the caster's level. Creatures standing on the site of the maw suffer a +3 penalty to Armor Class for purposes of this attack only. Creatures standing next to the maw suffer no AC penalty.

A successful hit inflicts 1d4 points of damage per level of the caster. An *unmodified* roll of 19 or 20 means the maw has swallowed the victim whole, burying the character 2d4 feet below ground. Victims can be dug out manually, with appropriate spells (such as *dig*), or with magical items (such as a *spade of colossal excavation*). A creature trapped underground will suffocate unless freed within a number of rounds equal to one-third its Constitution score.

Earthmaw may be cast on any area of loose or packed earth, sand, or vegetation-covered soil. It may be cast indoors on an earthen surface: for example, on the dirt floor of a barn or basement, but not on the marble floor of a home or temple. It may not be cast on an area containing a tree, any portion of a building, or any type of pavement.

An object present on the site of the maw (such as a campfire or a tent, etc.) counts as a creature of that object's size in attacks.

The material component is a tooth from any predatory creature.

Hunger (Alteration)

Sphere: Animal, Plant
Range: 10 yards
Components: V, S, M
Duration: 1 day/level of caster
Casting Time: 7
Area of Effect: 1 person
Saving Throw: Neg.

Those affected by *hunger* no longer gain sustenance from food. No matter how much they eat, they still feel hungry. If the spell did not end, victims eventually would starve, visibly wasting away.

After one day under the spell's effect, victims' concentration suffers (due to their preoccupation with their constant hungry feeling), causing them to suffer a –2 penalty to all ability and proficiency checks. On the eighth day without food, victims who have been maintaining normal activity levels lose 1 Strength point; on the ninth day, they lose 1 Constitution point. This alternating pattern continues until one of the character's ability scores falls to 3; at this point, the character becomes comatose. If a score reaches 0 before the *hunger* spell ends, the recipient dies. The victim regains lost points after the spell ends at a rate of 1 Strength and 1 Constitution point per day.

When casting the spell, the character secretly whispers a particular type of food; by eating the specified food, the victim breaks the spell. It must be a single, natural food (such as lamb, honey, or an apple) but can be exotic (dragon meat)—as long as the caster has tasted it personally at some point.

Hunger cannot be dispelled, but can be broken by the *remove curse* spell. Failing all else, a sufferer must wait to find relief until the spell's duration elapses.

The spell's material component is a pinch of the food that can end the spell.

Knurl (Alteration)

Sphere: Plant
Range: 5 yards/level of caster
Components: V, S, M
Duration: 1 turn/level of caster
Casting Time: 7
Area of Effect: 1 person
Saving Throw: Neg.

Casting a *knurl* spell transforms a creature's arm into a tree branch of the same thickness, covered with bark and twigs. The new limb possesses neither elbow nor wrist joints—not even a hand. The "arm" remains attached to the shoulder. The spell's recipient can use it as a club but not to manipulate tools, weapons, or spell components.

The caster chooses which of the recipient's arms to affect. A character could use multiple *knurl* spells to transform both arms of a humanoid. The arm is treated for all purposes as a tree branch: It becomes subject to fire, wood-altering spells, and tree diseases. *Dispel magic* ends the spell's effects.

The material component is a small twig.

Needlestorm (Alteration)

Sphere: Plant
Range: 60 yards
Components: V, S, M
Duration: Instantaneous
Casting Time: 7
Area of Effect: 1 tree or plant
Saving Throw: Save vs. spell for half damage

A favorite of cold-forest and desert druids, *needlestorm* causes the spines on any pine tree or similar needle-bearing plant to spray out in a deadly barrage. The shower of needles has a radius of approximately 1 foot for every 2 feet of the subject plant's height.

Everyone within this area suffers one attack, which inflicts 1d12 points of damage for every three full levels the caster has achieved. Thus, a spruce tree enchanted by a 7th-level character attacks with a THAC0 of 16 and inflicts 2d12 points of damage.

The material component is a spine from a needle-bearing tree or plant.

Fifth-level Spells

Cloudscape (Alteration)

Sphere: Weather
Range: 120 yards
Components: V, S
Duration: 3 turns/level of caster
Casting Time: 8
Area of Effect: 1,000 cubic feet/level of caster
Saving Throw: None

A character can cast *cloudscape* on a single cloud or part of a cloud bank, usually from a nearby mountaintop or while flying. It causes 1,000 cubic feet of cloud per level of the caster to become solid enough to support any weight. The solidified clouds remain airborne and feel like a thick carpet.

A creature that falls onto the magically strengthened cloud sustains falling damage per the *PH*, p. 104. An animal or individual that flies into the solidified cloud falls, stunned, for a round and must make a successful Dexterity check to recover. If a creature is flying through a cloud at the moment it becomes solidified, it may make a saving throw vs. petrification. Those who succeed escape the cloud in time. Creatures that fail the save become trapped as the cloud solidifies around them. However, as the cloud is porous, they can continue to breathe until the spell's duration elapses.

The solidified cloud itself continues to drift with the wind as usual. While the caster cannot use this particular spell to propel the cloud at all, a *control winds* spell can summon a great gust of air to turn the cloudscape into a unique flying conveyance easily enough.

Nature's Charm
(Enchantment/Charm)

Sphere: Elemental (earth, water)
Range: Touch
Components: V, S, M
Duration: 2 hours/level of caster
Casting Time: 1 round
Area of Effect: 15-foot radius/level of caster
Saving Throw: Creatures native to the area of effect are not affected.

Nature's charm causes a particular place to exert a special fascination beyond mere beauty to anyone entering the area except the spellcaster.

This spell must target a site of notable natural splendor that possesses both edible plants and fresh water. The spot may not be larger than the spell's area of effect. For instance, a 12th-level druid could cast this spell on a forest glade up to 360 feet across, with flowers and fruit-bearing trees centered around a waterfall.

Anyone coming upon the enchanted region must save vs. spell; those who fail invariably make up excuses to remain there long after they should have left. They say they want only to bathe, rest, admire the beauty a bit longer, eat the berries or fruit, paint a picture of the area, or defend the spot jealously from others.

Whatever the reason, those who fall victim to the enchantment forcefully resist all attempts to make them leave until the spell's duration ends.

The spell's material component is the druid's holy symbol.

Strengthen Stone (Alteration)

Sphere: Elemental (earth)
Range: 10 yards
Components: V, S, M
Duration: Permanent
Casting Time: 1 hour
Area of Effect: 1 building or wall
Saving Throw: None

Strengthen stone can reinforce any stone construction (house, tower, wall segment, aqueduct, etc.), against physical damage. The DM adds +4 to the structure's saving throw against any kind of damage, from siege engines to natural earthquakes. The stone object gains a saving throw vs. the *earthquake* spell. (See the *PH*, p. 233.) The spell may be cast only once on any stone object.

If a character casts this spell on a stone golem or other animated stone being (like one created by *animate rock*), the creature receives a –1 bonus to its Armor Class and adds a +1 bonus to its saving throws for the duration of the spell. *Strengthen stone* has no effect on earth elementals or galeb duhr.

The material component, a diamond chip worth at least 500 gp, must be crushed and sprinkled on the construction.

Thornwrack (Alteration)

Sphere: Plant
Range: Touch
Components: V, S
Duration: 1 thorn/level of caster
Casting Time: 8
Area of Effect: 1 person
Saving Throw: Neg.

Thornwrack causes long, painful thorns to grow out of the spell recipient's flesh, piercing the skin from the inside. One thorn appears each round, inflicting 1d3 points of damage, until all the thorns have appeared.

When the number of thorns exceeds the subject's experience level or HD, a victim still conscious becomes immobilized by the pain, unable to take any action.

One round after the last thorn erupts from the victim's flesh, the first one disappears. The thorns continue receding at a rate of one per turn. Immobilized subjects can move again once the number of thorns falls below their HD or experience level. For instance, say the body of a 4th-level character has seven thorns. After four turns had passed, only three thorns would remain, so the victim would no longer be immobile.

Cure spells can restore hit points but do not eliminate the thorns. *Dispel magic* will end the spell but prevents existing thorns from receding. A *heal* spell cancels the *thornwrack*, eliminates all existing thorns, and cures all damage. Without the benefit of magical remedies, the spell ends when the last thorn has receded.

Sixth-level Spells

Earthwrack (Alteration)

Sphere: Necromantic, Plant
Range: 20 yards/level of caster
Components: V, S, M
Duration: 2d4+10 years
Casting Time: 1 round
Area of Effect: 30-foot radius/level of caster
Saving Throw: None

This spell causes an area of soil to become barren and blighted. Healthy plants wither and die within 1d4 days of casting. No seed planted there will grow for the duration of the spell. Plant-based creatures entering the despoiled area can see the ruin and feel an intense "wrongness" within the soil. Each round they remain within the area, they suffer 1d4 points of damage.

The blight can be cured using a *limited wish*, a *wish*, or by casting a *remove curse* spell (at the 12th level of experience) and a *plant growth* spell simultaneously.

Most druids consider *earthwrack* an abomination, although some Shadow Circle druids use it as last-ditch "scorched earth" vengeance against an unruly hamlet.

The material component is the priest's holy symbol.

Ivy Siege (Enchantment)

Sphere: Plant
Range: 90 yards
Components: V, S, M
Duration: 6 turns
Casting Time: 9
Area of Effect: 1 building or similar structure
Saving Throw: Special

The *ivy siege* spell must be cast upon a stone or brick building constructed upon the earth; flying castles and the like remain unaffected. Immediately after casting, ivy begins to grow at a fantastic rate, climbing from the ground up the building's walls. At the end of one turn, the ivy has climbed the walls. At the end of the second turn, green creepers have covered the structure. On the third turn, the ivy has deepened to a black-green and begins to squeeze the building.

Starting on the third turn and every turn thereafter, the building must make a saving throw vs. siege damage, as if attacked by a small catapult (*DMG*, p. 76). Two cubic feet of the building crumbles away for each point by which the saving throw misses each turn. This cycle continues until the spell's duration expires or the building is destroyed. The ivy rots away instantly at the spell's end.

A druid can cast only one *ivy siege* per building at a time. After the ivy has rotted away, the druid may cast the spell on the same building again. However, multiple druids can cast several *ivy siege* spells on the

Druidic Magic • 95

same building. In the case of a large, interconnected series of buildings (like a castle), each casting affects only a single tower, keep, or wall segment, to a maximum of 1,000 cubic feet per level of the caster.

The DM may choose to prohibit arctic and desert druids from using this spell if they are not familiar with ivy.

The material component is an ivy leaf.

Seventh-level Spells

Tree Spirit (Necromancy)

Sphere: Plant
Range: Touch
Components: V, S
Duration: Permanent
Casting Time: 1 turn
Area of Effect: 1 tree
Saving Throw: None

Tree spirit permanently links the soul of the caster with a tree, usually chosen carefully for its health, vigor, and remote environment. Casting this spell joins the life force of the druid with that of the tree; as long as the tree lives, the caster ages at one-tenth the normal rate. (Because the spell causes the tree to devote all its energy to maintaining health rather than growth, it always remains exactly the size it was at the time of casting.) Moreover, the caster's spirit merges with the tree at the character's death. No form of reincarnation or resurrection (except a *wish*) on the character's body will work unless it lies within 10 feet of the tree.

One year after the caster dies, the druid's spirit animates the tree as a treant. (DMs should roll up treant statistics for the tree at the time the spell is cast, to determine the tree's Armor Class, Hit Dice, etc.) The chosen tree must be of treant height; the exact size determines the size of the new treant, which possesses the caster's memories and personality but has no granted powers or spellcasting ability. It must communicate as a treant.

The DM decides whether to consider this treant an NPC or allow the player to control it. (DMs should use the guidelines that apply to PCs who become lycanthropes or undead.)

However, when a druid uses *tree spirit* to link with a tree, the character suffers any physical damage inflicted on the tree. For instance, if someone hacks at the tree with an axe and causes 4 points of damage, the caster also loses 4 hit points; the druid knows the tree has been harmed, but does not know the nature of the injury.

If the tree dies but does not sustain enough damage to kill the caster, the character feels stunned for 1d6 rounds and must make a successful system shock roll to avoid death. Spells that heal the druid do not affect the tree.

Damage to the caster does not affect the tree, as the extra energy the tree expends on strength and health makes any damage the player sustains negligible to the tree. However, it's usually in the druid's best interest to have an animal friend or two guard the tree.

In addition, the druid should choose the tree carefully; if the surrounding land is cleared for construction work or lumber before the druid's prolonged life span finally ends, the character is in trouble.

Casting *tree spirit* first requires a full month's preparation. The druid lives near the tree during this time of prayer and mediation. Then the character conducts a private bonding ceremony at the height of a solstice. This spell often is cast by ancient druids, who wish to preserve their wisdom or make sure their groves remain defended even after their death.

Unwilling Wood (Enchantment/Charm)

Sphere: Plant
Range: 5 yards/level of caster
Components: V, S, M
Duration: Permanent
Casting Time: 1 round
Area of Effect: 10-yard radius
Saving Throw: Special

A caster can transform one or more living creatures within a 10-yard radius into *unwilling wood*, causing them to sprout roots, branches, and leaves. The victims become trees of a type native to the region and of the characters' age before the transformation. The spell works only if cast on beings occupying ground that could support a tree; recipients flying or suspended in water at the time of casting remain unaffected.

This spell can mutate a number of creatures equal in total Hit Dice (or levels) to the caster's level—within the area of effect, of course. If this area holds a group of creatures with Hit Dice (or levels) totaling a number greater than the caster's experience level, the character may decide the order in which the creatures become affected.

For instance, say a 14th-level druid casts *unwilling wood* into a target area containing a giant with 12 Hit Dice and two 3rd-level warriors. The druid can transform either the giant or two warriors, but not all three. "Leftover" Hit Dice or levels are lost.

Each creature affected may attempt to save vs. polymorph. The spell mutates all those failing their saving throw, along with any items they carry. A new tree has a height of 5 feet per level (or Hit Die) of the victim. The effect is permanent; a person transformed into a tree ages as a tree and dies as a tree. However, affected characters retain awareness, memories, personality, and intelligence. Only damage severe enough to kill the tree can kill an *unwilling wood* victim.

Druidic Magic • 97

Tree-characters can return to normal if a spellcaster of greater level than the original caster uses *remove curse*. The original caster can release a transformed entity at will.

The material components are a bit of tree root and the priest's holy symbol.

New Magical Items

Druid characters can use the magical items generally permitted priests except written ones, such as scrolls or books. They can wear magical armor only when it is natural, such as wooden shields. Any magical weapon a druid uses must be of a type permitted to priests, as well as by the character's druidic kit and branch.

This section contains new magical items that fit the druid's role of Nature priest, keeper of the balance, and dweller in the country. In addition, a small number of the items are designed for use against druids.

Although this listing contains some powerful items, many are fairly low-key. Items like the *bountiful spade,* or *seeds of plenty* represent the kind of magical item a high-level character would create as a gift for a favored farmer or lord. Druids might offer cursed items like the *necklace of beast speech* to someone as punishment for wronging the Order or the land.

Creating Magical Items

The normal rules for priests creating magical items (*DMG* pgs. 83–88) apply to druids as well. In almost all cases, gathering the rare, unique, or impossible components and combining them properly remains more important than purchasing expensive materials; quest and ritual take precedence over the depth of the druid's purse.

The personal touch is vital: Druids must make the vessels for enchantment using their nonweapon proficiencies. Characters needn't be expert artisans, but they cannot create a magical scimitar merely by enchanting a weapon someone else has made. As a result, a druid who completes an arduous series of tasks to collect the necessary components may not actually have to spend any money to build the item, although major magical items require components easily worth the 1,000 to 10,000 gp noted in the *DMG* (p. 87).

Priest characters must spend up to three weeks meditating, fasting, and purifying themselves before they can enchant an item. Druids must begin this process at a sacred time, like an equinox, for the enchantment to have any chance of success. Druids purify the vessel and pray for its consecration not at an altar, but at their grove.

Potions

Potion of Plant Health. This potion vitalizes a living plant when poured upon its roots. It cures the plant's illnesses and keeps it free from natural parasites and disease for a year. During this time, the plant grows 50% better than normal, and 10% better than normal the next year. Edible fruit, berries, or sap from the plant taste unusually succulent, while flowering plants bloom exceptionally well. If a vegetable monster such as a treant or shambling mound drinks this potion, treat it as a *potion of extra-healing*. XP value: 400.

Sap of the Eldest Tree. Usually found in an earthen flask, this potion resembles thick corn or maple syrup. Characters who drink the sap (or bake it in a cake and eat it) will not age a day for the next 10 years! However, unlike a *longevity* potion, it does not make the drinker any younger. A person must consume the entire potion to gain the full benefit; if five characters share the syrup, each stops aging for two years. Additional doses are not cumulative—later imbibings supplant earlier ones. XP value: 500.

Wands and Staves

Wand of Shape Binding. Characters often use this item *against* druids. When hit by its multicolored beam (projected up to 80 feet), beings with the ability to shapechange or polymorph must save vs. wands at a –3 penalty. Victims who fail cannot voluntarily alter shape for 2d10 turns. Attempts to shift shape using spells, magical items, or innate powers result in failure. A use of this rechargeable wand consumes one charge per 4 HD or levels of the subject. XP value: 800.

Wanderer's Staff. This resembles a stout oaken staff, which radiates magic and, in fact, functions as a *quarterstaff +1*. However, its primary power is locomotion. If carried as a walking stick, users hiking at a steady pace do not tire or need sleep. Any time spent walking counts as sleep for the purpose of resting the character. If desired, the character can walk night and day, taking only brief breaks for food, drink, etc. XP value: 2,000.

Rings

Ring of the Hierophant. Only druids can utilize this ring, which enables characters to speak the language of elementals. This, the ring's lesser power, uses up no charges.

More impressively, a druid wearing the ring may shapechange into an elemental. Druids in elemental form retain their own hit points and saving throws, but otherwise possess the characteristics of a 12 HD elemental. The transformation functions just like a druid's shapechanging power—this rechargeable ring even restores hit points when the druid changes back. However, transformations last only for a maximum of one hour. Each elemental form (air, fire, earth, and water) may be assumed only once per month. XP value: 4,000.

Weapons

Lunar Sickle. This weapon, a sickle crafted from silver and bound to the moon, may have been forged for druids as a symbol of the cyclic nature of time. The sickle boasts its greatest strength during the waxing moon. It has a +2 bonus from the new moon to half moon, a +3 bonus from the half moon to full moon, and +4 during the full moon. When the moon begins to wane, the *lunar sickle* drops to a +1 bonus. During the dark of the moon it loses all magical bonuses; until the new moon rises, it no longer affects creatures that can be hit only by magical weapons. XP value: 1,500.

Sickle of the Harvest. This sickle appears to be a normal farm implement, albeit of superior quality. If used in combat, it functions as a +1 weapon. However, its real power is as a magical harvesting tool.

Anyone who grasps the sickle and speaks in the secret language of the druids can order the sickle to harvest a field on its own. When so commanded, the sickle takes to the air and harvests up to half an acre of grain per turn. It can accept precise orders, such as, "Cut down all stalks of ripe grain within a mile, save for Farmer Dowd's field."

The sickle continues working until: three hours pass; its owner orders it to stop; or it moves a mile from its owner. Characters can also halt the sickle by destroying it or snatching it out of the air. Anyone trying to grab the sickle must make a successful attack roll against AC –4. Those who fail suffer 1d6+1 points of damage; success means a character grabs it and stops the harvesting.

Treat attacks on the sickle as attacks against a *sword of dancing*; the sickle, while physically unstoppable, can be affected by failing a saving roll against a spell such as *fireball, lightning bolt,* or *transmute metal to wood*. XP value: 1,300.

Heartwood Cudgel. This club, made from the heartwood of an oak, is a *club +1—club +2* in a druid's hands. XP value: 500.

Mistletoe Dart. The body and tip of this dart are fashioned from enchanted mistletoe. Magical armor, shields, or rings give no bonus protection against it; for example, a person wearing *chain mail +4* would have AC 5, not AC 1. Darts, while not innately poisonous, can be coated with any venom. Characters usually find these darts in groups of 2 to 8 (2d4). XP value: 50 each.

Armor

Antlered Helm. This metal-reinforced leather helm, adorned with a stag's antlers, allows the wearer to run like a deer, with a base movement rate of 18. Moreover, stags and deer see, hear, and smell wearers of an *antlered helm* as if they were stags, and react accordingly. This power makes the item very useful for hunting. XP value: 800.

Miscellaneous Magic

Bountiful Spade. Characters who use this enchanted farm implement to turn over the earth prior to planting a field receive a +3 bonus on their agriculture proficiency check for that year. XP value: 500.

Cloak of the Beasts. This plain brown cloak bears patches of many different animal skins. A character who speaks a word of command while wearing it instantly becomes transformed into a random animal for 1d6 hours. The cloak and the person's other clothing become part of the new form.

The type of animal varies with each use of the cloak's power—roll 1d100 on the *reincarnate* spell table (*PH*, p. 235), rerolling any nonanimal result. The nature of the change is identical to a druidic shapechange, except that wearers have no control over which animal form they take on and cannot change back until the enchantment wears off.

Upon returning to normal, the wearer regains 10% to 60% of any lost hit points (10d6). The cloak cannot be used again until 12 hours pass. XP value: 1,000.

Druid's Yoke. While this item looks like an ox yoke, it is small enough to fit a donkey or human. Worn by an animal, it offers no benefit. If fastened onto a human, demihuman, or humanoid, it transforms the wearer into a full-sized ox; the yoke expands to fit. The ox retains the wearer's mind, but cannot speak or use spells and becomes vulnerable to magic that affects normal animals. The effect lasts as long as the yoke stays on—the wearer can't remove it, but a friendly humanoid can. A character reverts back to normal immediately after the yoke comes off. Wearers killed in ox form die; their bodies revert back to humanoid form once the yoke is removed. XP value: 2,000.

Herbmaster's Pouch. This small bag of finely woven grass keeps herbs—including herbal magical ingredients—as fresh as if newly harvested. The –2 penalty for using preserved herbs to create magical herbal brews does not apply to ingredients kept in an *herbmaster's pouch*. XP value: 500.

Necklace of Beast Speech. This gold choker bears the image of a particular beast. To determine what kind, roll on the *reincarnate* table (*PH*, p. 235), rerolling any result that's not an animal.

Anyone who dons the device loses all power of speech, except with the animal species on the necklace. The character cannot remove the choker without a *wish* spell; a carefully worded *wish* might allow a wearer to retain the necklace and beast speech *and* regain human speech. XP value: 0.

Seeds of the Hedge. Usually found in a leather bag or pouch, these seeds resemble flower or grass seeds. A pinch of *hedge seed* sprinkled on earth or grass instantly causes a thorny hedge to grow. The user can decide to make this 10-foot × 10-foot × 5-foot hedge 5 feet long, 5 feet high, or 5 feet wide.

Creatures caught in the hedge's growth or trying to break through the hedge suffer 8 points of damage plus additional points equal to their Armor Class (excluding Dexterity adjustments). It takes two turns to safely cut through each 5-foot thickness. Normal fire does not harm it, but magical fire sets it ablaze in one turn, creating a temporary *wall of fire* effect (as if cast by a 9th-level wizard) of the same size. One bag of seeds sows three hedges. XP value: 600.

Seeds of Plenty. An ample sack holds magical seeds of the crop most important to local farmers—enough to sow a single large field. The only thing unusual about the seed is that it radiates magic (noticeable if a character checks). Fields sown with this seed produce superior crops: exceptionally large plants that prove resistant to disease.

Seeds of plenty double a normal harvest, increasing a typical farm family's income 50% to 100% for the year. Furthermore, products made from the crop are superior. Porridge or bread made from a grain harvest prove especially tasty and nutritious; clothes made from flax crops have exceptionally high quality; and so on. For this reason, a known sack of *seeds of plenty* sells for up to 2,000 gp.
XP value: 200 per sack.

Seeds of Doom. A sack holding these seeds appears identical to one filled with *seeds of plenty*. However, sowing a field with these seeds leads to disaster. The night after the planting, a dense field of noxious weeds springs up, each weed 5 to 7 feet high. Anyone less than giant size passing through the weeds can move only 10 feet per round. One turn after spending any time in the weeds, those not fully covered in armor (generally, anyone not wearing plate mail or better) must save vs. poison. Those who fail instantly develop a painful rash that lasts 2d6 days (–2 penalty to all attack rolls, as well as attribute and proficiency checks; –4 penalty if wearing armor or tight clothing).

Weeds set ablaze do burn, producing a foul stench that lasts 2d6 turns (equivalent to a *stinking cloud* spell over the field) and leaves a residual unpleasant smell for 2d6 days. Furthermore, the black ash left behind poisons the field so nothing will grow there for 2d6 years. Uprooting the weeds manually requires 100 people working for a week, due to the weeds' fast growth. XP value: 0.

Serpent Seeds. Normally available in a packet of 1d3 seeds, a *serpent seed* springs up into a 20-foot tree one round after being planted in an inch of dirt, watered, and told to grow in the druids' secret language. A serpent tree has no branches; its limbs are 1d8 brown serpents with green eyes, barklike skin, and wooden fangs dripping with poisonous white sap.

While the tree cannot move, its branches can reach out up to 20 feet and follow the druid's orders. Each serpent-branch's bite is poisonous. A person who fails to save vs. poison becomes incapacitated within one turn; the character does not die, but slowly becomes transformed into a "serpent of the tree," a nonpoisonous version of the branch-snakes.

Despite its barky appearance, this new creature resembles nonpoisonous snakes of the region in appetite and attacks. While serpents of the tree are not attached to the serpent tree, they remain subject to the druid's orders, just like the tree itself.

A victim can be restored with a *cure serious wounds* or *heal* spell administered within one day of the bite. On the second day, the transformation to a serpent of the tree is nearly complete; only a *wish* can return the victim to normal then.

The serpent tree remains permanently where planted and stays loyal to its maker as long as it exists. XP value: 1,000 per seed.

Serpent tree: Int Low (5); AL N; AC 6; MV 0; HD 6+6; THAC0 15; #AT 1/limb; Dmg 1d4/limb; SA poison changes victims into serpents of the tree; ML 8; SZ H; XP 875.

Serpent of the tree: Int Animal (1); AL N; AC 5; MV 15; HD 2+1; THAC0 19; #AT 1; Dmg 1; ML 8; SZ S (5 ft.); XP 90.

Stone of Lost Ways. This pebble might be mistaken for any other magical stone. However, those who carry it through trackless wilderness (not following a road or path) increase their chances of becoming hopelessly lost. Having a character with a *stone of lost ways* in a party adds 20% to the group's chance of becoming lost, in any terrain. (See Table 81 in the *DMG*, p. 128.) Furthermore, two checks instead of the normal one are needed, one for each half-day's travel. The stone affects only characters traveling on the ground. XP value: 0.

Swarm Queen's Crown. This dread item resembles a gold tiara set with a piece of amber encasing an insect—usually a queen bee. The crown has a value of 2,000 gp.

With a command word, a user's body mutates into a human-shaped mass of stinging, venomous wasps, bees, and spiders: a miniature, living *creeping doom*. The user's new "body" contains 10 insects per hit point. For example, a character with 10 hit points becomes a mass of 100 insects.

The user attacks by touching someone (a normal attack roll). After a hit, the user decides how many insects sting or bite the victim. Either 10, 20, or 30 insects may swarm over a victim per attack; for every 10 insects that hit, the victim loses 1d10 hit points, and the wearer of the crown loses 1 hp—each insect dies after its attack. So, a character may inflict up to 3d10 points of damage per attack at the cost of 3 hp.

While in insect form, the user has a move of 3, but can climb walls and ceilings. The user cannot employ any weapons, spells, magical items, tools, or armor. The swarm, which has AC 0, suffers no damage from piercing weapons (P), 1 point of damage from slashing weapons (S), and half damage from bludgeoning weapons (B). Magical bonuses and fire inflict full damage. Every point of damage to the wearer kills 10 insects. The user remains transformed as long as desired, but the crown can be used only once per day. XP value: 4,000.

Treeship. A living tree shaped like a currach (*PH*, p. 71), a *treeship* unites the magic of druids and the craftsmanship of elves. The mast is a magical tree, from which hang branchlike rigging and leaf-sails. The roots form the hull's ribs, covered by thick bark instead of hide. A ship carries up to eight people and 5 tons of cargo. While the vessel cannot sail by itself, a crew finds it quite seaworthy and swift (seaworthiness 80%, base move 3/6, emergency move 12).

Treeships can sail only in freshwater lakes, rivers, and seas; salt water poisons them within a week. When beached on grass or soil (not sand) for more than a week, they grow additional roots into the soil and require 1d6 days of pruning to become seaworthy again. XP value: 6,000.

Herbal Magic

A character with the herbalist proficiency may use herbs as an adjunct to the healing skill, as explained in Chapter 5 of the *PH* (p. 59). However, some druids possess exceptional herb lore, which enables them to produce magical herbal brews. Druids who devote at least three slots to the herbalism proficiency can create these brews.

An *herbal brew* is a concoction of several herbs (and sometimes fungi or tree bark) that produces exotic effects. The name of a brew does not refer to the herbs in it, but to its effects. Herbal brews require no magical plants; power comes from the combination of herbs and the secret techniques herbalist druids use in each stage of preparation.

Locating the Herbs

Finding an herbal brew's ingredients requires first locating the right place to look. The druid must search in the proper terrain for the time indicated in the brew's listing (starting on p. 105). Then, make an herbalism proficiency check, applying the brew's search modifier and a –4 penalty for snow-covered ground or darkness, if applicable.

Success means the druid locates enough herbs to produce one brew; failure means the character finds none. In either case, additional searches may be made, though a druid really should search only once per square mile of appropriate terrain. Repeated searches of an area carry a cumulative –2 penalty—there may be nothing there to find!

Some Common Herbs

Druids find these herbs especially useful in their magic. Others may be included, real or unique to your own campaign world.

Angelica root	Mustard seed
Anise seed	Myrrh gum
Cassia buds	Peppermint leaf
Chamomile flowers	Poppy seeds
Cloves	Sage leaf
Damiana leaf	Sarsaparilla root
Elder flowers	Thyme leaf
Gentian root	Valerian root
Marjoram leaf	Yerba mate leaf

Preserving Herbal Ingredients

Most herbs work best while fresh, but druids may wish to store some for future use rather than immediately turning them into brews. Preserving ingredients by drying, powdering, and packing the herbs takes six hours per set of ingredients (enough for one brew) and requires a successful herbalism check.

The DM makes this roll, informing the player whether the ingredients have spoiled only when the druid tries to use them in a brew. A successful roll ensures the herbs stay fresh while in a waterproof container. Failure indicates they will spoil in 1d6 days.

Making an Herbal Brew

To create an herbal brew, the druid must have the appropriate ingredients, either fresh or preserved. The brewing process requires a quiet place that fosters deep concentration. It involves both physical work (chopping and cleaning herbs, mixing the ingredients in proper portions, steaming them, etc.) and ritual gestures and prayer. As with granted powers and spells, if the druid has not remained faithful to the Order, the herbs fail to take on their magical properties.

After preparing the concoction as long as the brew's description requires, the druid rolls another herbalism proficiency check, using the modifiers shown. In addition, a –2 modifier applies if the druid used preserved rather than fresh herbs. A successful check means the druid creates the brew. Failure means the druid ruins the ingredients; a roll of 19 or 20 always fails.

A druid with several sets of ingredients for the same herbal brew may mix multiple batches at the same time. If the final proficiency check succeeds, the druid concocts all the batches; if it fails, the ingredients all go to waste.

Types of Herbal Brews

The next several pages offer descriptions of various herbal brews. Feel free to create new ones for your own druid characters.

Each brew entry includes these details:

Terrain tells where to find ingredients for the brew, as well as any special notes (gather only at night, etc.).

Search Time/Modifier indicates how many hours a druid must search for the brew's ingredients and offers a modifier to the herbalism proficiency check that determines whether the druid finds them.

Preparation Time/Modifier suggests how many hours it takes the druid to prepare the brew and offers a modifier to the herbalism proficiency check needed for successful brewing.

Application tells how to apply the brew: either as a tea, ointment, poultice, or vapor.

A *tea* consists of a mix of broken or crushed dried herbs infused into water. The rules for drinking potions apply to herbal teas, which keep indefinitely in dry form.

An *ointment* is a brew mixed with lard, beeswax, lanolin, or another similar base and rubbed onto skin. Treat it as a magical oil.

A *poultice* consists of a damp herbal brew bandaged onto a wound or area of skin. The contents of the poultice soaks into the skin gradually. Applying a poultice takes two rounds; it can be applied only to an unresisting or grappled subject.

A *vapor*, a mixture intended to be inhaled rather than drunk, usually affects an area. The dry ingredients must be stirred into boiling water so the brew's recipient can breathe in the steam. Administration requires two rounds and a source of hot water.

Effects describes what the brew does.

Save explains what kind of saving throw, if any, can resist the brew's effects. Most saving throws are against poison— even if a brew is not actually deadly.

Crawlbane
Terrain: Swamp and deep forest
Search Time/Modifier: 6/–1
Preparation Time/Modifier: 2/–1
Application: Ointment
Effects: This ointment strongly repels insects. Anyone covered head to foot in it remains unaffected by normal insects, even those summoned by spells such as *creeping doom* and *insect plague*. Giant insects still may attack the character, but do so at a –3 penalty, due to their revulsion.
Save: None

Darkweed
Terrain: Desert oasis
Search Time/Modifier: 6/–2
Preparation Time/Modifier: 10/–4
Application: Ointment
Effects: A character who smears this ointment over both eyes becomes blind within two rounds. However, the character can see invisible, astral, ethereal, or illusory objects as if they were real and fully visible.
Save: Neg. if save vs. spell

Deathmock
Terrain: Mountain slopes
Search Time/Modifier: 4/–3
Preparation Time/Modifier: 6/–3
Application: Tea
Effects: *Deathmock* causes drinkers to fall into a cataleptic trance; characters display muscle rigidity and do not appear to breathe or have a heartbeat. While injuries cause them little bleeding, they otherwise suffer normal damage. Those under the influence of this tea sleep for 2d4 days, during which time they need no food or water. They need only one-twentieth the air unaffected people do and can survive freezing temperature.
Save: Neg. if save vs. poison

Druidic Magic

Fiendflower
Terrain: Deep forest or jungle
Search Time/Modifier: 12/–4
Preparation Time/Modifier: 8/–3
Application: Tea
Effects: Characters who drink this bitter tea see horrifying visions that drive them temporarily mad. After 1d20 turns, drinkers suffer an episode of 2d6 minutes, during which they turn enraged, violent, and homicidal; such a PC should be played by the DM. Afterward, drinkers cannot recall what happened during the episode, which recurs once per day (at irregular intervals) for the next 2d4 days. A *neutralize poison* spell ends *fiendflower*'s effects.
Save: Neg. if save vs. spell

Ghostroot
Terrain: Old graveyards at night
Search Time/Modifier: 8/–4
Preparation Time/Modifier: 4/–6
Application: Vapor
Effects: This mixture's luminous vapors repel undead. Any undead attempting to draw near must save vs. spell. Failure prevents them from approaching within 10 feet of the steaming brew. Success allows them to ignore its effects; once they save, they remain immune to the brew for the rest of the day. The vapors last for one turn.
Save: Neg. if save vs. spell

Nevermind
Terrain: Forest clearings or caverns
Search Time/Modifier: 8/–3
Preparation Time/Modifier: 8/–7
Application: Tea
Effects: Characters develop amnesia one minute after drinking this tea, permanently forgetting all events since they last slept.
Save: Neg. if save vs. spell

Hushthorn
Terrain: Forests at night
Search Time/Modifier: 4/–3
Preparation Time/Modifier: 4/–3
Application: Tea
Effects: This tea causes drinkers to fall into a deep, natural sleep, from which they cannot be awakened for 2d10+13 hours.
Save: Neg. if save vs. poison

Snakesalve
Terrain: Jungle
Search Time/Modifier: 6/–1
Preparation Time/Modifier: 2/–1
Application: Poultice
Effects: If applied to a living snake-bite victim, this poultice neutralizes the poison.
Save: None

Springberry
Terrain: Moonlit spring meadows
Search Time/Modifier: 8/–3
Preparation Time/Modifier: 8/–7
Application: Tea
Effects: Within an hour of drinking the tea, characters fall in love with the first person of the opposite sex they see. The drinkers, while not *charmed*, act besotted and devote all efforts to wooing their love. The effects last for 2d4 days unless a player rolled a 20 on the save; in that case they are permanent.
Save: Neg. if save vs. spell

Wintersalve
Terrain: Mountain slopes or tundra
Search Time/Modifier: 6/–3
Preparation Time/Modifier: 6/–3
Application: Ointment
Effects: This ointment, when smeared over exposed body parts, provides the same protection against cold that a heavy fur coat would, but without the encumbrance. Combined with winter clothing, it allows for survival below zero and gives a +1 bonus to saving throws against cold-based attacks.
Save: None

CHAPTER 6

Sacred Groves

When not adventuring, druids prefer to live near a *sacred grove* and worship there as well. While the term "sacred grove" usually calls to mind a stand of trees within a forest, here it refers to any sacred place where druids worship Nature. All sacred groves are places of great natural beauty—and sometimes magical power. Areas with a history of druidic veneration tend to acquire wondrous abilities from their prolonged contact with druidic magic and rites.

Sometimes several druids share a single sacred grove. This arrangement enables them to take turns adventuring or traveling, leaving someone always on hand to protect and tend the grove. Druids occupying a sacred grove singly have to arrange for its safety before departing: setting various wards and traps, or arranging for allies to protect it in the druid's absence.

Features of a Sacred Grove

Each branch of the druidic order prefers certain sites for sacred groves. These include the woodland groves of the forest druids, the oases of the desert druid, the fungus-rich caves of the gray druid, and so on. In nearly every case, the overriding requirement is that the sacred grove possess a natural splendor. This splendor may range from the stark grandeur of a ring of standing stones atop a hill on a windswept moor to the gardenlike beauty of a tended forest glade.

A sacred grove is typically between 60 feet and 360 feet across (6d6 × 10 feet). Besides the expected grass, undergrowth, bushes, trees, or other local features, desirable groves share certain elements.

Distinct Boundaries

Sacred groves reveal themselves readily to those who know what to look for. A grove's boundary markers often result from the efforts of generations of druids. For example, the trees in a woodland grove may form concentric circles, the outermost layer reserved for the largest, most ancient trees.

Often the trees in a sacred grove are of an unusual size or a type distinct from others in the wood. For example, a sacred grove in a birch forest might have many oaks. Their branches may even entwine to form natural arches to welcome visitors. In more open terrains, sacred groves may surround themselves with high, thorny hedges or even a river. Some groves have artificial borders, such as an outer ring of standing stones. A few are small islands.

A Clearing

A quiet place of meditation blanketed with soft moss or grass lies in the center of the grove. Druids prefer groves carpeted with soft ground cover that encourages dancing over a floor of simple dirt or stone.

Source of Water

A spring, well, brook, or pool (often fed by a waterfall) provides the grove with pure, drinkable water. Druids use this water in their rituals and in their day-to-day life as well. Some druids prefer still water to a brook or spring, since the quiet water is less distracting during meditation and can prove useful in divination.

Central Feature

A commanding structure—perhaps the source of water—acts as a natural altar in the grove or as a focus for worship. Other common central features include a single great tree, a standing stone, or a fairy ring (a circle of toadstools or other fungi). These and other features sometimes possess magical powers, detailed in a later section.

Native Animals

An owl lives in a grove's great tree, a snake dwells under a stone—the druid is never really alone in a sacred grove. The place feels alive in every sense, and druids usually befriend a grove's inhabitants.

Living Quarters

While the druid and any servants or family members rarely live within the sacred grove proper, home lies not far away. A forest druid, for instance, generally has a stone, log, or sod cottage within a mile of the grove, with a vegetable and herb garden, and perhaps a few domestic animals.

Stewardship

Although druids do not claim to "own" sacred groves, they take responsibility for them very seriously. The druid associated with a grove normally goes by the title of steward, keeper, or caretaker. Stewardship of a sacred grove is traditional: Keepers always designate their successors.

Guards and Wards

The steward of a sacred grove is first and foremost responsible for the grove's safety, especially if the grove has "awakened" with magical powers (explained later in this chapter) or if beings such as dryads live there. Therefore, druids devote considerable effort to protecting a sacred grove—in some cases, through secrecy. Only a few trustworthy people and creatures know the grove's location. A druid obscures the pathway to the grove, while *hallucinatory forest* spells and better-cleared false trails twist away from it, leading a searcher astray.

More active defenses include pits covered with branches and leaves (perhaps sharp stakes, poisonous spiders, or snakes). Druids of at least 5th level use the *snare* spell liberally, as its defenses remain fixed until triggered. Using *plant growth* to set up permanent dense barriers around the grove is a very good strategy, especially if a druid plans to lace the obvious paths through these barriers with traps and snares, leaving only one or two concealed "safe" passages.

If enemies are on their way, the druid should strive to prevent them from using fire to damage the grove. Controlling weather to create a rainstorm before foes even reach the grove keeps the enemy miserable and stops the grass, bushes, and wood from igniting. Of course, one of the best ways a druid can defend a grove is to discover potential enemies and strike before they even reach the sacred natural site. (See "Eyes in the Wilderness," Chapter 4.)

Tending the Grove

While safeguarding the grove remains most important, stewards must not neglect regular care. This day-to-day work involves tending the plants and animals in the grove, talking to them, and dealing with illnesses or parasites that might appear. In addition, if a druid prefers a gardenlike appearance to a wild one, the steward cleans up loose branches, prunes trees and bushes, and so on. Druids should devote 12 days per month to this job, or about three days per week. If a druid fails in this duty, the DM can assume the sacred grove's health and appearance deteriorates (as does the magic of awakened groves, lesser powers first). Deterioration is immediately obvious to any visiting druid.

Several druids may use the same sacred grove as a place of worship, sharing the work detailed above, but only one is its steward; the others usually consider themselves the sacred grove's tenders. By tradition, if the keeper dies or retires, one of the tenders takes over the stewardship.

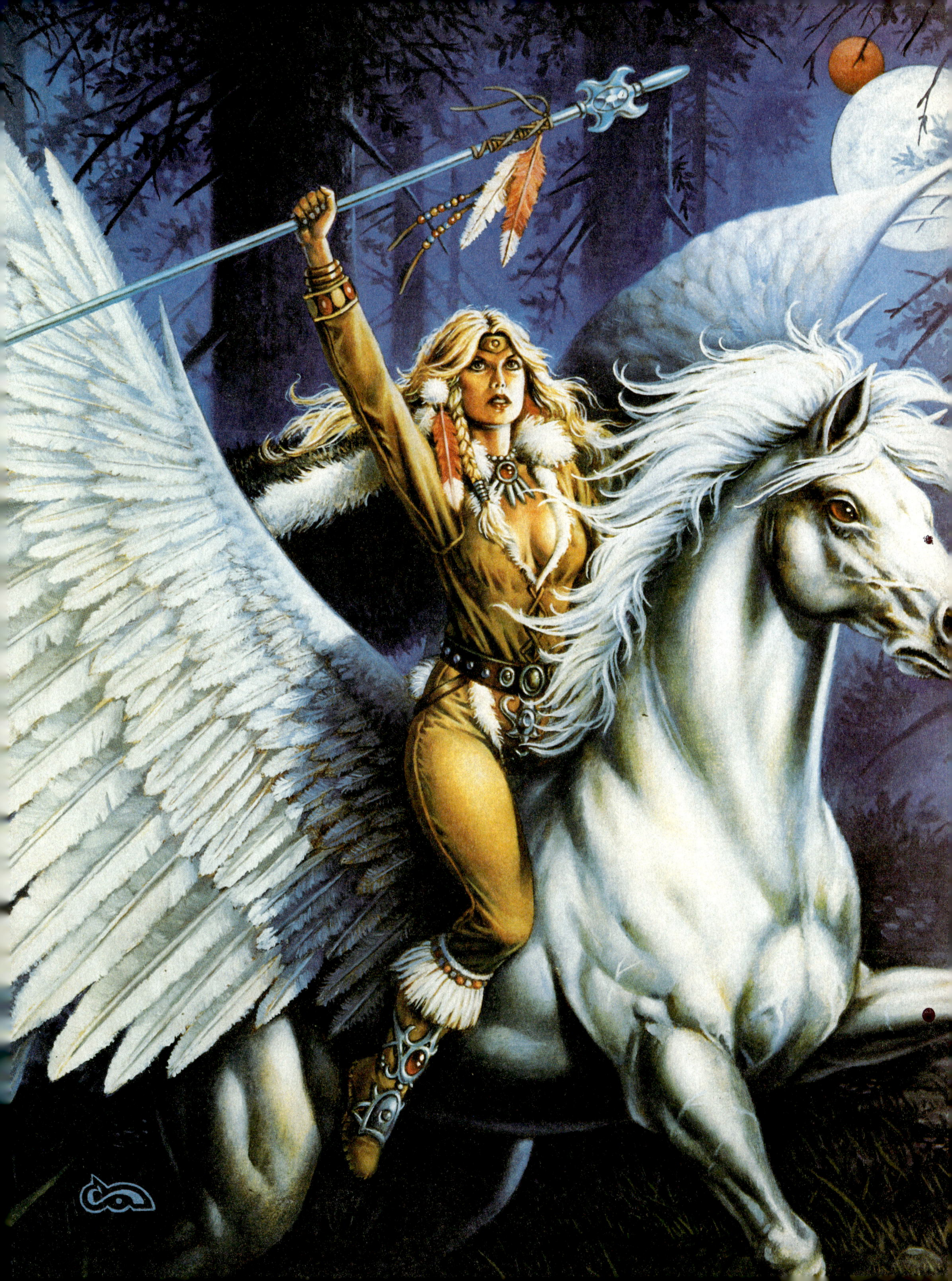

It is considered a crime for one druid in the Order to forcibly displace another from a stewardship. Such an incident, when reported to the great druid, constitutes grounds for the ban. In response, several druids will join together to expel the offender from the grove, finding a more suitable replacement—the original steward, if that druid did not die in the grove's defense.

An exception is allowed when a druid's negligence results in the deterioration or defilement of a sacred grove. In this case, an inner circle druid or the great druid appoints a new keeper for the grove. It becomes that druid's responsibility to reclaim the grove, by force if necessary, from its inept steward.

Grove Law

Druids, far stricter about protecting their sacred groves than any other wilderness area, have established a law to safeguard these special sites. The following points make up the law of the grove, upheld by all except the steward and those with special dispensation from the steward:

• No trees or plants within the grove may be harmed, cut, or pruned. No one may pick or cut branches, berries, nuts, or fruit, either; visitors can eat or otherwise use only that which has fallen to the ground.

• No one may fight within the grove.

• No bird or animal within a sacred grove may be harmed. If a hunted creature flees into the grove, hunters must break off the chase; they cannot shoot at the beast from outside the grove once it enters.

• No one may fish in the waters of a grove, nor foul these waters in any way.

• None may light a fire within a grove's bounds—not even tinder or a pipe.

The maximum penalty for violating the law of the grove is death, though a druid may apply a lesser penalty in certain cases. The punishment for violating these rules—or for more serious defilement of a sacred grove—depends on the offender's motives, the damage, and the druid's inclination. If a cruel wizard damaged a sacred grove with a *fireball* in an attack on the steward, the druid would think death a proper punishment— preferably death by fire. On the other hand, if a careless toddler did the same damage by accidentally setting fire to the grove, the druid seeks a more suitable punishment: kidnaping the child to raise as a druid. Thus the child devotes a lifetime to atonement.

Note that there is no law against folk entering the grove. While some druids keep visitors away, others welcome people and animals who come to admire the grove or worship, and even shelter needy travelers. Similarly, the steward may allow visitors to collect fallen deadwood, fruits, nuts, and berries. Since druids usually can speak with the animals, plants, and (sometimes) stones in their grove, they can determine easily how a person acquired suspicious bounty.

Becoming a Steward

A druid player character can acquire stewardship of a sacred grove in four ways:

First, the keeper of a grove might nominate the PC to become the successor to the stewardship. This tactic allows the PC to take over when the existing steward dies, disappears, or decides not to care for the grove any longer. The successor must have the current steward's trust and respect, and usually has spent time worshiping in the grove and tending it under supervision. Most of all, the nominee must prove worthy to defend the grove. If the grove has magic, the character should have reached at least 7th level to deserve consideration. However, young sacred groves lacking magic often receive the protection of lower-level druids.

Second, a player character can find an abandoned sacred grove and reclaim it. Sometimes a powerful monster or other foe eliminates both the steward of a sacred grove *and* the chosen successor. Such groves often are cursed, haunted by undead, or frequented by local monsters. But a druid who overcomes these obstacles and reclaims the grove proves worthy of the stewardship.

Third, a stewardship may come with a title, although this practice varies from circle to circle. For instance, a circle may award the responsibility for certain sacred groves to its archdruids or great druid, and—unlike a normal grove—this stewardship changes hands as new druids assume the high ranks. At the DM's discretion, the world might even hold a wondrous "high sacred grove"— the responsibility of the Grand Druid.

Fourth, a PC can find a virgin grove site and sanctify it. Virgin groves match the physical requirements listed earlier for a sacred grove, but have no magical powers and have never been tended. Finding such a spot is simply a matter of the druid's knowledge of local geography. A virgin grove rarely has clear boundaries, so the druid may make "improvements," such as planting a circle of trees or erecting standing stones to mark the new grove's borders.

Sanctifying and Awakening a Grove

Druids may wish to consecrate a sacred grove, perhaps awaken it to its magical properties. To this end, they must find a suitable natural site with the features described earlier.

After preparing a site, the druid performs a ritual to sanctify it. This ceremony, a blessing and invocation of Nature—takes a day of uninterrupted prayer. Once sanctified, a site becomes a sacred grove—a living shrine to Nature, where druids can perform their rites.

As druids worship there over the years, a sacred grove tends to absorb power from the rituals, becoming a holier place. If druids consistently venerate a grove, it may awaken to the magical powers described earlier. Venerating a grove means that druids (not necessarily just the one who sanctified it) pray and meditate there on a regular basis. Furthermore, the druid appointed the grove's steward must faithfully tend it.

A sanctified sacred grove actively visited and tended for seven years has a chance to gain magical powers. This time need not be contiguous—that is, a sacred grove can be active for five years, then abandoned, then active for another two years. After the seven years have passed, the DM begins rolling 1d10 each spring. On a roll of 10, the grove "awakens." Awakened groves gain the basic powers of a lesser sacred grove and a special ability (Table 3).

Sacred groves with a long history of druidic use become the most potent, their power slowly increasing over the ages as a result of continued exposure to druidic magic. For every seven years an awakened grove remains active, it has a further 10% chance of gaining additional powers, to a maximum of six powers. Roll on Table 3 at each success, rerolling duplicated powers.

A lesser magical sacred grove becomes a greater grove only through millennia of use by druids or direct divine intervention. DMs may assume a 10% chance of gaining greater grove status (and 1d4 such powers) per thousand years of veneration by druids.

Magical Sacred Groves

Not all sacred groves have magical powers, but many of them do. A grove may have been innately magical since the creation of the world or have gained its magic through an unusual event, such as a visit by a deity, the birth of a unicorn, or a dryad or nymph's long-time residence in the grove.

Lesser Magical Groves

An enchanted lesser sacred grove always radiates magic, although never good or evil. It has the following properties:

• Druids entering the grove feel a watching presence and a sense of power. For every three rounds they spend within its boundaries they learn one power of the sacred grove, through a vision or intuition.

• All druids receive a +1 bonus to saving throws vs. spell, death magic, and wands while within a lesser magical grove. The grove's steward receives a +2 bonus.

• All in the grove are rendered immune to magical *fear* while within it.

• *Dig* spells never work within a grove.

• Natural (nonmagical) lightning never strikes trees or beings in the grove.

• Evil enchanted creatures cannot enter the grove unless it has been defiled. (See "Defiled and Cursed Groves" in this chapter.)

In addition to these abilities, lesser magical sacred groves may possess other powers. To quickly create a grove the PCs might stumble upon while adventuring, the DM first decides how many lesser powers the grove has (chooses or rolls 2d4–2). Then, the DM selects the powers from Table 3 or rolls 1d10 to pick from the table randomly. (Descriptions of the powers follow.)

TABLE 3: Lesser Grove Powers

d10	Power
1	Awakened plants
2	Bountiful
3	Control temperature
4	Faerie fire
5	Healing
6	Prophecy
7	Protective aura
8	Still winds
9	Sweet water
10	Special

Awakened Plants. The grove's magic has "awakened" 1d3 10-foot-square patches of weeds, creepers, or bushes with semi-intelligence, 4 Hit Dice, AC 10, and the ability to attack as an *entangle* spell. They will act to protect themselves and defend the grove.

Bountiful. If the sacred grove contains plants that produce edible fruit, nuts, or berries, 3d6+20 enchanted examples sprout each spring along with the usual crop. The magic fruit, nuts, or berries—the largest and most healthy of their species—confer the benefits of a *goodberry* spell's products on the characters who eat them. Once picked, no more will grow until the following year.

Control Temperature. Any Nature worshiper in the grove may make a grove's temperature rise or fall within 30 degrees. This ability, possible once per day, affects the entire grove. Arctic or desert groves commonly feature this power, which enables those in the grove to survive brief climatic extremes, especially combined with the power to still winds (below).

Faerie Fire. A Nature worshiper (even a nonpriest) may cause a *faerie fire* luminance to appear, centered on the character or upon any of the trees, rocks, or standing stones in the grove. The *faerie fire*, which lasts one turn per level of the caller, can be summoned once per person in a given day. *Faerie fire* that druids call endures for two turns per level of the druid and can flicker about the grove at will. When a druid casts a *faerie fire* spell within the grove, its duration triples.

Healing. Beings of neutral alignment or those allied to the druid may heal wounds at twice the rate of natural healing while in the magical sacred grove. Healing-related spells produce the maximum benefits; for instance, *cure light wounds* restores 8 points of damage.

Prophecy. A druid who spends the night sleeping in the grove may receive a magical portent in a dream concerning the past, present, or future. The nature of the prophecy remains the DM's decision, but it should never contain more information than would come to light using a properly cast *commune with nature* spell. The portent usually warns of danger or hints at a task Nature wishes the druid to perform.

Protective Aura. Any creature but a druid, dryad, or nymph who sees the grove must save vs. spell. Those who fail perceive the grove as nothing other than a normal clearing (or the like) until they are led into it. The sacred grove also generates a continual protective field similar to *protection from evil, 10' radius*, except it covers the entire grove and has the powers of both *protection from evil* and *protection from good* spells.

Still Winds. Worshipers of Nature in the sacred grove (even nonpriests) can cause winds to calm for up to one turn per level, as long as they concentrate on maintaining this power. Triple the duration when a druid invokes it. This power, possible once per day, is quite common in desert, mountain, and arctic groves, as it protects the sacred grove and those in it from sandstorms, tornadoes, or snowstorms, and the like.

Sweet Water. Water from a source within the grove or dew gathered from the grass in the area has the properties of *sweet water*, but loses these special properties as soon as it is removed from the site.

Special. The DM can create a power associated with the branch or kit of the druid that sanctified this grove. For instance, the grove of a Hivemaster might contain a wasp's nest or beehive from which a druid could call an *insect plague* once per day, while a swamp druid's grove could feature a patch of firm ground that turns suddenly to quicksandlike mud (as in a *rock to mud* spell).

Greater Magical Groves

A greater magical sacred grove possesses exceptional enchantments. Each domain includes fewer than a score of such groves, most of which fall under the control of druids of 12th or higher level.

A greater grove has all the basic powers of the lesser grove, mentioned earlier. In addition, druids who sleep overnight in the grove before praying for spells receive an extra spell. Thus, a druid who chooses two 1st- and one 2nd-level spell receives another 1st- or 2nd-level spell of the DM's choice.

A greater magical sacred grove has 2d4 lesser grove powers (rolled on Table 3) and 1d4 greater grove powers (rolled on Table 4). Descriptions of the greater powers follow.

TABLE 4: Greater Grove Powers

d12	Power
1	Awakened tree
2	Beast speech
3	Concealment
4	Earthpower
5	Know alignment
6	Peaceful
7	Reincarnation
8	Waters of life
9	Scrying pool
10	Magic fruit
11	Forbiddance
12	Special

Awakened Tree. A large, ancient tree living in the grove gains Intelligence and Wisdom (2d6+6), the spellcasting ability of a 3rd-level druid, and the power of speech. It can use any two of its branches at once like arms. It speaks —in a deep, slow voice—in the secret language of the druids. In combat, treat it as a treant created by the *liveoak* spell. Roots bind it to the earth like a normal tree.

Beast Speech. Any normal or giant animal with an Intelligence score between animal and low can speak and understand the secret language of the druids for as long as it remains within the sacred grove. The animal's Intelligence does not increase. Also, casting *animal summoning* calls a 50% greater number (or Hit Dice) of animals than usual.

Concealment. All mobile beings (not normal plants) within the grove when this power is invoked become *invisible* for three turns per level of the druid or until they leave the grove. This power, possible once a day, ceases to conceal anyone who attacks.

Earthpower. When druids in the sacred grove cast a Plant or Earth Elemental sphere spell within its boundaries, they double the spell's duration, area of effect, and range.

Know Alignment. A druid may know the alignment of others in the sacred grove by concentrating one round. (The druid and subject must remain in the grove during this time.) This spell-like power can be used any number of times. Nonpriest worshipers of Nature can use this power after two rounds of concentration (and two successful Wisdom checks), but can make only one attempt.

Peaceful. Anyone entering this grove may notice odd sights, like predators and prey playing together. Those who make a successful attack against another within this grove must make a saving throw vs. wands. Attackers who fail suffer all the damage themselves; the wounds they meant to inflict appear on their own bodies. If they save, they suffer only half damage.

Reincarnation. If a druid's ashes or remains are buried in the sacred grove, the character becomes reincarnated (per the priest spell). The new incarnation appears within a mile of the grove in 1d6 days.

Waters of Life. Any source of water within the grove has unusual healing properties. Anyone bathing in the water (maximum of once per day per person) gains the benefit of simultaneous *neutralize poison, cure disease,* and *cure serious wounds* spells. The water loses all special properties outside the grove's boundaries, however, so characters cannot use it as a *healing* potion.

Scrying Pool. A source of still water within the grove, such as a pool or well, may be used for divination. Once per day a druid can command the pool or well to act as a *reflecting pool* cast at the druid's level.

Magic Fruit. The grove has a tree whose fruit or berries have a magical effect when eaten. In a given year, 1d6 fruits ripen, each with a distinct appearance to set it apart from common fruit—lustrous golden apples, for example. The magic fruit's effects are equivalent to one of the following:
- *Potion of animal control*
- *Potion of heroism*
- *Potion of longevity*
- *Potion of treasure finding*
- *Philter of love*
- *Philter of glibness*.

Forbiddance. A druid can invoke the *forbiddance* power (per the spell) to cover the boundaries of the grove. The effects can be called up only once per day and, once called, last one hour per level of the druid.

Special. The DM should devise a power associated with the branch or kit of the first steward of the greater magical sacred grove.

Defiled and Cursed Groves

Some sacred groves tell a tragic story: Their plants have been dug up, trees burned or chopped down, water sources fouled, or standing stones overturned and broken. Perhaps their clearings once served as altars to other priests in the worship of strange gods. Such groves have been defiled, stripped of all their powers until druids reclaim them (described below).

Other events may result in a still worse fate—a grove becoming cursed. For instance:
- A terrible event takes place within the grove's boundaries: Someone reads a cursed scroll, a deity's avatar passes through, a druid dies violently, or another highly charged event takes place.
- The grove is deliberately defiled but not destroyed. When plants begin to grow back, the grove may retain some twisted vestige of its original power.
- If the druid who sanctified the grove strays badly from the neutral alignment, abandons the Order, or takes up the path of the Lost Druids, the grove's beauty and powers may become warped—perhaps as a warning to the erring steward.

To determine what curse has struck a particular sacred grove, the DM may roll on Table 5. A druid who discovers a cursed grove nearly always tries to find a way to lift the curse and ultimately resanctify the land. Some typical curses are described below.

TABLE 5: Properties of Cursed Groves

d6	Property
1	Entrancing
2	Poisoned ground
3	Haunted
4	Perpetual season
5	Hungry trees
6	Special

Entrancing. This curse can apply to any grove containing a source of water or plants bearing fruit, nuts, or berries. Those who eat natural fruits of the grove or drink its water must save vs. spell or become charmed: They refuse to leave the grove, claiming they must defend this beautiful place. They resist forcefully if anyone tries to harm the grove or take them from it. The charm is broken if those it has entranced leave the grove, or it can wear off, per the *charm person* spell.

Poisoned Ground. A terrible poison lives within the ground, although the plants in the grove are immune. Those who touch the vegetation (including grass) with bare skin must save vs. poison each round of contact or suffer 1d6 points of damage. Characters who eat fruits, etc., from the grove must save vs. poison or die.

Haunted. The life forces of people who die in a haunted grove or within a mile of its boundaries are drawn into one of the grove's trees or standing stones. The trunks of the trees or the surfaces of the stones contain twisted images of the dead trapped within. While trapped, these souls cannot be raised, resurrected, or reincarnated.

To defend itself, the grove can summon any of its prisoners' spirits as ghosts or banshees (described in the *Monstrous Manual*™). Each summoning takes two rounds, but only one ghost or banshee can exist at any time. Resanctifying the grove (described below) ends the curse and frees the trapped spirits, who now may be reincarnated, raised, or resurrected. Destroying the grove before resanctifying releases all the trapped spirits as malevolent ghosts or banshees to haunt the region henceforth.

Perpetual Season. The grove, locked into a single season, never experiences a change in climate. Though a grove locked into winter isn't ever popular, a grove of perpetual spring or summer may seem like a blessing. While winter blizzards rage outside, the day is warm and sunny within a grove of perpetual summer; grass is always green, trees always leafy, and flowers ever blossoming. Nevertheless, druids consider this redundant setting horribly unnatural.

Hungry Trees. The trees in this grove have been animated by a hunger for flesh. Treat the 2d8 hungry trees of this cursed grove as evil treants. Masquerading as normal trees, they suddenly attack anyone entering the grove. They never cross its borders unless attacked from outside the grove, though; in that case, they re-enter the grove after defeating (and consuming) foes.

Reclaiming Cursed or Defiled Groves

Druids whose sacred grove becomes defiled or destroyed must perform a ritual of atonement, plus find and punish the guilty party. Failing deprives druids of all granted powers and major access to priestly spheres.

The first step in reclaiming a defiled grove involves repairing any damage it has sustained: planting new trees, restoring damaged standing stones, and so on. Then, a druid must perform an uninterrupted day-long ceremony within the grove to ask for the renewed blessings of Nature.

Reclaiming a cursed grove poses additional difficulties. After performing the above steps, the druid must complete a task to balance the forces behind the curse. The nature of the task is up to the DM, but it usually involves a dangerous quest in a real or symbolic attempt to "undo" the curse, punish those who caused it, or make amends for the act that led to it. After concluding the task, the druid must return to the grove to invoke Nature and cast a *remove curse* spell.

Standing Stones

Standing stones are large, shaped stones that rise from the ground to towering heights. In some cases, their presence in a forest, on a bleak moor, or atop a lonely hill automatically qualifies an area as a sacred grove, even if it lacks other natural beauty. Druids may have erected the standing stones, or they may mark a holy place that predates the druids' arrival in the area— perhaps a site sacred to prehuman peoples (elves, for instance) or prehistoric tribes.

Though sometimes stones stand alone, they more often join together to form various arrangements. A single standing stone is called a *megalith*—either a shaped slab or a more natural, tapering *obelisk*. Two shaped stones placed upright with a third laid across their tops constitutes a *trilithon*. Several megaliths or trilithons frequently form patterns, usually circles or horseshoe shapes.

Individual stones may weigh 5 to 25 tons each and stand 10 to 30 feet tall. A large circle may take a generation to build, unless powerful earth magic or suitable monsters (treants, earth elementals, or giants) help in the construction. Because druids possess the necessary magic, they often create these monuments for their sacred groves.

Standing stones fall into one of two categories: magical and nonmagical.

Nonmagical Standing Stones

Many standing stones have no innate magical properties, although they may have been built by magic. In "awakened" groves, these nonmagical stones may share in the general magic of the grove. The DM decides on the purpose, type, and number of stones.

Boundary Markers. Stones can simply mark the grove's borders, a common practice when a circle of trees is inappropriate. Mountain druids, in particular, use stone circles to mark borders.

Natural Observatory. The stones might serve as a primitive astronomical calculator (as in the case of Stonehenge), their positions marking eclipses, equinoxes, and other important solar and lunar dates whose exact times remain important for religious reasons and for maintaining the agricultural calendar. Usually one such astronomical circle of stones exists in every major druidic domain. Creating such a circle requires two proficiencies: astrology and engineering. In some cases, these circles are relics left behind to mark the visits (and predict the eventual returns) of spelljamming space druids.

Monuments. The lives of particularly notable historical figures can merit great megalith memorials. Sometimes treasure or a body lies buried under the stone. In rare instances, although the stone has no magic, the body beneath it rests in magical suspended animation—think of King Arthur, waiting for Merlin to awaken him.

Magical Standing Stones

Magical standing stones can serve any of the nonmagical variety's purposes. Lesser magical sacred groves containing standing stones possess a 10% chance of having one with magical powers. This chance increases to 20% for groves with five or more stones, and 30% for groves with 25 or more stones. Standing stones within greater groves have triple the chance of being magical.

Standing stones may become magical through association with druidic rites, divine intervention, or via the normal process used to create druidic magical items. DMs deciding that a stone has magic either pick its powers from those described below or roll on Table 6. Add a +1 bonus to rolls for standing stones that help form a trilithon.

TABLE 6: Powers of Standing Stones

d4	Power
1	Petrified entity
2	Stone guardian
3	Peaceful stones
4	Speaking stones
5	Trilithon gate

Petrified Entity. The magical stone is actually a huge being—often a giant or titan—that has been so weathered and overgrown with moss or ivy over the years its original humanoid form is no longer discernable. It radiates magic and may return to life if a *dispel magic* or *stone to flesh* spell succeeds. Depending on its alignment and the reason it became petrified, the creature may feel either grateful or hostile to its rescuer. A petrified entity usually points to the work of dual-class wizard/druid.

Stone Guardian. Once per day, the steward of the grove can order the stone to come to life for one turn per level of the druid. The animated stone fights as a 16 HD earth elemental, but if it leaves the grove it reverts to a normal stone and may not be reanimated until returned to the grove—a herculean task, since it weighs several tons! If injured, the magical stone heals at a rate of 1 hit point per turn—within the grove only.

Peaceful Stones. The standing stones exert a calming influence on the earth. No *earthquake* spells may succeed within a radius that measures (in feet from the center of the stone or cluster) a distance equal to the number of stones in the circle. Since no earthquakes or volcanic eruptions occur in this area, peaceful stones often stand near volcanoes or faults. Removing them could spell disaster for nearby forests and towns!

Speaking Stones. Any druid can cause any standing stones in the grove to speak, per the *stone tell* spell. Characters can use this power as often as desired, but the stones speak for no more than three rounds per day. Stewards use this power to learn whether intruders have visited the grove while they were away; druids who find a strange grove could use it to become familiar with the grove's history and keepers (if any).

Trilithon Gate. Characters passing under the stones may emerge from any other sacred grove in the world that also has a trilithon gate, no matter how distant. Those who have a particular gate in mind reach it; otherwise, characters come through a random gate. Anyone can travel via trilithon gate only once per day; it is impossible to go through and return again immediately.

APPENDIX A

AD&D® Original Edition Druids

The following represents a summation of information on druids from the AD&D Original Edition Player's Handbook and the Unearthed Arcana reference book. Some of these rules may not coincide with the rules for druids in the AD&D 2nd Edition game.

The druid is a subclass of the cleric, a neutral priest of nature who views good and evil, law and chaos, as necessary and vital balancing forces. Druids hold trees (especially ash and oak) sacred, venerate the sun(s) and the moon(s), and serve as protectors of forests, wild plants, crops, and—to a lesser extent—animals and the human followers of their religion. They never destroy woodlands or crops, no matter what the situation (although druids could act to change the *nature* of an evil enchanted wood, for instance, without destroying it). Similarly, they avoid slaying wild or domestic animals, except as necessary for self-preservation and sustenance. However, druids rarely risk their lives to prevent damage to woodlands or animals—instead, they favor retribution after the fact, in a manner, time, and place of their own choosing.

To become a druid, a character must have a minimum Wisdom of 12 and Charisma of 15; if both these scores exceed 15, the druid gains a 10% bonus on earned experience. Human, elven, half-elven, and halfling PCs may be druids, although halflings and some types of elves are subject to level restrictions.

Druids fight and save as clerics, but get a +2 bonus to save vs. fire or vs. electrical attacks. They can wear only leather armor and use only wooden shields. Their weapon options are limited to club, dagger, dart, hammer, khopesh, scimitar, scythe, sickle, sling, spear, and staff.

A druid can use those magical items permitted to clerics, except for written items (books and scrolls) and weapons and armor forbidden to their class.

General Abilities

All druids speak their own secret language. Upon reaching 3rd level, and each level thereafter, a druid gains the language of one of the following creatures: centaur, dryad, elf, gnome, green dragon, hill giant, lizard man, manticore, nixie, pixie, satyr, sprite, treant.

Druids gain powers as they rise in level.

At 3rd level:
• Identify plant type.
• Identify animal type.
• Identify pure water.
• Pass through overgrown areas without leaving a trail and at the normal movement rate.

At 7th level: (in addition to above)
• Immune to *charm* spells.
• Shapechange into a bird, reptile, and animal, each form once per day.

High-level Druids

The number of druids above 11th level in a given land is limited. (See Table 7.)

Druid. A land can have only nine 12th-level Druids; when druids earn enough experience to achieve 12th level, they gain this level's powers only if the land presently has fewer than nine 12th-level Druids. A character also could gain the level by defeating one of the land's nine Druids in magical or hand-to-hand combat. Losers that survive must drop just enough experience points to place them at the beginning of the next lower level (11th).

Archdruid, Great Druid. The same procedure applies when a 12th-level Druid gains enough experience to become an Archdruid, and when an Archdruid reaches Great Druid level. There are only three positions for Archdruids in a given region, and only one Great Druid.

AD&D® Original Edition Druids • 119

Table 7: Original Druid Experience Points

Experience Points	Experience Level	Accumulated hp	Qty./Land	Level Title
0—2,000	1	1	any	Aspirant
2,001—4,000	2	2	any	Ovate
4,001—7,500	3	3	any	Initiate of the 1st circle
7,501—12,500	4	4	any	Initiate of the 2nd circle
12,501—20,000	5	5	any	Initiate of the 3rd circle
20,001—35,000	6	6	any	Initiate of the 4th circle
35,001—60,000	7	7	any	Initiate of the 5th circle
60,001—90,000	8	8	any	Initiate of the 6th circle
90,001—125,000	9	9	any	Initiate of the 7th circle
125,001—200,000	10	10	any	Initiate of the 8th circle
200,001—300,000	11	11	any	Initiate of the 9th circle
300,001—750,000	12	12	9	Druid
750,001—1,500,000	13	13	3	Archdruid
1,500,001—3,000,000	14	14	1	Great Druid
3,000,001—3,500,000	15	15	*	The Grand Druid

* Only one Grand Druid governs all the lands of the world.

Grand Druid. Ranking above the Great Druids stands a single Grand Druid, the ultimate overseer of all a world's druids. Besides knowing six spells of each level, the Grand Druid has the ability to cast up to six spell levels (as one additional spell or in any combination that totals six levels—one 6th-level spell, six 1st-level spells, one 4th- and one 2nd-level spell, etc.).

Hierophant. The Grand Druid has an essentially political job, and most adventurers eventually tire of it. After attaining 500,000 experience points as a Grand Druid, the character may appoint any worthy Great Druid with 1,500,001 or more experience points as the successor. The former Grand Druid then rises to the 16th experience level, becoming a Hierophant.

As a Hierophant, the character relinquishes the Grand Druid's six bonus spell levels and, furthermore, loses all but 1 experience point (yet remains at 16th level). The character then begins counting experience points again and progressing using Table 8 (next page).

Attendants. Each 12th- or higher-level druid acquires an entourage of devoted lower-level druids. The least experienced 12th-level druid has three 1st-level aspirants, the next has three 2nd-level ovates, and so on. The most experienced has as followers three initiates of the 7th circle. Three 10th-level initiates of the 8th circle always serve Archdruids, while three 11th-level initiates of the 9th circle attend the Great Druid.

The Grand Druid is attended by nine druids unattached to any specific land. Any character of at least Druid level may seek out the Grand Druid and offer service. Three of these servants, Archdruids, roam the world as the Grand Druid's personal agents and messengers. Each has four additional spell levels, as explained above.

Table 8: Original Hierophant Experience Points

Experience Points	Experience Level	Accumulated hp	Level Title
1—500,000	16	15+1	Hierophant Druid
500,001—1,000,000	17	15+2	Hierophant Initiate
1,000,001—1,500,000	18	15+3	Hierophant Adept
1,500,001—2,000,000	19	15+4	Hierophant Master
2,000,001—2,500,000	20	15+5	Numinous Hierophant
2,500,001—3,000,000	21	15+6	Mystic Hierophant
3,000,001—3,500,000	22	15+7	Arcane Hierophant
3,500,001 and up	23	15+8	Hierophant of the Cabal

Hierophant Abilities

No bonus spells are awarded to Hierophants (as above for the Grand Druid and attendants), but they do receive additional, cumulative spell-like powers.

At 16th level:
- Immune to all natural animal or vegetable poisons, including those of monsters, but not mineral or gaseous poisons.
- Blessed with extra longevity equal to experience level times 10 years. For instance, a 16th-level druid lives 160 extra years.
- Maintains vigorous health (prime of life) regardless of actual age.
- Alters appearance at will in only one-tenth of a round. Hierophants can alter their facial and body features to those of any human or humanoid, change their height and weight by up to 50%, and alter their apparent age to anything from child to old. This non-magical power cannot be detected except by *true seeing* or similar magic.

At 17th level:
- Hibernate for a number of years equal to experience level times 10. For instance, a 17th-level druid can hibernate 170 years in suspended animation (without aging).
- Enter the Plane of Elemental Earth.
- Conjure water elemental.

At 18th level:
- Enter the Plane of Elemental Fire.
- Conjure air elemental.

At 19th level:
- Enter the Plane of Elemental Water.
- Conjure magma/smoke para-elemental.

At 20th level:
- Enter the Plane of Elemental Air.
- Conjure ice/ooze para-elementals.

At 21st level:
- Enter the para-elemental planes.

At 22nd level:
- Enter the Plane of Shadow.

At 23rd level:
- Enter any of the Inner Planes.
- Roam the Inner Plane probability lines (the 7th dimension).
- Enter the Plane of Concordant Opposition.

Entering Other Planes. It takes the druid one round to shift into a plane (or back to the Prime Material Plane), but the character can stay there as long as desired. The ability to enter a plane also confers the ability to survive there. So, a druid who can enter the Plane of Elemental Water will not drown during the visit, one entering the Plane of Elemental Fire will not burn, etc.

Conjuring Elementals. This ability works like a *conjure fire elemental* spell, but it calls for a percentile dice roll when the druid makes a conjuration attempt. If the roll is equal to or less than the character's experience level, use Table 9 to choose which elemental creature appears. Otherwise, roll on Table 9 to see what the druid summoned.

TABLE 9: Elemental Conjurings

Fire:
01–85	16 HD fire elemental
86–94	1d3+1 salamanders
95–98	efreeti
99–00	21–24 HD fire elemental

Earth:
01–85	16 HD earth elemental
86–94	1d3+1 xorn
95–98	dao
99–00	21–24 HD earth elemental

Water:
01–85	16 HD water elemental
86–94	1d6+6 tritons (5th–8th level) riding hippocampi
95–98	marid
99–00	21–24 HD water elemental

Air:
01–85	16 HD air elemental
86–94	1d3+1 invisible stalkers
95–98	djinni
99–00	21–24 HD air elemental

Para-elemental, any:
01–85	16 HD para-elemental
86–95	Special*
96–00	21–24 HD para-elemental

* Special: Choose 1d4+4 lava children, 1d4+4 winter wolves, 1d4+20 mud-men, 1d4+20 vapor rats, or similar creatures associated with the appropriate para-element.

A single entity, when conjured, has as many extra hit points added to its total as the druid has levels; it may not exceed its maximum hit points, though.

All conjured creatures serve the Hierophant selflessly and obediently, regardless of their alignment and temperament.

Druidic Spells

Druids use mistletoe as their religious symbol when casting spells, though holly and oak leaves both hold lesser mystic power for them as well.

All druidic spells with a material component assume the caster uses greater mistletoe. Druids seek the mistletoe themselves on Midsummer's Eve, cut it with a gold or silver sickle, and catch the cuttings in a golden bowl before they touch the ground. Lesser mistletoe results when druids harvest the plant themselves in any other fashion. Borrowed mistletoe is any mistletoe not cut personally by the druid casting the spell.

If a druid does not use greater mistletoe, the effectiveness of the character's spell is reduced as follows:

- Lesser mistletoe: 75% duration*.
- Borrowed mistletoe: 75% range*, 50% duration**.
- Holly: 75% range*, 50% duration**, 75% area of effect*.
- Oak leaves: 50% range**, 50% duration**, 50% area of effect**.

* or +1 bonus to saving throw if category not applicable.
** or +2 bonus to saving throw if category not applicable.

Table 10: Druidic Spells by Class and Level

Druid Level	Spell Level 1	2	3	4	5	6	7
1	2	—	—	—	—	—	—
2	2	1	—	—	—	—	—
3	3	2	1	—	—	—	—
4	4	2	2	—	—	—	—
5	4	3	2	—	—	—	—
6	4	3	2	1	—	—	—
7	4	4	3	1	—	—	—
8	4	4	3	2	—	—	—
9	5	4	3	2	1	—	—
10	5	4	3	3	2	—	—
11	5	5	3	3	2	1	—
12	5	5	4	4	3	2	1
13	6	5	5	5	4	3	2
14	6	6	6	6	5	4	3
15+	6	6	6	6	6	6	6

1st-level spells: *Animal friendship, ceremony, detect balance, detect magic, detect poison, detect snares and pits, entangle, faerie fire, invisibility to animals, locate animals, pass without trace, precipitation, predict weather, purify water, shillelagh, speak with animals.*

2nd-level spells: *Barkskin, charm person or mammal, create water, cure light wounds, feign death, fire trap, flame blade, goodberry, heat metal, locate plants, obscurement, produce flame, reflecting pool, slow poison, trip, warp wood.*

3rd-level spells: *Call lightning, cloudburst, cure disease, hold animal, know alignment, neutralize poison, plant growth, protection from fire, pyrotechnics, snare, spike growth, starshine, stone shape, summon insects, tree, water breathing.*

4th-level spells: *Animal summoning I, call woodland beings, control temperature, 10' radius, cure serious wounds, dispel magic, hallucinatory forest, hold plant, plant door, produce fire, protection from lightning, repel insects, speak with plants.*

5th-level spells: *Animal growth, animal summoning II, anti-plant shell, commune with nature, control winds, insect plague, moonbeam, pass plant, spike stones, sticks to snakes, transmute rock to mud, wall of fire.*

6th-level spells: *Animal summoning III, anti-animal shell, conjure fire elemental, cure critical wounds, feeblemind, fire seeds, liveoak, transport via plants, transmute water to dust, turn wood, wall of thorns, weather summoning.*

7th-level spells: *Animate rock, changestaff, chariot of sustarre, confusion, conjure earth elemental, control weather, creeping doom, finger of death, fire storm, reincarnate, sunray, transmute metal to wood.*

APPENDIX B

A good many works of modern fantasy fiction deal with druids or druidlike figures who act to magically preserve and protect Nature. Some of the best are listed below, but many more Arthurian (Merlin was a druid!) or Celtic-inspired fantasies await in bookstores and libraries.

Novels and Series

The Mists of Avalon, Marion Zimmer Bradley. The story of King Arthur, Merlin, and Morgan le Fay told from Morgan's point of view. Beautifully written.

The Dreamstone, C. J. Cherryh. Arafel, the last of the Sidhe and immortal protectress of the wood, makes a good model for an eccentric Guardian druid. Sequel: *The Tree of Swords and Jewels.*

Moonheart, Charles De Lint. This novel has a modern setting, but its compelling tale of bards, druids, shamans, and the meeting of Celtic and Amerind magic has relevance to any fantasy campaign—as do most of De Lint's other novels (especially *Greenmantle*).

The Chronicles of Thomas Covenant the Unbeliever series, Steven R. Donaldson. An outcast from our world becomes drawn reluctantly into a struggle to save the magical Land from evil. The forces rallied in defense of the Land hold ideas usable in a druidic campaign. Also relevant is the theme of protecting a world against a corrupting evil.

Moon of Gomrath, Alan Garner. This tale, regarding the return of "wild magic" to England, contains useful enchantments.

Mythago Wood, Robert Holdstock. This award-winner full of powerful images brims with druidic magic and ancient mystery in England's woods. The Mythago Wood is the archetypal primal forest; mythagos themselves would make an exciting mystery encounter—and an interesting alternative to avatars. Sequel: *Lavondyss.*

Druid, Morgan Llywelyn. Clearly, this novel is superior historical fantasy.

Nausicaa and the Valley of the Wind, Hayao Miyazaki. Nausicaa, the heroine of this excellent science-fantasy comic (and movie), resembles a gray druid with the Hivemaster kit.

Moonshae and *Druidhome* trilogies, Douglas Niles. These six books center around a druid who worships the Earthmother in the FORGOTTEN REALMS setting.

The Forest of Forever, Thomas Burnett Swann. This is one of several novels by Swann that focuses on sylvan folk, dryads, and the like within an ancient setting.

Lord of the Rings, J. R. R. Tolkein. The encounters with the Old Forest, Tom Bombadil, Radagast, and Treebeard contain many ideas usable within a druidic campaign. Some think Gandalf resembles a druid far more than a wizard.

The Seedbearers trilogy, Peter Valentine. This series postulates a druid migration to Great Britain following the sinking of Atlantis. Its action continues up to Rome's destruction of the druids.

Game Supplements

Halls of the High King (FA1), Ed Greenwood. This FORGOTTEN REALMS adventure contains information on druidic groves in the Realms, including their unique "moonwells."

Celts Campaign Sourcebook (HR3), Graeme Davis. This book provides rules on how the very different Celtic druids of ancient Britain, Gaul, and Ireland can work within a historical fantasy AD&D game. It has a useful bibliography on historical druids.

Character _____
Alignment _____
Class _____
Player's Name _____
Sex _____ Age _____ Ht. _____
Wt. _____ Hair _____ Eyes _____
Appearance _____

Race _____
Level _____
Branch _____
Kit _____

Druid

Personality Type _____

ABILITIES

	STR	Hit Prob	Dmg Adj	Wgt Allow	Max Press	Op Drs	B B/L G
	DEX	Rctn Adj		Missle Att Adj		Def Adj	
	CON	HP Adj	Sys Shk	Res Sur	Pois Save		Regen
	INT	No of Lang	Spell Lvl	Lrn Sp	Spells/Level		Spell Immun
	WIS	Mag Def Adjus	Bonus Spells		Spell Fail		Spell Immun
	CHR	Max No Hench		Loy Base		Rctn Adj	

MOVEMENT

Base Rate [ ]
Light ( )
Mod ( )
Hvy ( )
Svr ( )
Jog (×2)
Run (×3)
Run (×4)
Run (×5)

SAVING THROWS

_____ Paralyze Poison _____
_____ Rod, Staff or Wand _____
_____ Petrify Polymorph _____
_____ Breath Weapon _____
_____ Spells _____
Modifier   Save

ARMOR

AC

Adjusted AC   Armor Type (Pieces)
Surprised _____ _____
Shieldless _____ _____
Rear _____ _____
_____

Defenses _____

HIT POINTS | **Wounds**

WEAPON COMBAT

Weapon	#AT	Attack Adj/Dmg Adj	THAC0	Dam (SM/L)	Range	Weight	Size	Type	Speed
				/					
				/					
				/					
				/					
				/					

Special Attacks _____
_____
_____

Ammunition _____ _____ ☐☐☐☐
☐☐☐☐☐ ☐☐☐☐☐ _____ ☐☐☐☐
☐☐☐☐☐ ☐☐☐☐☐ _____ ☐☐☐☐

Granted Powers

_____ _____
_____ _____
_____ _____
_____ _____
_____ _____
_____ _____
_____ _____
_____ _____

Spheres
Major Access: _____
Minor Access: _____
_____ _____
_____ _____
_____ _____

Proficiencies/Skills/Languages

_____ (/) _____ (/)
_____ (/) _____ (/)
_____ (/) _____ (/)
_____ (/) _____ (/)
_____ (/) _____ (/)
_____ (/) _____ (/)
_____ (/) _____ (/)
_____ (/) _____ (/)
_____ (/) _____ (/)
_____ (/) _____ (/)
_____ (/) _____ (/)
_____ (/) _____ (/)
_____ (/) _____ (/)

**Kit Benefits
and Hindrances**

This form may be photocopied for personal use in playing AD&D® games.

©1994 TSR, Inc. All Rights Reserved.

Gear

Item	Location	Wt.	Item	Location	Wt.	Item	Location	Wt.

Supplies
Water/Wine
☐☐☐☐☐ ☐☐☐☐☐
☐☐☐☐☐ ☐☐☐☐☐

Rations
☐☐☐☐☐ ☐☐☐☐☐
☐☐☐☐☐ ☐☐☐☐☐
☐☐☐☐☐ ☐☐☐☐☐
☐☐☐☐☐ ☐☐☐☐☐

Feed
☐☐☐☐☐ ☐☐☐☐☐
☐☐☐☐☐ ☐☐☐☐☐
☐☐☐☐☐ ☐☐☐☐☐

Experience

Treasure

Coins

Gems

Other Valuables
_____
_____
_____
_____
_____
_____
_____
_____

Miscellaneous Information

(Magical Items, Command Words, Small Maps, etc.)

Spheres _____
_____
_____
_____

Henchmen/Animal Companions

Druid Character Kit Design Sheet

Character Class: _____
Campaign: _____
Player: _____
Dungeon Master: _____

OVERVIEW:
Forbidden branches: _____
ROLE: _____

WEAPON PROFICIENCIES
Required: _____
Recommended: _____

NONWEAPON PROFICIENCIES
Bonus Proficiencies: _____
Required Proficiencies: _____
Recommended, General: _____
Recommended, Warrior: _____
Recommended, Priest: _____
Recommended, Wizard: _____
Recommended, Rogue: _____
Forbidden: _____

EQUIPMENT: _____
_____

SPECIAL BENEFITS: _____
_____
_____
_____
_____
_____
_____
_____
_____
_____
_____
_____
_____
_____
_____
_____

SPECIAL HINDRANCES: _____
_____
_____
_____
_____
_____

WEALTH OPTIONS: _____
_____
_____
_____

Advanced Dungeons & Dragons® Game

Great campaigns don't just happen!

They take imagination, knowledge, and skill. These five AD&D® game fundamentals are a "must-own" for your adventuring party.

AD&D® Player's Handbook
It's the indispensable encyclopedia of adventure gaming, with everything players need to know: how to create characters, differences between races, mapping and combat rules, and more.
TSR #2101
Sug. Retail $20.00
ISBN 0-88038-716-5

Character Record Sheets
Quick! Your hero is face-to-face with a dragon... what will he do? For faster, more spontaneous play, record ability scores, possessions, background, and much more on these sheets!
TSR #9264
Sug. Retail $8.95
ISBN 0-88038-152-1

DUNGEON MASTER™ Guide
The more versatile and knowledgeable the DM™, the livelier the adventure! The *DUNGEON MASTER™ Guide* is your complete source of information on how to be the best leader of the game!
TSR #2100
Sug. Retail $18.00
ISBN 0-88038-729-7

DUNGEON MASTER™ Screen
The easy-to-use charts of the *DUNGEON MASTER™ Screen* organize all the statistics and figures the DM™ must have to run a quality AD&D® campaign. Includes a 16-page mini-adventure.
TSR #9263
Sug. Retail $6.95
ISBN 0-88038-747-5

Monstrous Manual
The ultimate monster reference! Descriptions and full-color illustrations for over 600 monsters, including all the creatures from MONSTROUS COMPENDIUM® Volumes 1 and 2, and many more beasties.
TSR #2140
Sug. Retail $24.95
ISBN 1-56076-619-0

Available at book, game, and hobby stores everywhere!

ADVANCED DUNGEONS & DRAGONS, AD&D, and MONSTROUS COMPENDIUM are registered trademarks owned by TSR, Inc. DUNGEON MASTER, DM, and the TSR logo are trademarks owned by TSR, Inc. © 1994 TSR, Inc. All Rights Reserved.